Contents

For Boris Dolingo, on the line between Europe and Asia, who knows a good story can be found on either side

EXCEPTIONS TO

STORIES

REALITY

ALAN DEAN FOSTER

BALLANTINE BOOKS · NEW YORK

A Del Rey Mass Market Original

Copyright © 2008 by Thranx, Inc.

Published in the United States by Del Rey Books, an imprint of The Random House Publishing Group, a division of Random House, Inc., New York.

DEL REY is a registered trademark and the Del Rey colophon is a trademark of Random House, Inc.

Some of the stories contained in this work were originally published as follows:

"The Muffin Migration" previously appeared in *Star Colonies*, DAW Books, 1999.

"Chauna" previously appeared in *Far Frontiers*, DAW Books, 2000.

"At Sea" previously appeared in *Warriors Fantastic*, DAW Books, 2000.

"The Killing of Bad Bull" previously appeared in the original anthology *The Mutant Files*, DAW Books, 2001.

"Rate of Exchange" previously appeared on AOL Online, 2001.

"Wait-a-While" previously appeared in *Realms of Fantasy*, Aug. 2001.

"The Short, Labored Breath of Time" previously appeared in *Darkling Plain*, Vol. 1 #2, 2001.

"A Fatal Exception Has Occurred at . . ." previously appeared in *Children of Cthulhu*, Del Rey Books, 2002.

"Basted" previously appeared in *Pharoah Fantastic*, DAW Books, 2002.

"Serenade" previously appeared in *Masters of Fantasy*, Baen, 2002.

"Redundancy" previously appeared in *Space Stations*, DAW Books, 2004.

"Panhandler" previously appeared in *Little Red Riding Hood in the Big Bad City*, DAW Books, 2004.

"The Last Akialoa" previously appeared in *Fantasy & Science Fiction*, Dec. 2005.

ISBN 978-0-345-49604-1

Printed in the United States of America

www.delreybooks.com

OPM 9 8 7 6 5 4 3 2 1

EXCEPTIONS TO
REALITY

By Alan Dean Foster
Published by The Random House Publishing Group

The Black Hole
Cachalot
Dark Star
The Metrognome and Other Stories
Midworld
Nor Crystal Tears
Sentenced to Prism
Splinter of the Mind's Eye
Star Trek® Logs One–Ten
Voyage to the City of the Dead
... Who Needs Enemies?
With Friends Like These ...
Mad Amos
The Howling Stones
Parallelities

Stories:
Impossible Places
Exceptions to Reality

The Icerigger Trilogy:
Icerigger
Mission to Moulokin
The Deluge Drivers

The Adventures of Flinx of the Commonwealth:
For Love of Mother-Not
The Tar-Aiym Krang
Orphan Star
The End of the Matter
Bloodhype
Flinx in Flux
Mid-Flinx
Reunion
Flinx's Folly
Sliding Scales
Running from the Deity
Trouble Magnet
Patrimony

The Damned:
Book One: A Call to Arms
Book Two: The False Mirror
Book Three: The Spoils of War

The Founding of the Commonwealth:
Phylogenesis
Dirge
Diuturnity's Dawn

The Taken Trilogy:
Lost and Found
The Light-years Beneath My Feet
The Candle of Distant Earth

Introduction

There was a time when writers of short fiction used to be able to make a living at it. Back in the heyday of the slicks and pulps, the 1930s and '40s, magazines vied with radio, sports, and going out to the movies as a major arena of popular entertainment. Nowadays magazines containing fiction are an endangered species. Shifting short fiction to websites has not proven the savior of the genre some thought it might be. It may yet turn out to be the case, perhaps when soundtracks and illustrations are added. But at present the auguries are not good, the entrails being read less than sanguine.

While novels remain highly popular, the market for short fiction of every kind appears to be on the wane. I find this surprising. Today's denizens of planet Earth, raised on ever-briefer and more compacted bursts of information delivered via the Net and the ever-accelerated editing of the visual image, would seem ideally conditioned to accept their printed fiction in equivalently more concise packages. Yet the fantasies that sell best have mutated into gargantuan doorstops spanning multiple volumes. As for science fiction, it largely continues to resist the trend toward obesity, though the spawning of sequels (an inclination to which I, too, must plead guilty) continues unabated.

Therefore whence then the short story, that polished gem so demanding of readers' attention but not of their time?

It has been saved for now, not by the brave magazines that continue to hang on in the face of ebbing coteries of truly dedicated readers, but by the anthology. Buyers who shun the magazine section of a bookstore, and never seek out magazines online, who don't want to be bothered with subscribing to *anything* anymore, be it *Analog* or the Fruit-of-the-Month Club, will find anthologies of short fiction conveniently included alongside the monolithic novels on bookstore racks and available in the book section of their favorite Web retailer. That is where short fantasy and science fiction continues to survive and, on a modest scale, even prosper.

I love the magazines. I miss the illustrations they provide (why can't we have illustrated anthologies in the United States as they do in Europe?) and their sense of immediacy. But they do not wear well, they don't fit on bookshelves cleanly alongside all those bloated epics (where are the magazine publishers who have modified the size of their 'zines to match that of the standard hardbound novel?), and their built-in impermanence makes them look and feel cheap. Readers today like their purchases to have heft and solidity. Books continue to provide that extra tactile bonus. Magazines do not.

Marketing isn't my job, though. I just continue to write short stories and hope that whatever the venue, readers will continue to find them.

I'm pleased that you found these.

ALAN DEAN FOSTER,
Prescott, Arizona, 2006

The Muffin Migration

Deep-space explorers struggling to survive on a new world. Bizarre alien life-forms, sometimes friendly, often-times not. Issues of survival, interpersonal conflict, mal-functioning equipment, the impossibility of rescue in the event of harrowing circumstances—all these are tropes of the adventure science-fiction story that existed even before the arrival of Amazing Stories in 1926. That they are old, even hoary, does not automatically render any of them invalid or useless as plot points in the telling of a tale. Or as John W. Campbell, editor of Astounding/Analog, used to prefer to say when he found a good old-fashioned story that he liked, "I think you've got a pretty good yarn here."

A good story is a good story. I see the proof of it in the faces of very young readers whenever the occasion arises for me to read to them. They respond to the same ele-ments as their ancestors have down through the millen-nia. Danger, new discoveries, the need to cooperate in order to survive—these are fundamentals of adventure storytelling that have existed since Ur-storyteller Norg first enthralled listeners around the cave fire with tales of what really lay behind those mysterious lights that ap-peared in the sky every night.

Today we look up at those very same stars with a good deal more understanding of their true nature. But our science is not yet all-encompassing, our knowledge far from absolute. Those stars still hold many mysteries, *and where there is mystery there is always room for adventure. We know now for a certainty that around those stars orbit other worlds. Perhaps some that are much like our own. On those planets we can yet hope to experience the adventures that Norg and his fellow mythspinners first began to envision.*

We might even imagine that one of those still-unknown alien worlds could be home to creatures as strange as muffins . . .

It was a beautiful day on Hedris. But then, Bowman reflected as he stood on the little covered porch he and LeCleur had fashioned from scraps of shipping materials, every day for the past four months had been beautiful. Not overwhelming like the spectacular mornings on Barabas, or stunningly evocative like the sunsets on New Riviera; just tranquil, temperate, and bursting with the crisp fresh tang of unpolluted air, green growing grasses, and a recognition of the presence of unfettered, unfenced life-force.

In addition to the all-pervasive, piquant musk of millions of muffins, of course.

The muffins, as the two planetary advance agents had come to call them, were by incalculable orders of magnitude the dominant life-form on Hedris. They swarmed in inconceivable numbers over its endless grassy plains, burrowed deep into its unbelievably rich topsoil, turned streams and rivers brown with their bathing, frolicking bodies. Fortunately for Bowman and LeCleur, the largest of them stood no more than fifteen centimeters high, not counting the few thicker, lighter-hued bristles that protruded upward and beyond the otherwise dense covering of soft brown fur. A muffin had two eyes, two legs, a short fuzzy blob of a tail, and an oval mouth filled with several eruptions of tooth-like bone designed to make short work of the diverse variety of half-meter-high grass in which they lived. They communicated, fought, and cooed to one another via appealing sequences of chirruping, high-pitched peeping sounds.

It was a good thing, Bowman reflected as he inhaled deeply of the fresh air that swept over the benign plains of Hedris, that the local grasses were as fecund as the muffins, or the planet would have been stripped bare of anything edible millions of years ago. Even though a patient observer could actually watch the grass grow, it remained a constant source of amazement to him and his partner that the local vegetation managed to keep well ahead of the perpetually foraging muffins.

The uncountable little balls of brown-and-beige fur were not the only native browsers, of course. On a world as fertile as Hedris, there were always ecological niches to fill. But for every kodout, pangalta, and slow-moving, thousand toothed jerabid, there were a thousand muffins. No, he corrected himself. Ten thousand, maybe more. Between the higher grass and the deeper burrows it was impossible to get an accurate account, even with surveys conducted with the aid of mini-satellites.

Such qualified stats filled the reports he and LeCleur filed. They had another five months in which to refine and perfect their figures, hone their observations, and codify their opinions. The House of Novy Churapcha, the industrial-commercial concern that had set them up on Hedris, was anxious to put together a bid and stake its claim in front of the Commonwealth concession courts before any of the other great trading Houses or public companies got wind of the new discovery. By keeping their outpost on Hedris tiny, isolated, and devoid of contact for almost a year, the managers hoped to avoid the unwanted attention of nosy competitors.

So far the strategy seemed to have worked. In the seven

months since the fabrication crew, working around the clock, had erected the outpost, not even a stray communication had come the way of the two agents. That was fine with Bowman. He didn't mind the isolation. He and LeCleur were trained to deal with it. And they were very well compensated for maintaining their lack of offworld contact.

A few clouds were gathering. There might be an afternoon rain shower, he decided. If it materialized, it would be gentle, of course, like everything else on Hedris. No dangerous lightning, and just enough distant thunder to be atmospheric. Then the sun would come out, attended by the inevitable rainbow.

The smoky-sweet smell of muffin on the grill reached him from inside, and he turned away from the brightening panorama. It was LeCleur's week to do the cooking, and his partner had long since mastered multiple ways of preparing the eminently edible little indigenes. Not only were the multitudinous muffins harmless, cute beyond words, and easy to catch, but their seared meat was tender and highly palatable, with a sugary, almost honeyed flavor to the whitish flesh that was nothing at all like chicken. Tastewise, it easily surpassed anything in their store of prepackaged concentrates and dehydrates. There wasn't a lot of meat on a muffin, but then, neither was there a shortage of the hopping, preoccupied, forever foraging two-legged creatures.

The slim, diminutive humanoid natives who were the dominant species on Hedris virtually lived on them, and lived well. Only their metabolism kept them thin, Bowman reflected as he closed the front door of the station behind him. Overawed by the far more massive humans, the native Akoe were occasional visitors to the outpost. They were invariably polite, courteous, and quietly eager to learn all they could about their extraordinary visitors. Their language was a simple one. With the aid of electronic teaching devices, both experienced field agents had soon mastered enough of it to carry on a rudimentary conversation. The Akoe were always welcome at the outpost, though sometimes their quiet staring got on Bowman's nerves. An amused LeCleur never missed an opportunity to chide him about it.

"How's it look outside?" LeCleur was almost as tall as Bowman, but not nearly as broad or muscular. "Let me guess: clear and warm, with a chance of a sprinkle later in the day."

"What are you, psychic?" Grinning, Bowman sat down opposite his friend and partner. The platter of grilled muffin, neatly sliced, sizzled atop a warmer in the center. It was ringed by reconstituted bread, butter, jams, scrambled rehydrated eggs from three different kinds of fowl, and two tall self-chilling pitchers flamboyant with juice. Coffee and tea arrived in the form of the self-propelled carafes that approached the men whenever they verbally expressed their individual thirst.

"Thought we might run a predator census between rivers Six EW and Eight NS today." Having finished his meal, LeCleur was adding sweetener to his hot mug of high-grown tea.

Bowman was amenable to the suggestion. "Maybe we'll see another volute." They'd only encountered one of the pig-sized, loop-tailed carnivores so far, and that from a distance.

The agent was smearing rehydrated blackberry jam on his toast when the perimeter alarm went off. Neither man was alarmed.

"I'll get it." A resigned LeCleur rose from his seat. "My turn."

While Bowman finished the last of his breakfast, LeCleur activated the free-ranging heads-up. A cylindrical image appeared in the middle of the room, a perfect floating replica in miniature of a 360-degree view outside and around the outpost. A spoken command from LeCleur caused the image to enlarge and focus on the source of the alarm. This was followed by an order to shut down the soft but insistent whine.

The agent chuckled into the ensuing silence as he recognized the slender standing figure that had set off the alert. A combination of experience and study allowed him to instantly recognize the expression on the alien's face: slight bewilderment. "It's only Old Malakotee."

Wiping his mouth, Bowman rose. "Let him in and we'll see what he wants." It was always interesting and instructive to observe the elderly native's reaction to the many miracles the outpost contained. Also fun. He and LeCleur had few enough diversions.

Precisely enunciated directives caused the circumferential viewer to be replaced by a floating command board. In seconds LeCleur had shut down the station's external defenses, rotated the bridge to cross the deep artificial ravine that encircled the outpost, and opened the front door. By the time Bowman was finishing up the dishes, the Akoe elder had arrived at the entrance.

Old Malakotee was a venerable leader among his people, wizened and much respected. The Akoe were led not by one chief but by an assembly of elected seniors. Decisions were made by group vote. All very democratic, LeCleur mused as he greeted the alien in his own language. Malakotee responded in kind but declined to enter, though he could not keep his eyes from roving. Nor did he accept the offer of one of the chairs that sat invitingly on the porch. His much slighter, smaller body and nearly nonexistent backside tended to find themselves engulfed by the massive human furniture. Also, he never knew quite what to do with his tail. It switched back and forth as he chattered, the tuft of kinky black hair at the tip swatting curious flying arthropods away.

Dark intelligent eyes peered out from beneath smooth

brows. The alien's face was hairless, but the rest of his body was covered with a fine charcoal-gray down. When he opened his mouth, an orifice that was proportionately much wider than that of a comparably sized human, LeCleur could see how the stubby incisors alternated with flattened grinding teeth. In place of a nose was a small trunk with three flexible tips that the Akoe could employ as a third, if very short, hand.

A cloak comprising the skins of many native animals, especially that of the ubiquitous muffin, was draped loosely over his slim form. The garment was decorated with bits of carved bone, handmade beads of exceptional quality—the two humans had already traded for samples—and shiny bits of cut and worked shell. The Akoe were very dexterous and possessed substantial artistic skill. Necklaces hung from Old Malakotee's throat while bracelets jangled on his wrists. He leaned on a ceremonial kotele staff, the wood elaborately garnished with feathers, beads, and paint.

"Thanking you for offer to come into your hut." The native had to tilt his head back to meet the much taller human's eyes. "I not stay long today. Come to tell you that my people, they are moving now."

LeCleur was openly surprised. Recovering from their initial shock and stupefaction at the humans' arrival, the Akoe had been a fixture on the shores of River One NS ever since. Calling for his partner to join them, the agent pressed their visitor for an explanation.

"The Akoe are moving? But where, and why?"

Raising his primitively florid staff, the elder turned and pointed. "Go north and west soon. Long trek." Bowman appeared on the porch, wiping his hands against his pants as Malakotee finished. "Find safety in deep caverns."

"Safety?" Bowman made a face. "What's this about 'safety'? Safety from what?"

The elder turned solemn eyes to the even bigger human. "From migration, of course. Is time of year. When migration over, Akoe come back to river."

The two men exchanged a glance. "What migration?" LeCleur asked their pensive visitor. "What is migrating?" Uncertain, he scanned the vast, barely undulating plain that extended in all directions beyond the outpost's perimeter.

"The muffins. Is time of year. Soon now, they migrate."

A modest herd of less than a hundred thousand of the small brown browsers was clustered in the grass in front of the outpost, grazing peacefully. Their familiar soft peep-peeping filled the morning air. LeCleur watched as several, each no bigger than his closed fist, hopped as close as they dared to the edge of the steep-sided ravine that surrounded the station to graze on the ninicumb flowers that were growing there.

"We'll see you when you come back, then."

"No, no!" Old Malakotee was uncharacteristically insistent. "I come warn you." He gestured emphatically. "You come with Akoe. You big skypeople good folk. Come with us. We keep you safe during migration."

Bowman smiled condescendingly to the native, whose appearance never failed to put him in mind of an anorexic Munchkin. "That's very kind of you and your people, Malakotee, but Gerard and I are quite comfortable here. We have protections you can't see and wouldn't understand even if I tried to explain them to you."

The miniature tripartite snout in the center of the Akoe's face twitched uneasily. "Malakotee know you skypeople got many wondrous things. You show Malakotee plenty. But you no understand. This is ixtex," he explained, using the native word for the bipedal muffins, "migration!"

"So you've told us. I promise you, we'll be all right.

Would you like some tea?" The chemical brew that was
Terran tea had been shown to produce interesting,
wholly pleasurable reactions within the Akoe body.

Ordinarily Old Malakotee, like any Akoe, would have
jumped at the offer. But not this morning. Stepping
down from the porch, he gestured purposefully with his
staff. Beads jangled and bounced against the rose-hued,
dark-streaked wood.

"I tell you. You come with Akoe, we take care of you.
You stay here"—he made the Akoe gesture for despair—
"no good." Reaching the ground, he promptly launched
into a slow-spinning, head-bending, tail-flicking tribal
chant-dance. When he was through, he saluted one
final time with his ornamented staff before turning his
back on them and striding deliberately away from the
outpost.

As LeCleur called forth the heads up and rotated the
bridge shut behind the retreating native, Bowman pondered what they had just seen. "Interesting performance. Wonder if it had any special significance?"

LeCleur, who was more of a xenologist than his partner, banished the command panel display with a word
and nodded. "That was the 'Dance for the Dead.' He
was giving us a polite send-off."

"Oh." Bowman squinted at the sky. Just another
lovely day on Hedris, as always. "I'll get the skimmer
ready for the census."

The Akoe had been gone for just over a week when
LeCleur was bitten. Bowman looked up from his work
as his partner entered. The bite was not deep, but the
thin bright line of blood running down the other man's
leg was clearly visible. It emerged from beneath the hem
of his field shorts to stain his calf. Plopping himself
down in a chair, LeCleur put the first-aid kit on the

table and flicked it open. As he applied antiseptic spray and then coagulator, Bowman looked on with casual interest.

"Run into something?"

A disgruntled, slightly embarrassed LeCleur finished treating the wound with a dose of color-coded epidermase. "Like hell. A damn muffin bit me."

His partner grunted. "Like I said: run into something?"

"I did not run into it. I was hunting for burrowing arthropods in the grass over in the east quad when I felt something sharp. I looked back, and there was this little furry shitball gnawing on my leg. I had to swat it off. It bounced once, scrambled back to its feet, and shot off into the grass." He closed the first-aid kit. "Freakish."

"An accident, yeah." Bowman couldn't keep himself from grinning. "It must have mistaken your leg for the mother of all casquak seeds."

"It wasn't the incident that was freaky." LeCleur was not smiling. "It was the muffin. It had sharp teeth."

Bowman's grin faded. "That's impossible. We've examined, not to mention eaten, hundreds of muffins since we've been here. Not one of them had sharp teeth. Their chewing mechanism is strictly basal molaric dentition, evolved to grind up and process vegetation."

His partner shook his head slowly. "I saw the teeth, Jamie. Sharp and pointed. Saw them and felt them. And there was something funny about its eyes, too."

"That's a description that'll look nice and formal in the records. 'Funny' how?"

Clearly upset, LeCleur pursed his lips. "I don't know. I didn't get a good look. They just struck me as funny." He tapped his leg above the now hermetized bite. "This didn't."

"Well, we know they're not poisonous." Bowman turned back to his work. "So it was a freak muffin. A break in the muffin routine. An eclectic muffin. I'm sure it was an isolated incident and won't happen again."

"It sure won't." LeCleur rose and extended his mended leg. "Because next time, you're doing the periphery arthropod survey."

It was a week later when Bowman, holding his coffee, walked out onto the porch, sat down in one of the chairs, and had the mug halfway to his lips when something he saw made him pause. Lowering the container, he stared for a long moment before activating the com button attached to the collar of his shirt.

"Gerard, I think you'd better come here. I'm on the porch."

A dozy mumble responded. The other agent was sleeping in. Bowman continued to nag his partner until he finally appeared, rubbing at his eyes and grumbling. His vision and mind cleared quickly enough as soon as he was able to share his partner's view.

On the far edge of the ravine, muffins were gathering. Not in the familiar, tidily spaced herd cluster in which they spent the night seeking protection from roving carnivores, nor in the irregular pattern they employed for browsing, but in dense knots of wall-to-wall brown fur. More muffins were arriving every minute, crowding together, filling in the gaps. And from the hundreds, going on thousands, there rose an unexpectedly steady, repetitive peep-peeping that was somehow intimidating in its idiosyncratic sonority.

"What the hell is going on?" LeCleur finally murmured.

Bowman remembered to take a drink of his coffee before pulling the scope from its pocket on the side of the chair. What he saw through the lens was anything but reassuring. He passed it to his partner. "Take a look for yourself."

LeCleur raised the instrument. The view it displayed resolved into groups of two to three muffins, bunched so tightly together it seemed impossible they could breathe, much less peep. Each showed signs of swelling, their compact bodies having puffed up an additional 10 percent, the brown fur bristling. Their eyes—LeCleur had seen harbingers of that wild, collective red glare in the countenance of the one that had bit him a week ago. When they opened their mouths to peep, the change that had taken place within was immediately apparent. Instead of a succession of smooth, white eruptions of bone, the diminutive jaws were now filled with a mixture of grinding projections and triangular, assertively sharp-edged canines. It was as if the creatures had visited en masse some crazed muffin cosmetic dentist.

He lowered the scope. "Christ—they're metamorphosing. And moving. I wonder how extensive the metamorphosis is?"

Bowman already had the command heads-up in place. A few verbal directives were sufficient to materialize an image. Atop the single-story station, remote instrumentation was responding efficiently.

The plain around the outpost was alive with rustling, festering movement. Come midday they no longer needed the instruments to show them what was happening. The two men stood on the porch, seeing with their own eyes.

All around them, as far as they could see and beyond, the grass was coming down, mowed flat by a suddenly ravenous, insatiable horde. Within that seething, frenzied mass of brown fur, red eyes, and munching teeth, nothing survived. Grass, other plants, anything living was overwhelmed and consumed, vanishing down a sea of brown gullets. From the depths of the feeding frenzy arose an unsettling, relentless, ostinato peeping that drowned out everything from the wind to the soft hum of the outpost's hydrogen generator.

Bowman and LeCleur watched, recorded, and made notes, usually without saying a word. By evening the en-

tire boundless mass of muffins had begun advancing like
a moving carpet in a southeasterly direction. The Akoe,
Bowman suddenly recalled, had gone northwest. The
two agents needed no additional explanation of the phenomenon they were observing.

The migration was under way.

"I suppose we could have offered to let the Akoe stay
here," he commented to his partner.

LeCleur was tired from work and looking forward to
a good night's sleep. It had been a busy day. "I don't believe it would've mattered. I think they would have gone
anyway. Besides, such an offer would have constituted
unsupported interference with native ritual. Expressly
forbidden by Church protocols."

Bowman nodded. "You check the systems?"

His friend smiled. "Everything's working normally.
Wake-up alarm the same time tomorrow?"

Bowman shrugged. "Works for me." He spared a final
glance for the heaving, rippling sea of brown. "They'll
still be here. How long you estimate it will take them to
move on through?"

LeCleur considered. "Depends how widespread the
migration is." Raising a hand, he pointed. "Check that
out."

So dense had the swarm become that a number of the
muffins at its edge were being jostled off into the ravine.
The protective excavation that ringed the station was
ten meters deep, with walls that had been heat-sealed to
an unclimbable slickness. A spider would have had trouble ascending those artificial precipices. The agents re-
tired, grateful for the outpost soundproofing that shut
out all but the faintest trace of mass peeping.

The station AI's pleasant, synthesized female voice
woke Bowman slightly before his partner.

"Wha . . . ?" he mumbled. "What's going on?"

"Perimeter violation," the outpost AI replied, in the same tone of voice it used to announce when a tridee recording was winding up or when mechanical food pre-prep had been completed. "You are advised to observe and respond."

"Observe and respond, hell!" Bowman bawled as he struggled into an upright position. Save for the dim light provided by widely spaced night illuminators, it was dark in his room. "What time is it, anyway?"

"Four AM, corrected Hedris time." The outpost voice was not abashed by this pronouncement.

Muttering under his breath, Bowman shoved himself into shorts and shirt. LeCleur was waiting for him in the hall.

"I don't know. I just got out of bed myself," he mumbled in response to his partner's querulous gaze.

As they made their way toward outpost central, Bowman queried the AI. "What kind of perimeter violation? Elaborate."

"Why don't you just look outside?" soft artificial tones responded. "I have activated the external lights."

Both men headed for the main entrance. As soon as the door opened, Bowman had to shield his eyes against the artificial brightness. LeCleur's vision adjusted faster. What he exclaimed was not scientific, but it was certainly colorful.

Bathed in the bright automated beams positioned atop the roof of the outpost was a Dantean vision of glaring red eyes, gnashing teeth, and spattering blood; a boiling brown stew of muffins whole, bleeding, dismembered, and scrambling with their two tiny legs for a foothold among their seething brethren. Presumably the rest of the darkened plain concealed a similar vision straight out of Hell. Presumably, because the astounded agents could not see it. Their view was blocked by the tens of thousands of dead, dying, and feverish muffins that had filled the outpost-encircling ravine to the brim with their bodies. At the same time, the reason for the transformation in the aliens' dentition was immediately apparent.

Having consumed everything green that grew on the plains, they had turned to eating flesh. And one another.

Bulging eyes flared, tiny feet kicked, razor-sharp teeth flashed and ripped. The curdling miasma of gore, eviscerated organs, and engorged muffin musk was overpowering. Rising above it all was the stench of cooked meat. Holding his hand over mouth and nose, LeCleur saw the reason why the outpost had awakened them.

Lining the interior wall of the artificial ravine was a double fence of waved air. Frenzied with instinct, the muffins were throwing themselves heedlessly into the lethal barrier, moving always in a southeasterly direction. The instant it contacted the electrically waved air, a scrambling muffin body was immediately electrocuted. As was the one following behind it, and the next, and the next. In their dozens, in their hundreds, their wee corpses were piling up at such a rate that those advancing from behind would soon be able to stumble unhindered into the compound. Those that did not pause to feast on the bodies of their own dead, that is.

"I think we'd better get inside and lock down until this is over," LeCleur murmured quietly as he stood surveying the surging sea of southeastward-flowing carnage.

An angry Bowman was already heading for the master console. Though it held an unmistakable gruesome fascination, the migration would mean extra work for him and his partner. The perimeter fence would have to be repaired. Even with automated mechanical help it would take weeks to clear out and dispose of the tens of thousands of muffin corpses that had filled the ravine and turned it into a moat full of meat. They would have to do all that while keeping up with their regular work schedule. He was more than a little pissed.

Oh well, he calmed himself. From the first day they had occupied the outpost everything had gone so smoothly, Hedris had been so accommodating, that it would be churlish of him to gripe about one small, unforeseen difficulty. They would deal with it in the morning. Which was not that far off, he noted irritably. As soon as the greater part of the migration had passed them by or settled down to a more manageable frenzy, he and LeCleur could retire for an extended rest and leave the cleaning up to the station's automatics. Surely, despite the muffins' numbers, such furious activity could not be sustained for more than a day or two.

His lack of concern stemmed from detailed knowledge of the station's construction. It had been designed and built to handle and ride out anything from four-hundred-kilometer-an-hour winds to temperatures down to 150 below and the same above. The prefab duralloy walls and metallic glass ports were impervious to windblown grit, flying acid, ordinary laser cutters, micrometeorites up to a diameter of two centimeters, and solid stone avalanches. The interior was sealed against smoke, toxic gases, volcanic emissions, and flash floods of water, liquid methane, and anything else a planet could puke up.

Moving to a port, he watched as the first wave of migrating muffins to crest the wave fence raced toward the now impervious sealed structure. Their small feet, adapted for running and darting about on the flat plains, did not allow them to climb very well, but before long, sufficient dead and dying bodies had piled high enough against the northwest side of the outpost to reach the lower edge of the port. Raging, berserk little faces gazed hungrily in at him. Radically transformed teeth gnawed and bit at the window, their frantic scrabbling sounds penetrating only faintly. They were unable even to scratch the high-tech transparency. He watched as dozens of muffins smothered one another in their driven desire to sustain their southeasterly progress, stared as tiny teeth snapped and broke off in futile attempts to penetrate the glass and get at the food within.

LeCleur made breakfast, taking more time than usual. The sun was rising, casting its familiar benign light over a panorama of devastation and death the two team members could not have imagined at the height of the worst day they had experienced in the past seven halcyon, pastoral months. As for the migration itself, it gave no indication of abating, or even of slowing down.

"I don't care how many millions of muffins there are inhabiting this part of the planet." Seated on the far side of the table, LeCleur betrayed an uncharacteristic nervousness no doubt worsened by a lack of sleep. "It has to slow down soon."

Bowman nodded absently. He ate mechanically, without his usual delight in the other man's cooking. "It's pitiful, watching the little critters asphyxiate themselves like this, and then resort to feeding on one another's corpses." He remembered cuddling and taking the measurements of baby muffins while others looked on, curious but only mildly agitated, peeping querulously. Now that peeping had risen to a tyrannical, pestilential drone not even the outpost's soundproofing could mute entirely.

"It's not pitiful to me." Eyes swollen from sleeplessness, LeCleur scratched his right leg where he had been assaulted earlier. "You didn't get bit."

Holding his coffee, Bowman glanced to his right, in the direction of the nearest port. Instruments told them the sun was up. They could not confirm it directly because every port was now completely blocked by an unmoving mass of accumulated muffin cadavers.

Still, both men were capable of surprise when the voice of the outpost AI announced later that evening that it was switching over to canned air. Neither man had to ask why, though Bowman did so, just to confirm.

The station was now completely buried beneath a growing mountain of dead muffins. Their accumulated tiny bodies had blocked every one of the shielded air intakes.

The men were still more aggravated than worried. They had enough bottled air for weeks, along with ample food, and they could recycle their wastewater. In an emergency, the station was almost as self-sufficient a closed system as a starship, though quite immobile. Their only real regret was the absence of information, since the swarming bodies now also obstructed all the outpost's external sensors.

Three days later a frustrated LeCleur suggested cracking one of the doors to see if the migration had finally run its course. Bowman was less taken with the idea.

"What if it's not?" he argued.

"Then we hit the emergency door close. That'll shut it by itself. How else are we going to tell if the migration's finally moved on and passed us by?" He gestured broadly. "Until we can get up top with some of the cleaning gear and clear off the bodies, we're sitting blind in here."

"I know." Bowman found himself succumbing to his partner's enticing logic. Not that his own objections were vociferous. He knew they would have to have a look outside sooner or later. He just was not enthusiastic about the idea. "I don't like the thought of letting any of the little monsters get inside."

"Who would?" LeCleur's expression was grim. "We'll draw a couple of rifles from stores and be ready when the door opens, even though the only thing that's likely to spill in are dead bodies. Remember, the live muffins are all up top, migrating southeastward. They're traveling atop the ones that've been suffocated."

Bowman nodded. LeCleur was right, of course. They had nothing to fear from the thousands of compressed muffins that now formed a cocoon enclosing the outpost. And if anything living presented itself at the open door, the automatic hinges would slam the barrier shut at a word from either man. They would not have to go near it.

With a nod, Bowman rose from the table. After months of freely roaming the plains and rivers beyond the outpost, he was sick and tired of being cooped up inside the darkened station. "Right. We'll take it slow and careful, but we have to see what's going on out there."

"Migration's probably been over and done with for days, and we've been wasting our time squatting in here, whining about it."

The rifles fired needle-packed shells specifically designed to stop dangerous small animals in their tracks. The spray pattern that resulted subsequent to triggering meant that those wielding the weapons did not have to focus precisely on a target. Aiming the muzzles of the guns in the approximate direction would be sufficient to ensure the demise of any creature in the general vicinity of the burst. It was not an elegant weapon, but it was effective. Though they had been carried on field trips away from the outpost by Bowman and LeCleur as protection against endemic carnivores both known and unknown, neither man had yet been compelled to fire one of the versatile weapons in anger. As they positioned themselves five meters from the front door, Bowman hoped they would be able to maintain that record of non-use.

Responding to a curt nod from his partner signifying that he was in position and ready, LeCleur gave the command to open the door exactly five centimeters. Rifles raised, they waited to see what would materialize in response.

Seals releasing, the door swung inward slightly. Into the room poured a stench of rotting, decaying flesh that the outpost's atmospheric scrubbers promptly whirred to life to neutralize. A column of solid brown revealed itself between door and reinforced jamb. Half a dozen or so crushed muffin corpses fell into the room. Several exhibited signs of having been partially consumed.

After a glance at his partner, LeCleur uttered a second command. Neither man had lowered the muzzle of his weapon. The door resumed opening. More small, smashed bodies spilled from the dike of tiny carcasses to build a small sad mound at its base. The stink grew worse, but not unbearably so. From floor to lintel, the doorway was blocked with dead muffins.

Lowering his rifle, Bowman moved forward, bending to examine several of the bodies that had tumbled into the room. Some had clearly been dead much longer than others. Not one so much as twitched a leg.

"Poor little bastards. I wonder how often this migration takes place?"

"Often enough for population control." LeCleur was standing alongside his partner, the unused rifle now dangling from one hand. "We always wondered why the muffins didn't overrun the whole planet. Now we know. They regulate their own numbers. Probably store up sufficient fat and energy from cannibalizing themselves during migration to survive until the grasses can regenerate themselves.

"We need to record the full cycle: duration of migration, variation by continent and specific locale, influencing variables such as weather and availability of water, and so on. This is important stuff." He grinned. "Can you imagine trying to run a grain farm here under these conditions? I know that's one of the operations the company had in mind for this place."

Bowman nodded thoughtfully. "It could be done. This is just a primary outpost. Armed with the right information and equipment, I don't see why properly prepared colonists can't handle something even as expansive as this mass migration."

LeCleur agreed. That was when the wall of cadavers exploded in their faces. Or rather, its center did.

Continuing to sense the presence of live food beyond the door, the muffins had swiftly dug a tunnel through their own dead to get at it. As they came pouring into the room, Bowman and LeCleur commenced firing frantically. Hundreds of tiny needles bloomed from dozens of shells as the rapid-fire rifles took their toll on the rampaging intruders. Dozens, hundreds, of red-eyed, onrushing muffins perished in the storm of needles, their diminutive bodies shredded beyond recognition. A frantic LeCleur screamed the command to close the door, and the outpost did its best to comply. Unfortunately, a combination of deceased muffins and live muffins had now filled the gap. Many died as they were crushed between the heavy-duty hinges as the door swung closed. But—it did not, could not, shut all the way.

A river of ravenous brown flowed into the room, swarming over chairs and tables, knocking over equipment, snapping and biting at everything and anything within reach, including one another. Above the fermenting chaos rose a single horrific, repetitive, incessant sound.

PEEP PEEP PEEP PEEP . . . !

"The storeroom!" Firing as fast as he could pull the trigger, heedless of the damage to the installation stray needle-shells might be doing, Bowman retreated as fast as he could. He glanced down repeatedly. Trip and fall here, now, and he would disappear beneath a tsunami of teeth and tiny clawing feet. LeCleur was right behind him.

Stumbling into the main storeroom, they shut the door manually, neither man wanting to take the time to issue the necessary command to the omnipresent outpost pickups. Besides, they didn't know if the station voice would respond anymore. In their swarming, the muffins had already shorted out a brace of unshielded, sensitive equipment.

The agents backed away from the door as dozens of tiny thudding sounds reached them from the other side. The storeroom was the station's most solidly constructed internal module, but its door was not made of duralloy like the exterior walls. Would it hold up against the remorseless, concerted assault? And if so, for how long?

Then the lights went out.

"They've ripped up or shorted internal connectors," Bowman commented unnecessarily. Being forced to listen to the rapid-fire pounding on the other side of the door and not being able to do anything about it was nerve-racking enough. Having to endure it in the dark was ten times worse.

There was food in the storeroom in the form of concentrates, and bottled water to drink. They would live, LeCleur reflected—at least until the air was cut off, or the climate control shut down.

Bowman was contemplating a raft of similar unpleasant possibilities. "How many shells you have left, Gerard?"

The other man checked the illuminated readout on the side of his rifle. It was the only light in the sealed storeroom. "Five." When preparing to open the front door, neither man had, reasonably enough at the time, considered it necessary to pocket extra ammunition. "You?"

His partner's reply was glum. "Three. We're not going to shoot our way out of here."

Trying to find some kind of light in the darkness,

LeCleur commented as calmly as he could manage, "The door seems to be holding."

"Small teeth." Bowman was surprised to note that his voice was trembling slightly.

"Too many teeth." Feeling around in the darkness, LeCleur located a solid container and sat down, cradling the rifle across his legs. He discovered that he was really thirsty, and tried not to think about it. They would feel around for the food and water containers later, after the thudding against the door had stopped. Assuming it would.

"Maybe they'll get bored and go away," he ventured hopefully.

Bowman tried to find some confidence in the dark. "Maybe instinct will overpower hunger and they'll resume the migration. All we have to do is wait them out."

"Yeah." LeCleur grunted softly. "That's all." After several moments of silence broken only by the steady thump-thumping against the door, he added, "Opening up was a dumb idea."

"No, it wasn't," Bowman contended. "We just didn't execute smartly. After the first minute, we assumed everything was all right and we relaxed."

LeCleur shifted his position on his container. "That's a mistake that won't be repeated, but it doesn't matter. I don't care how benign the situation appears—I'll never be able to relax on this world again."

"I hope we'll both have the opportunity not to." Bowman's fingers fidgeted against the trigger of the rifle.

Eventually they found the water and the food. The latter tasted awful without machine pre-prep, but the powder was filling and nourishing. Unwilling to go to sleep and unable to stay awake, their exhausted bodies finally forced them into unconsciousness.

LeCleur sat up sharply in the darkness, the hard length of the rifle threatening to slip off his chest until he grabbed it to keep it from falling. He listened intently for a long, long moment before whispering loudly.

"Jamie. Jamie, wake up!"

"Huh? Wuzzat . . . ?" In the dim light provided by the illuminated rifle gauge, the other man bestirred himself.

"Listen." Licking his lips, LeCleur slid off the pile of containers on which he had been sleeping. His field shorts squeaked sharply against the smooth polyastic.

Bowman said nothing. It was silent in the storeroom. More significantly, it was equally silent on the other side of the door. The two men huddled together, the faces barely discernible in the feeble glow of the gauge lights.

"What do we do now?" LeCleur kept glancing at the darkened door.

Bowman considered the situation as purposefully as his sore back and unsatisfied belly would permit. "We can't stay cooped up in here forever." He hesitated. "Anyway, I'd rather go down fighting than suffocate when the air goes out or is cut off."

LeCleur nodded reluctantly. "Who's first?"

"I'll do it." Bowman took a deep breath, the soft wheeze of inbound air echoing abnormally loud in the darkness. "Cover me as best you can."

His partner nodded and raised the rifle. Positioning himself at the most efficacious angle to the door, he waited silently. In the darkness, he could hear his own heart pounding.

Holding his weapon tightly in his left hand, Bowman undid the seals. They clicked like the final ticks of his internal clock counting down the remainder of his life. Light and fresher air entered the room as the door swung inward. Exhaling softly, Bowman opened it farther. No minuscule brown demons flew at his face, no nipping tiny teeth assailed his ankles. Taking a deep breath, he wrenched sharply on the door and leaped back, raising the muzzle of his weapon as the badly dented barrier pivoted inward. Light from the interior of the station made him blink repeatedly.

It was silent inside the outpost. A ridge of dead muffins nearly a meter high was piled up against the door. None of the little horrors moved. Rifles held at the ready, the two men emerged from the storeroom.

Light poured down from the overheads. They still had power. The interior of the outpost was rancid with tiny cadavers. There were dead muffins everywhere: on the dining table, in opened storage cabinets, under benches, beneath exposed supplies, and all over the kitchen area. They were crammed impossibly tightly together in corners, in the living quarters, on shelves. Their flattened, furry, motionless bodies had clogged the food prep area and the toilets, filled the showers and every empty container and tube.

Bright daylight poured in through the still-open front door. Scavengers, or wind, or marauding muffins had reduced the avalanche of dead creatures on the porch to the same height of a meter that had accumulated against the storeroom portal. The exhausted agents could go outside, if they wished. After weeks of unending peep-peeping, the ensuing silence was loud enough to hurt Bowman's ears.

"It's over." LeCleur was scraping dead muffins off the kitchen table. "How about some tea and coffee? If I can get any of the appliances to work, that is."

Setting his rifle aside, Bowman slumped into a chair and dropped his head onto his crossed forearms. "I don't give a damn what it is or if it's ice cold. Right now my throat will take anything."

Nodding, LeCleur waded through dunes of dead muffins and began a struggle to coax the beverage maker to life. Every so often he would pause to shove or throw dead muffins out of his way, not caring where they landed. The awful smell was little better, but by now the agents' stressed systems had come to tolerate it without comment.

A large, mobile shape came gliding through the gaping front door.

Forgetting the beverage maker, LeCleur threw himself toward where he had left his rifle standing against a counter. Bowman reached for his own weapon, caught one leg against the chair on which he was sitting, and crashed to the floor with the chair tangled up in his legs.

Gripping his staff, Old Malakotee paused to stare at them both. "You alive. I surprised." His alien gaze swept the room, taking in the thousands of deceased muffins, the destruction of property, and the stench. "Very surprised. But glad."

"So are we." Untangling himself from the chair, a chagrined Bowman rose to greet their visitor. "Both of those things: surprised and glad. What are you doing back here?"

"I know!" A wide smile broke out on the jubilant LeCleur's face: the first smile of any kind he had shown for days. "It's over. The migration's over, and the Akoe have come back!"

Old Malakotee regarded the exultant human somberly. "The migration not over, skyman Le'leur. It still continue." He turned to regard the confused Bowman. "But we like you people. I tell my tribe: We must try to help." He gestured outside. Leaning to look, both men could see a small knot of Akoe males standing and waiting in the stinking sunshine. They looked healthy, but uneasy. Their postures were alert, their gazes wary.

"You come with us now." The elder gestured energetically. "Not much time. Akoe help you."

"It's okay." Bowman gestured to take in their surroundings. "We'll clear all this out. We have machines to help us. You'll see. In a week or two everything here will be cleaned up and back to normal. Then you can visit us again, and try our food and drink as you did before, and we can talk."

The agent was feeling expansive. They had suffered through everything the muffin migration could throw at them, and had survived. Next time, maybe next year, the larger, better-equipped team that would arrive to relieve them would be properly informed of the danger and could prepare itself appropriately to deal with it. What he and LeCleur had endured was just one more consequence of being the primary survey and sampling team on a new world. It came with the job.

"Not visit!" Old Malakotee was emphatic. "You come with us now! Akoe protect you, show you how to survive migration. Go to deep caves and hide."

LeCleur joined in. "We don't have to hide, Malakotee. Not anymore. Even if the migration's not over, the bulk of it has clearly passed this place by."

"Juvenile migration passed." Stepping back, Old Malakotee eyed them flatly. Outside, the younger Akoe were already clamoring to leave. "Now adults come."

Bowman blinked, uncertain he had heard correctly. "Adults?" He looked back at LeCleur, whose expression reflected the same bewilderment his partner was feeling. "But—the muffins." He kicked at the half a dozen quiescent bodies scattered around his feet. "These aren't the adult forms?"

"They juveniles." Malakotee stared at him unblinkingly. His somber demeanor was assurance enough this was not a joke.

"Then if every muffin we've been seeing these past seven months has been a juvenile or an infant . . ." LeCleur was licking his lips nervously. "Where are the adults?"

The native tapped the floor with the butt of his staff. "In ground. Hibernating." Bowman struggled to get the meaning of the alien words right. "Growing. Once a year, come out."

The agent swallowed. "They come out—and then what?"

Old Malakotee's alien gaze met that of the human. "They migrate." Raising a multifingered hand, he pointed. To the southeast. "That way."

"No wonder." LeCleur was murmuring softly. "No wonder the juvenile muffins flee in such a frenzy. We've already seen that the species is cannibalistic. If the juveniles eat one another, then the adults . . ." His voice trailed off.

"I take it," Bowman inquired of the native, surprised at how calm his voice had become, "that the adults are a little bigger than the juveniles?"

Old Malakotee made the Akoe gesture signifying concurrence. "*Much* bigger. Also hungrier. Been in ground long, long time. Very hungry when come out." He started toward the doorway. "Must go quickly now. You come—or stay."

Weak from fatigue, Bowman turned to consider the interior of the outpost: the ruined instrumentation, the devastated equipment, the masses of dead muffins. Juvenile muffins, he reminded himself. He contemplated the havoc they had wrought. What would the adults be like? Bigger, Old Malakotee had told them. Bigger and hungrier. But not, he told himself, necessarily cuter.

Outside, the little band of intrepid Akoe was already moving off, heading at a steady lope for the muffin-bridged ravine, their tails switching rhythmically behind them. Standing at the door, Bowman and LeCleur watched them go. What would the temperature in the deep caves to the northwest be like? How long could they survive on Akoe food? Could they even keep up with the well-conditioned, fast-moving aliens, who were, in their element, running for days on end over the grassy plains? The two men exchanged a glance. At least they had a choice. Didn't they? Well, didn't they?

Beneath their feet, something moved. The ground quivered, ever so slightly.

Chauna

"*What do you give the man who has everything?*"

It's a phrase you hear constantly at gift-giving time: birthdays, holidays, special occasions. To me the answer always seemed relatively simple and straightforward: ask him.

With the very rich and powerful, the reply is apt to b? predictable: more. More of everything. More wealth, more control, more toys, more possessions. And most especially, more than the next guy. The typical billionaire's wishes are fundamental enough to border on the jejune. If the other guy has a hundred-foot yacht, you want a hundred-meter yacht. If his is bigger than a hundred meters, you have to have one with a helicopter, or a private submersible, or a Michelin-blessed chef concocting five-star meals in the galley.

But what if there were a truly wealthy and powerful dreamer or two whose imaginings vaulted beyond the merely materialistic and puerile? What if there were an individual whose dreams matched his bank account? What might he seek? Would it be possible that he might even read science fiction, and have science-fiction dreams? What if he determined to put all his vast wealth and power at the disposal of those who might help him to fulfill such a yearning, even at the risk of being laughed at?

It takes a strong billionaire indeed who can stand being laughed at.

Carl Sagan's Contact *is one of the best books (and movies) about science and what motivates scientists. For most viewers of the film, the most sympathetic character was that of Jodie Foster's Dr. Ellie Arroway. While I empathized fully with her hunger for knowledge, the individual I most strongly sympathized with was that of the reclusive, Howard Hughes–like billionaire S. R. Hadden (a sly and knowing John Hurt), who desperately wanted to take her place for that first contact with intelligent alien life, but whose failing health allowed him only to finance such an endeavor and not participate in it. Though few and far between, such people are not isolated examples.*

Even billionaires can have dreams.

"Mr. Bastrop, sir—we're looking for something that doesn't exist."

Slowly, painfully, Gibeon Bastrop lifted his gaze to meet that of the master of the *Seraphim*. It was a gaze that had once struck those upon whom it had fallen with awe or fear, envy or unbounded admiration or a host of other strong emotions. Nowadays it most often inspired only pity. Inwardly, Gibeon Bastrop raged. He could only do so inwardly. It had been nearly two decades since he had been physically capable of expressing extremes of emotion.

He was not even sure how much of him was original Gibeon Bastrop anymore. So many parts had been replaced; cloned, regrown from his own reluctant tissues, or, where necessary, replaced with synthetics. The brain was still all Gibeon Bastrop, he felt, though even there the physicians and engineers had been forced to tweak and adjust and modify to keep everything functioning properly. They were very good at their work. Gibeon Bastrop could afford the best. If you couldn't, you were unlikely to live to be 162—next April, Bastrop mused. Or was it May?

"Mr. Bastrop?"

"What?" It was Tyrone, badgering him again. Always wanting to give up, that Tyrone. Give up, turn around—although they were so far out now that *around* no longer had any real meaning—and go home. A fine Shipmaster, Tyrone, but easily discouraged. How long had they been searching now? Barely two years, wasn't it? The youth of today had no patience, Bastrop reflected. None at all. Why, Tyrone was barely in his eighties, far too young to be complaining about time. Let him reach triple digits; these days, you had to earn the right to complain.

"Mr. Bastrop." Contrary to the owner's belief, the Shipmaster possessed considerable patience. He was exercising some of it now. "The Chauna doesn't exist. It's bad enough to take us chasing after a fairy story—but an *alien* fairy story?"

"It is not a fairy story." Gibeon Bastrop might no longer be capable of raging, but he could still be adamant. "The Cosocagglia are insistent on that point."

Shipmaster Tyrone sighed. Outside, beyond the great convex port that fronted on Gibeon Bastrop's ornate stateroom, stars and nebulae gleamed in other-than-light profusion. There wasn't a one among them the Shipmaster recognized, and he had been journeying among the starways for more than half a century. The Old Man was taking them farther and farther into the void, closer and closer to nowhere.

"The Cosocagglia are an ancient species existing in a state of advanced decline. Now if the Vuudd, or even the redoubtable Paquinq, had vouchsafed the existence of the mythical Chauna, I would be more inclined to grant the remote possibility of its existence." He smiled in what he hoped was a sympathetic manner. "But the Cosocagglia?"

Gibeon Bastrop's voice dropped to a mutter. He was tired, even more so than usual. "The Cosocagglia were a great race."

"Once." Tyrone was no longer in any mood to coddle his employer. Like the rest of the crew, he had been too long away from home, was too much in need of blue skies and unrecycled air. "That was tens of thousands of years ago." He sniffed scornfully. "They no longer even go into space. They have forgotten how, and travel between worlds only when they can book or beg passage on a ship of one of the younger species, like the Helappo or ourselves. They have hundreds of legends from those days. The Chauna is just one of many."

He felt sorry for the Old Man, marooned in his motile, no longer able to stand erect even with the aid of neurorganetics. For a hundred years, the name of Gibeon Bastrop had been one to be reckoned with throughout the sapient portion of the galaxy. Inventor, engineer, industrialist, megamogul; his influence and his fame were known even on nonhuman worlds. Now he was a shadow of the self he had been, mentally debased, poor at advanced cogitation, unable to survive more than a few days at a time without an immoderate amount of medicinal attention. The medical provisions and personnel he had brought with him on the *Seraphim* could have equipped a hospital sufficient to serve a good-sized conurbation. It was all for him. Everything and everyone on the ship existed to keep Gibeon Bastrop functioning and his every need looked after.

What must it be like, the Shipmaster mused, to live out your last days knowing that being the richest human alive no longer meant anything?

"The Chauna is not a fancy!" Gibeon Bastrop pounded

the arm of his motile with suddenly surprising strength. "The Chauna is real!"

"Far more so the people on board this ship, sir. They have lives, too. And families, and careers, and needs and desires. All of which they have left behind so that you could follow this whim of yours."

"They are being well-paid to do so."

"Extremely well-paid." Tyrone was willing, as always, to concede the obvious. "But I'm afraid that's no longer enough, sir." Taking a step forward, he gestured at the port and the magnificence of the drive-distorted starfield. "They've been away from home for too long. We're not talking a month or two. Almost two years in Void is enough to drive anyone crazy."

The hoverchair hummed softly as Bastrop pivoted to face the same sweeping galactic panorama. "I haven't changed—but then, you all think I was insane when I began this expedition. Why should you think differently of me now?"

The Shipmaster's tone was kindly. Like nearly every other member of the crew, he genuinely liked the Old Man. It was Bastrop's obsession that was hated, not the individual behind it. Nor was great wealth, as is so often the case, an issue. Gibeon Bastrop was admired for starting from nothing and making his mammoth fortune through the astute application of genius and plain hard work.

"We don't think you're crazy, Mr. Bastrop. Just in thrall to a falsehood."

Gibeon Bastrop looked up at the younger man. "Is that a crime?"

"No sir," Tyrone replied patiently. "But you must realize that your obsession is not shared by your crew. Initial enthusiasm gave way to tolerance, then to grudging compliance, and most recently to exasperation. I have worked hard to keep it from progressing to the next step." He leaned toward the floating chair that kept Gibeon Bastrop not only mobile, but alive. "Word that we have finally struck for home would immediately alleviate any potential problem and eliminate tension among discontented personnel."

Bastrop nodded thoughtfully. Even his enfeebled voice, when he replied, was one that could still command fleets and minions. "We've come to find the Chauna. We will search until we do so."

Tyrone's lips tightened. His response was devoid of insolence, but firm. "At the risk of voicing a cliché, sir, money can't buy everything. It can't buy you people."

"No, but it can damn well rent them for me," Bastrop declared with knowing confidence.

"It can't buy you a myth."

"That remains to be seen. You are dismissed, Mr. Tyrone."

The Shipmaster nodded imperceptibly and bowed out. Wakoma and Surat were waiting for him on the bridge.

"What did he say?" Surat was small and dynamic, like a puppy perpetually kept on a too-short leash. She was also the finest navigator Tyrone had ever worked with. "Did you make your point?" Her expression was no less eager than Wakoma's.

"I made it." The Shipmaster brushed past them. "And he ignored it. Stand by for downslip." He settled into place in front of his bank of readouts.

Crestfallen but hardly surprised, the two seconds in command parted, each to their own station. Tyrone's words meant that more weeks, maybe months, of pointless wandering lay before them. Like the rest of the crew, they were beyond homesick. If this kept up, the *home* portion of their condition would begin to slough away for real.

"Maybe he'll die." Wakoma struggled to concentrate

on his work. Like everyone else on board the *Seraphim,* he was an exceedingly competent professional.

"Not likely." The tech seated alongside him kept his voice down. "There's enough advanced medical technology on this ship to allow an amoeba to operate a *torkue* projector. With the medics caressing his carcass twenty-four seven, I'll bet the old bastard's got another twenty years in him before he slides into complete senility."

The ship plunged out of OTL to emerge in the vicinity of Delta Avinis. It was the forty-third multiple-star system the *Seraphim* had visited since leaving home. According to the elaborate Cosocagglia mythology, the Chauna was only to be encountered in multiple-star systems. Why this should be, no one knew—not even the Cosocagglia themselves. It did not matter, Tyrone grumbled silently as coordinates were checked and confirmed, because there was no such thing as a Chauna. They might as well be searching single-star systems, or dark wanderers, or the ghostly gray silverstone spheres known as stuttering molters.

"Something beautiful." That was how the Cosocagglia legends identified the Chauna. A stellar phenomenon that was supposedly unsurpassingly beautiful. That was about all the fable had to say about it, too. Tyrone had seen the translations, laboriously performed by the xenologists who worked with nonhuman species, like the Cosocagglia. Where the Chauna was concerned the Cosocagglia could supply reams of adjectives but nothing in the way of specifics. A Chauna was no more, no less, than a beautiful thing.

They had encountered the phenomenon but rarely; a millennia ago, when the Cosocagglia had been in their prime: a youthful, expansionist, vital race. To see a Chauna, it was said, was to be blessed forever with knowledge of what real beauty was. Any individuals so

consecrated by the vision were held up to be the most
fortunate of travelers. But for all its supposed wonder,
there remained in the crumbled lore of the species not a
single description of the Chauna itself.

How exceptional could it be, anyway? Tyrone mused.
Even if it existed, it was hardly likely to be a previously
unobserved phenomenon. In the course of the past thousand years humankind had identified an enormous
range of stellar objects and events, from X-ray bursters
to miniature ambling pulsars to Möbius black holes.
Some were so esoteric, the always busy astrophysicists
had not found time to name them. Some were even
beautiful, like the tornadic nebulae and the gamma-ray
ropes. But none, according to the Cosocagglia who had
been shown imagings of them, were Chauna.

Delta Avinis was an impressive, but not unprecedented, double-star system. There were half a dozen
planets, all sere, all lifeless. Their orbits were erratic,
their gravitational grip on continued existence uncertain.

As soon as he was confident that downslip had been
finalized and that the system held no navigational sur-
prises, Tyrone rose from his seat, formally relinquished
control of the ship to Wakoma and Surat, and announced that he was going on sleeptime. Two months
ago such announcements by the Shipmaster had been
greeted with unified protest. Now people simply muttered to themselves in his absence. Everyone was too
tired to remonstrate loudly. Resigned to a seemingly in-
terminable fate, they had not yet decided what to do
about it, or what to do next. That eventuality might
manifest itself at the next star system, the Shipmaster
knew, or the one after that. He would keep things going
for as long as he could. It was part of his job.

Surat waited for several minutes until she was sure her

superior was gone before rising from her position. "I'm going to talk to Gibeon Bastrop."

One of those who served under her looked up in alarm. "Are you sure that's wise, Anna?"

The navigator shrugged slim shoulders. "What can the Old Man do—fire me? I'm not refusing to perform my duties. Maybe later, but not yet. Not today." Such a refusal, they both knew, could result in a hearing board denying recompense to the perpetrator. Angry and frustrated as they were, no one aboard the *Seraphim* wanted to sacrifice two years' accumulated pay in order to make a point.

No one challenged Surat as she made her way through the ship toward the Old Man's quarters. The *Seraphim* was a sizable vessel, with a crew of several hundred. Everyone was too busy or too apathetic to confront her. They knew they had arrived at yet another system. There was no sense of excitement, no joy of discovery. Next week, the procedure would be repeated. As it had been now for nearly twenty-four months. As it might be for another twenty-four. No one wanted to think about it.

Well, Anna Surat was thinking about it, and she intended to give full voice to her thoughts.

There were guards posted outside Bastrop's quarters. They had been there since Tyrone had mobilized them four months ago, when the first serious rumblings of discontent had begun to make themselves known among the crew. Everyone was aware that if Gibeon Bastrop died, his crazed quest across the cosmos would die with him, and they could all go home. No one had tried to hurry the process along—yet. Surat knew that they were hoping time and accumulating infirmities would do for them what none of them could do for themselves.

She was admitted without having to wait. Depending on his mood and health, Gibeon Bastrop liked company. Long journeys in Void were lonely matters at best.

She found him seated before his dog. At the moment, the obedient sphere was taking dictation. Bastrop pivoted his motile to greet her. As he did so he essayed the shadow of a smile. Once, that expression had charmed millions. Now it was all the Old Man could do to induce the muscles in his face to comply with the simple physical demand.

"You're looking well today, sir." The polite mantra fooled neither of them.

Bastrop waved the dog away. It drifted off to sulk in a corner, powering down as it did so. "I'm always up for a visit from an attractive woman, Anna Surat. To what do I owe the pleasure of your company?"

When was the last time he had a woman? she found herself wondering perversely. Does he even remember what it was like? So old—he was so old! If not for the dozens of doctors and billions of credits at his beck and call, he would have been dead thirty or forty years ago. Instead, he had bought himself an extra lifetime. And for what? So he could spend it like this, visibly decomposing in an expensive hospice motile that every month had to take over more and more of his own failing bodily functions? She resolved never to allow herself to be placed in such a situation. Not that she really needed to worry about it. She was about a hundred billion short of qualifying for that level of care.

"Mr. Bastrop, I know that Shipmaster Tyrone has been to see you . . ."

At her opening words his expression fell. His voice dropped to a raspy whisper. "Oh. That again. I was hoping . . ." His words trailed away.

Hoping what? she wondered. That I was coming for the pleasure of your selfish, semi-senile company? She forced herself to smile engagingly, wondering even as she did so if he was capable of responding to such gestures.

"You can't subject us to this any longer, Mr. Bastrop. It isn't reasonable. It isn't fair."

From the depths of memory the parchment-like substance that formed his face twisted into a semblance of a grin. "The search for beauty is never reasonable or fair, my dear. Being beautiful yourself, you should know that."

Damn him, she cursed silently. She had been determined that nothing the aged industrialist did was going to affect her. But even the shadow of that smile was capable of lighting something within her. It was no comfort to know that it had done likewise to thousands who had been subjected to it before her.

"You can't distract me with words, sir."

"Pity." He turned slightly away from her. "There was a time when I could have done so with a simple phrase. Long ago, that was."

Feeling sympathy in spite of herself, she advanced to rest a hand on his shoulder. Beneath the synsilk lay very little flesh and much narrow bone. The feel of it made her want to pull her hand away, but she did not.

"You are unloved here, sir. I realize you know that, and don't care. I can't change that. Not even you can change that." Her words came a little faster. "But by turning for home now you can regain their respect! You can finish this in a way that will be remembered with pride instead of animosity."

He turned back toward her. Not by pivoting the chair this time, but by making an actual uncommon physical effort to rotate the upper portion of his remaining body. "And what about you, Anna Surat? Do *you* hate me for what I've done?"

"No, Mr. Bastrop. I don't hate you. I just want to go home. I have a husband, you know. At least, I hope I still have a husband."

"You are a starship navigator. He knew what he was

getting into when he married you. Everyone knows. I've been married myself, so even if you think otherwise, I do understand. Outlived most of them." He shook his head slowly. "They were all comely, in their own way. But they were not the Chauna."

Surat knew she was out of line in speaking this way to her admittedly generous if stubborn employer, but the time for overindulgence was past. "*Nothing* is the Chauna, Mr. Bastrop! They say that you were once the smartest man in the galaxy. What happened to that person? Did he—?"

"Get senile?" Gibeon Bastrop chuckled. "I don't think so—but then if I was, I wouldn't know it, would I? I don't think the pursuit of ultimate beauty stamps me as mad, Anna. I think it marks me as sane. Saner than most, I should say. Ultimately, what else is there but beauty? Beauty of discovery, beauty of thought, beauty of soul. It's one thing I've never been able to buy, navigator. Now it is all I want. The last thing I want. No other human being has seen it. We will be the first."

"Many myths are highly attractive, Mr. Bastrop. Seductive, even. But in the end they're only myths. Isn't the loveliness of legend enough? Can't you leave it at that?"

"Maybe the Chauna is a world, Anna Surat. Have you thought of that?" Excitement danced in eyes that had been thrice replaced. "A world so wonderful even the Cosocagglia have no words for it. Can you imagine the reaction such a discovery would trigger? A world even more captivating than Earth, empty and waiting for us. Or maybe it's a gas giant with multiple rings that glow like gold in the light of triple suns. But most likely it's something we cannot imagine."

"Neither can the Cosocagglia," she responded, "because it doesn't exist. Anything of absolute beauty has to be imaginary, or it ceases to be exceptional and becomes just one more item in the always expanding stellar pantheon."

He started to reply, stopped, and began to wheeze softly. She ought to call somebody, she knew. She ought to summon help. Instead, loathing her deliberate inaction, she stood and watched, silent and hopeful. No such luck. The hospice motile did things with tubes and probes, and in less than a couple of minutes the Old Man was breathing normally again. Shallow, but normal.

"That was unpleasant." His eyes met hers. "You really think I'm being unreasonable, Anna Surat? To want, after more than a century and a half, this one last thing? To view beauty that no one else has seen?"

Her attitude softened. He was working his wiles on her, she knew. A hundred years of practice gives a man certain skills. But she could only be manipulated to a limited degree.

"No, Mr. Bastrop. It's not unreasonable to want such a thing. But it is unreasonable to want to see that which does not exist. If you would only—"

A voice entered the room via an unseen synthetic orifice. "Mr. Gibeon Bastrop. Mr. Gibeon Bastrop, sir!" She recognized Tyrone's commanding tones. What was he doing awake? Sleeptime was precious to every crewmember, from the lowliest to the Shipmaster. What had wrenched him back to alertness? "Are you awake?"

She responded for him. "Yes, he's awake."

"Navigator Surat? What are you . . . ? Never mind. Mr. Bastrop, I'm rotating the *Seraphim* on her axis. Look to your port and viewers."

"Why?" The transformation that abruptly overcame the Old Man was astonishing to behold. Suddenly he looked barely a hundred. "What's happening?"

"Something—we're not sure, sir. An energetic transmutation of a level—Berkowski and her people are working on an analysis, but the field changes and fluctuations are—"

The Shipmaster broke off. Perhaps he was too busy to continue. Or perhaps he was simply, like everyone else on board the *Seraphim* who was at that moment in a position to view the event, too overwhelmed to continue.

The enormous expanse of the two-story-high port polarized automatically as the twin suns of Delta Avinis revolved into view. Nearby, one of the dead planets that orbited the twin stars took a shadowed, heavily cratered bite out of Void. Anna wondered at the Shipmaster's words until the second, lesser sun slowly hove into view. Then she pointed and her lips moved slowly.

"Oh! Look at it. Just *look* at it!"

Gibeon Bastrop had displaced the hoverchair forward until it could no longer advance. It was right up against the port, pressing against the thick transparency. Had Bastrop been able to continue, the navigator had no doubt he would have done so, right out into the vacuum of space itself.

"Look at what, Anna Surat? At that? At the Chauna?"

Something had materialized *between* the two suns. Hitherto invisible, the extraordinary ephemeral shape was rapidly becoming visible as it drew energy from the nearest star. One gigantic jet of roiling plasma after another burst from the surface of the smaller sun to be drawn across many AUs into the larger. Each jet was several hundred times the diameter of the Earth, infinitely longer, with an internal temperature rated in the thousands of degrees Celsius.

And each time a violent, spasming plasma jet erupted between the two stars, a portion of it illuminated the Chauna. The legend of the Cosocagglia was not a wandering planet, or a lost ship of profound dimensions, or a streak of natural phenomena as yet unidentified by science. It was at once something less, and much, much more.

"My God," Anna Surat whispered in awe, "it's alive!"

There were two wings, each ablaze with lambent energies of wavelengths as yet unidentified. They rippled and flamed across the firmament, faint but unmistakable, like bands of energized nebulae ripped loose from their primary cloud. Nearby stars were clearly visible through them, but they were substantial enough to hold color. With each massive emission from the smaller star, the Chauna partook a little of the enormous energies that were passing between the two suns. The central portion of the event—creature? spirit?—was sleek and slightly less pellucid than the wings. No other features were visible: no limbs, no face, no projections of any kind. No other features were necessary.

"It looks," an awestruck Anna observed almost inaudibly, "like a butterfly. But what's going on? What is it doing?" She had to strain to make out the Old Man's reply.

"It's feeding, Anna. Though it's millions of kilometers across, it's too fragile a structure to pull energy from a star itself. So it waits for one star to move near enough to another, for all that great deep gravity to do the job for it. When it senses what's going to happen, it places itself between the two and filters what it needs from the fleeting eruptions of plasma, like a great whale feeding on plankton. Neutrinos, cosmic rays, charged particles—who knows what it ingests and what it ignores? How would you, how could you possibly study such an entity? We can only watch and marvel. In the process, it apparently acquires throughout the length and breadth of its otherwise imperceptible substance a little ancillary coloration."

"A little!" The tenuous but vast extent of the Chauna was already greater than both suns. She continued to stare—what else could one do?—even as the *Seraphim*'s

instruments methodically registered the immense strength
of the repeated solar outbursts while her screens fought to
shield her frail, vulnerable, minuscule organic occupants
from the effects of all that energy being blasted into space.

On other worlds, instruments would register the
pulsar-like outburst and place it in the accepted category
of celestial disturbances. They would not note the presence of a third object drawing upon a tiny portion of the
expelled energies. Though of unimaginable size, that object was far too ephemeral to be perceived by distant instruments.

The feeding of the Chauna was an infrequent event, or
it would have been noticed before. The Cosocagglia had
noticed it, in their thousands of years of space-faring.
Now it was, at last, the turn of humans to do so. The
myth had been made real. And it was a discovery that
could be shared and supported. The *Seraphim*'s battery
of recorders would see to that.

When those incredibly attenuated sun-sized wings
moved, there was a collective gasp among the crew of
the witnessing vessel. Nothing like a Chauna had ever
been seen before, and nothing like a Chauna in motion
had ever been imagined. It was beyond imagining, past
belief, a magnificent violation of established astrophysi-
cal doctrine. With that movement, no one questioned
any longer if the phenomenon was alive. It was visible
for another minute or two, a colossal undulation of energized color rippling against the starfield, a million billion times vaster than any aurora. Then it was gone, the
life sustaining solar energy it had assimilated dispersed
throughout its incomprehensibly vast incorporeality.

For a long time the navigator stood staring out the
lofty port, aware she had been witness to one of the
greatest sights—if not *the* greatest sight—the galaxy had
yet placed before a captivated humankind. Then she was
reminded that her hand was still resting on the sharp

shoulder of the man who had made it possible for her to experience the inconceivable wonder. The man who had insisted it was real, that it existed, and that if they persisted long enough and looked hard enough, the tiny wandering creatures called humans might actually be able to descry such a marvel. Who had insisted despite the protests and disapproval of his fellows.

Suddenly she understood a little of what had made Gibeon Bastrop the singular individual he was. Suddenly she understood something of the source of his remarkable ability and drive and power. It made her wish she could have known the *man,* and not simply the pitifully weakened and aged husk that presently occupied the motile.

"You were right, Mr. Bastrop. You were right all along. You and the Cosocagglia. And everyone else was wrong. Mr. Bastrop?" Her hand slid gently along the bony shoulder until it made contact with the leathery neck. The head reacted by falling forward, stopping only when the strong chin made contact with the all-but-exposed sternum. The neck did not pulse against her hand. When she shifted it, no air moved from the open mouth against her palm. She drew her hand back slowly.

"You were right," she repeated. "It was beautiful. As beautiful as you had hoped.

"And so were you."

At Sea

The juxtaposition of entirely different story ideas is one of the joys of writing. This is especially true of science fiction and fantasy, wherein the writer has access to absolutely anything that can be conjured, no matter how seemingly unrelated. The only rule is that the final result has to make sense as a story. You can mix together all manner of ingredients, but the result has to be something palatable to the mind.

Grounding fantasy in the real world is always fun. You have the opportunity to upset all manner of perceptual applecarts. If your concept works well, you also enjoy the pleasure of surprising the reader. Sometimes the most disparate notions will come together to produce a viable tale. Once the story is plotted and the rough draft completed, the writer then has the fun of sprinkling it with details, like adding lace and sequins to a dress. The design of women's earrings, for example, is not something I often find myself having to ponder when putting in those little touches that add verisimilitude to a fantasy. Nor are the minutiae of drug-running, commercial fishing, and Scandinavian mythology.

Especially not in the same story . . .

"Hoy, Cruz—there are five horses on the stern!"

Sandino was a big man with a squinched puss and huge arms the color of aged bratwurst. Right now his expression was slowly subsiding into his face, like a backstreet into a Florida sinkhole, swallowing his features whole. It was left to his voice, which had the consistency of toxic cheese-whip, to convey his confusion.

Although he was onboard a modern longline fishing boat, Cruz did not know much about fishing. This did not matter, because he did not care much about fishing. Boats, however, were something else. Boats could go where planes and cars could not. As far as fishing boats were concerned, the best thing about them was that they stank. The big swordfish boat reeked of blood, guts, fish oil, and sea bottom. This made it perfect for Cruz's purpose. This was his ninth run on the *Mary Anne*, and there was no reason to believe it would be any less successful than the previous eight. No one suspected she carried any cargo beyond the limp mass of dead billfish in her hold. No one suspected that one particular dead swordfish contained twenty million dollars' worth of pure top-grade Bolivian cocaine that did not normally form part of a billfish's diet. Compressed and packed into dozens of waterproof, odor-proof, break-proof packages, this highly inhalable product of the Andean hinterland fit neatly into the honored fish's hollowed-out body cavity.

Cruz did know enough to realize that the presence of five horses on the stern of the *Mary Anne*, 120 miles out from Providence, Rhode Island, was not in accord with normal commercial fishing procedure. Even if the horses had been dumped at sea, they could not have climbed aboard. Since he had not heard the metallic bang-and-rattle of the big winch that was used to haul in the longlines, they could not somehow have been lifted aboard.

It occurred to Cruz that Sandino might be enjoying a joke at his expense. A single hard stare was enough to put that possibility to rest. There was a lot of meat on Sandino, but not much of it was gray matter. Nor was it the sort of gag that Truque or Weatherford would concoct. Lowenstein—now, he was different. The computer and communications expert was clever. Cruz's brows furrowed. Too clever to come up with a dumb line about horses on the stern.

"I don't have time for stupid shit now, Sandino. We'll be having to look out for Coast Guard soon."

Cruz turned back to the thick port glass that looked out over the foredeck of the *Mary Anne*. Sullen and silent as they always were in the presence of their unwanted passengers, the crew of the fishing boat went about the business of securing their vessel for the night. They didn't like Cruz and his unpleasant companions; did not like the way they comported themselves while onboard. Didn't like the way they hectored and taunted Captain Red and his son David. Did not like the way they acted as if they owned the *Mary Anne*. Why the captain tolerated their presence on so many trips even his closest friends did not know. But when asked about it, Red just stared off into the distance and mumbled something about old obligations, and told the questioners to carry on. Because they loved Red, and because he always found swordfish and made them money, the crew ground their teeth and held their peace.

"Nice cloud cover," Cruz declared conversationally to Gunnar "Red" Larson as he peered up at the night sky. "Fog would be better."

"For you. Not for me." Larson kept his gnarled fisherman's hands on the ship's wheel and his eyes straight ahead. He strove to focus only on his instruments: the radar, the GPS, the depth finder, and the weather scan. Most of the devices arrayed across the broad, glowing console he could ignore, knowing as he did the way back to the *Mary Anne*'s home berth the way a puffin knows its flight path back to the North Sea cliffs of its birth. He hated the wiry, soft-talking son-of-a-bitch standing next to him. Hated the man's face, his manner, his clothing, the smelly Indonesian clove cigarettes he chain-smoked, and his friends. Most of all, he hated Cruz's business.

No, he told himself as the ulcer-sparked pain that would not go away spasmed his gut and made him wince imperceptibly. There was one more thing he hated: the old gambling debt that had put him in bondage to Cruz more than six years ago. The debt he could not seem to satisfy. The debt from which he had begun to fear he would never emerge.

Three years ago he had stumbled drunkenly out of Portuga's Bar and Grill on Sixth Street, his arm around David's shoulder, and on a quiet night in the middle of the river park, had broken down and confessed all to his only son. David, fine young college-educated boy that he was, had listened in stony but sympathetic silence while he waited for his tough-as-hooks father to stop sobbing. Then he had proposed that Red immediately repeat the story to the police. The old man had violently demurred. He knew people like Cruz, he explained. Had known them most of his life. Lock up Cruz and his minions, and others of his filthy kind would take vengeance. Not out of any love for Cruz, who after all was a sly and successful competitor, but as a warning to others. To keep their mouths shut. To pay their debts.

Besides, old man Larson had mumbled, it was only one or two trips a year. Just one or two trips. Meet the courier boat in the open Atlantic, transfer the noisome illegal cargo, stuff it in a conscripted sacrificial swordfish, and it was done. No violence, no confrontations. At the wharf, that one fish would be purchased by a certain buyer from New York, and that was the end of it. Year after year. Soon the debt would be paid, he had assured a dubious David. Soon they would be free of Cruz and his grinning, scornful face. Soon, soon . . .

Was *soon,* Red Larson reflected as he stared resolutely out the port at his sulking crew and the gathering night, ever to come?

"Fog is better for you," he repeated. "Not for me. I am responsible for the boat."

Puffing on one of his sweet, execrable cigarettes, Cruz looked away and tittered. "'Horses on the stern.' You'd think Lowenstein, that squeaky little nerd asshole, could come up with something better."

Unconsciously Larson looked away from the black water athwart the bow and over at his noxious passenger. "What the devil are you talking about?"

"I know what he is talking about. The brigand is insulting our mounts."

Uttered in a most distinctively steely feminine voice, the observation was bizarre enough. Turning simultaneously there on the bridge of the *Mary Anne,* the sight that Cruz and his sulky captive captain beheld was stranger still. But not, a captivated Cruz reflected, in any way unpleasant. So taken was he by the unexpected vision that he barely gave a thought to the notion that it might somehow be connected to the putative presence of multiple horses on the stern.

Crowding onto the bridge were five of the most simply stunning, utterly gorgeous women Cruz or Larson or Nick Panopolous, who was standing with his mouth open at the far side of the chart table, had ever seen. All of them were blond. Startlingly blond, except for one scintillating redhead, and all had eyes of electric blue, save for two who flashed green, the redhead among them. Variously attired, none was dressed for open-ocean deep-sea fishing. Common to all of them, though visible more on some than on others, was scarlet underwear. One wore a severe off-the-shoulder black dress suitable for performance with a symphony orchestra. She was carrying a violin case. Despite this, her appearance was no more incongruous than that of her four companions. Lost in the rear of the crowd, though not unhappily so, was a visibly dazzled David Larson.

"Hi, Dad," the young fisherman called out. "I'd like you to make the acquaintance of some new friends of mine."

Before a flabbergasted Red Larson could reply, the suddenly animated Cruz stepped forward. "It is lovely to meet you all, senoritas. Though I have no idea how you come to be here, on this miserable boat in the middle of the open ocean, I gladly welcome you aboard." He leered unashamedly at the nearest woman. She wore a comfortable brown business suit, practical flats, and stood five-nine, maybe five-ten. She was also the shortest member of the group. "I assure you I was not intentionally insulting your mounts. Though I am always available to such charming company to discuss matters of mounting."

Pushing past him without a word, the blonde confronted the bewildered captain. Hands on hips, she looked him slowly up and down, leaned forward to peer deep into his eyes, reached out to take several of the thinning hairs atop his head and rub them between thumb and forefinger, all the while sniffing at him with a nose that was as pert and perfect as the rest of her. She smelled, old man Larson decided, of wild honey and expensive leather, of crisp fresh air and slow-warmed Cognac. Married for thirty-six years to the same woman, he nonetheless felt dizzy in the presence of this impossibly flawless golden goddess.

"Do not be alarmed," she told him forthrightly. "My name is Herfjötur."

"Say what, girl?" Even though she was facing away from him, Cruz continued to stare at her, and not at the back of her head.

She spun around to confront the smirking Colombian.

"'War-Fetter' to you, blackguard." Raising a hand, she gestured at her watchful companions. "These are my sisters. That's Sigrdrifa. Next to her are Hrist and Róta. The tall one behind them in the evening gown is Skeggjöld." The "tall one," Red Larson noted, towered over his son, who stood six-foot-one in his stocking feet. "When in his misery and desperation a true scion of the Old Believers called out to us"—she indicated David Larson—"we came as soon as we could. The others would have come as well, but they are presently occupied." She glanced enigmatically back at the confounded captain. "We are wiring Asgard, you know. Being on another temporal plane creates problems that most installers cannot imagine."

"War-Sister is too modest," declared Róta. "In this plane she works for Nokia, you know."

The one called Sigrdrifa nodded. "Having companies like hers and Ericsson right in our ancestral backyard has helped immensely."

Hrist was shaking her head slowly. "Between battles, Odin insists on being online. And Freyja is simply impossible."

It was a tentative Gunnar Larson who stuck his head around Herfjötur to inquire cautiously, "You're not . . . ?" Beneath bushy brows his eyes grew a little wider. "By my grandfather's honored soul, you *are*, aren't you?"

The spectacular blonde who was resting an elbow on David Larson's shoulder essayed a divine smile. "Don't you recognize us? Of course, we have to adopt our dress to the present time, or we would draw the stares of the meddlesome curious while living and working among them."

As if you don't draw stares as you are now, the old captain mused.

With a polished fingernail painted fire-engine red,

Skeggjöld flicked one of the long earrings that dangled alongside her neck. It took the form of a pendulant hatchet fashioned from rubies and diamonds. "These sign my name, fisherman. Can you know it?"

Larson struggled to remember the old tales his grandmother had told him over hot cocoa beside crackling fires on midwinter New England nights. He nodded. "Yes, I know you, 'Wearing-a-War-Ax.'"

Skeggjöld shrugged exquisitely. "I do what little I can with what contemporary fashion allows."

Cruz, who had been watching and listening to the meaningless wordplay, was interested in only one thing. Well, two things. But matters of paramount importance must perforce come first.

"How did you get on this ship?" He glanced through a port. Outside, it was now black as the inside of a deserted Bronx tenement. "I didn't hear or see another boat pull up alongside."

"We did not come by boat," Róta informed him coolly. "We flew."

"Low," Hrist added. "You have to, these days, to stay under the coastal radar."

Cruz frowned. A glance at the stupefied Sandino showed that no plane or copter had been observed approaching. The smuggler was not entirely displeased with the attempted subterfuge. It would be a pleasure to pull the truth out of liars as attractive as these.

"I don't know why you're telling me these loco stories. You've been on the *Mary Anne* all along, haven't you? That's it!" His gaze narrowed, and the false veneer of good humor vanished. "I could almost think you were agents, planted here for purposes of entrapment. But why only women? And in such clothing?"

"Maybe," Sandino rumbled from beside the starboard doorway, "they're hiding something."

"*Seguro* . . . sure." Cruz's smile returned. Sandino

was a good man. Dedicated, loyal. It was time to reward him. "Why don't you have a look and see? But pick on one your own size."

A wide, wicked grin of realization slowly oozed across the face of the muscle. Advancing, he unhesitatingly extended a hand in the direction of the bodice of Skeggjöld's elegant evening gown. As he did so, she reached down and lifted the hem of the exquisite dress, in the process exposing more leg than Cruz or both Larsons or Nick Panopolous had ever seen in their lives.

She also revealed, running from hip to knee, a custom-fitted leather scabbard on which was embossed the cognomen GUCCI. From this she drew a mirror-bright short sword with bejeweled pommel. Bringing it around and down in a single incredibly swift, smooth arc, she hacked off the impertinent approaching forearm of the shocked Sandino. Screaming like a baby, he staggered backward, clutching at the stump of his arm as blood fountained across the bridge. Some of it spattered Róta, who brushed at it in obvious displeasure.

"For damn! This has to be dry-cleaned."

All thoughts of mastery of the situation and any ancillary activities fled from Cruz's mind as quickly as his balls shriveled inside his scrotum. Fumbling for the pistol he always kept holstered beneath his weather jacket, he shouted for help. In moments the interior of the bridge became bedlam.

Clutching his AK-47, Truque came hurtling through the rear door. As he tried to bring the weapon to bear on Skeggjöld, Róta ("She-Who-Causes-Turmoil") removed from the violin case she had been holding a double-bladed ax that could have done duty in a television commercial for men's razors. Her howl of battle reverberated through the enclosed space as she leaped into the air, kicked with both feet off the chart table as a stunned

Panopolous fell backward out of his chair, and brought the ax down blade-first.

"Skull-splitter eats!" she screamed, in a piercing but not unattractive soprano.

Falling from Truque's suddenly limp fingers, the automatic rifle fell to the floor. It was followed by a substantial portion of his brains. Behind him, Weatherford came barreling in, a pistol clutched in each hand. One blew a hole through the center foreport just as Red Larson dove for the deck. The other dropped from the big man's fingers as he felt himself lifted off the floor in Hrist's astonishing grasp. Long ago Weatherford had played a couple of seasons of semi-pro football, before finding out that he could make a lot more money in a game with far fewer rules. He weighed well over three hundred pounds.

Hrist banged him headfirst into the ceiling, then rammed his flailing form into the nearest port. The thick, storm-resistant glass did not give. Not right away. When it finally did, Weatherford was already unconscious, his skull crushed by "The Shaker."

Of Cruz's people, only Lowenstein had enough sense to avoid the furious cataclysm that filled the bridge. It did him no good. Perceiving the advent of most welcome sea change aboard the *Mary Anne*, members of the long-quiescent crew chased the terrified computer specialist twice around the ship, finally cornering him on the bow. There was no need to weight the screaming, kicking passenger when they threw him overboard. It was over a hundred miles to the nearest landfall, and even in the tepid Gulf Stream, the open Atlantic at night is not a kind place to weak swimmers.

Though he held his pistol tightly, Cruz had yet to fire a shot. The fight had ended so quickly and so spectacularly that he had been stunned into immobility. Shocking enough it was to see his handpicked, street-hardened professionals disposed of by a bunch of tall blondes (and one redhead), but the manner of their dispatch had been so brutal as to scarcely be believed. He felt as if he were partaking of a bad dream from which he would soon awaken.

Something hit him in the middle of his back and pushed him forward. Behind him, teeth clenched, Red Larson had taken out six years' worth of frustration in that single shove.

"Paid off," the captain growled. "My debt is paid, Cruz. Go back to New York. Tell your people to leave me and my family alone." His eyes glistened as he regarded the five women: all beautiful, all breathing hard, and all drenched in the blood of his enemies. Behind them he could see concerned members of his crew, good friends all, bunching up in the ship's corridor as they tried to steal a glimpse of the bridge.

Cornered in the center, Cruz had nowhere to turn. That these women were rather more than what they appeared to be was now brutishly self-evident. That he could not fight them, when experienced killers like Truque and Sandino had failed, was equally apparent. But he had not survived in his chosen profession for as long as he had by turning pussy in the face of adversity. Whirling, he stepped behind the old captain and put the pistol in his right hand against the other man's temple.

"All right now! I don't know who you are or what you are, but I have a cargo to deliver." His voice was threatening, steady. "Don't think you can frighten me, because there are people I work for who are more terrible than you can imagine. If I fail, they will kill me slowly. So—put down your weapons and back out of this bridge, now. Stay below, out of my way." He pressed the muzzle of the pistol harder into Larson's temple, so that it forcefully dimpled the flesh. "Otherwise this man dies before you can do anything to me."

Exchanging glances, the women did as they were told. Ax followed sword in clattering to the floor. Cruz started to relax a little. Whatever these bitches were, they were not omnipotent. He only had to stay awake until they made port. Another day and night. He could do that. He had done similar things before, on other desperate occasions, and had always survived. Did they have any idea who they were dealing with?

One by one, the women started to file off the bridge. David Larson would not go with them, would not leave his father. That was fine with Cruz. Two hostages were better than one.

A sudden coldness brushed the smuggler's face, chilling his skin. It was unusual to feel such on the bridge, which was always kept warm in defiance of the sometimes brutal cold outside. Taking his eyes off the doorway for just an instant, he glanced upward in the direction of the breeze.

The needle-pointed icicle that fell from the ceiling—it had been flash-frozen by Sigrdrifa, alias "Victory Blizzard"—went right through his left eye.

Staggering and screaming, he stumbled away from old man Larson, who perceptively fell to the deck as several shots from the agonized smuggler's pistol rang out wildly. They hit nothing but a framed antique chart on the wall and a surprisingly sturdy metal purse that Hrist thrust forward to shield the younger Larson. Striding over to the wildly sobbing figure that was now rolling about uncontrollably on the deck, Sigrdrifa dispatched the half-blinded Cruz with a single swift, quick slice of the sharply curved blade she took from her elegant attaché case. The drug-runner's legs kicked out violently several times before quivering to a halt.

"So perish all enemies of good fisherfolk." Turning, she ululated a victory cry that was taken up and amplified by her sisters. The *Mary Anne* shuddered with the force of it, and members of the crew who were used to hauling in longlines in howling Atlantic gales found themselves covering their ears.

Reassembling on the bridge, with the wide-eyed crew once more crowding as close as they could to the gore-soaked scene of battle, the quintet of bloodied blondes (and one redhead) confronted Red Larson and his son.

"We have to go now," the indifferently blood-soaked Róta informed them.

"Yes." Hrist checked her Patek Philippe chronometer. "I have a meeting in Zurich tomorrow at nine, and with the time difference I will get little enough sleep as it is."

Sigrdrifa nudged Cruz's body with a high-heeled shoe. "Sorry about the mess. It was not exactly Ragnarok, but it is good to still be able to do battle on behalf of a noble cause now and then." Raising her stained short sword, she sensuously licked blood from the flat of the blade. "Keeps a girl in shape."

Red Larson swallowed hard. "I hardly know what to say, how to thank you . . ."

Herfjötur smiled. Stepping over Truque's body, she put a reassuring hand on the captain's shoulder. "Thank your son, who, in a moment of desperate need, had the foresight to call upon those of us who have watched over your tribe for millennia." Leaning forward, she gave him an encouraging peck on the cheek. The old man did not blush, but he was glad his wife was not present.

As for David Larson, he was the dazed recipient of kisses from every one of the women. It was enough to make a weaker man succumb, but David had been toughened by years of hard work on the *Mary Anne*. Still, when she bent him back to buss him most soundly, Skeggjöld nearly sprained his spine. Her ax earrings fell forward, tickling his cheeks as he felt the salt of her tongue slide into his mouth. The salt, he knew, came from the blood she had licked off her sword. This realization somewhat mitigated his otherwise complete enjoyment of the moment.

Too awestruck to talk among themselves, the crew gathered on the stern's deck to watch as, one by one, the women mounted their snow-white steeds. With a kick and a leap, they soared away from the *Mary Anne,* calling out boldly to one another as they rose into the night sky. Most prominent among them was the beauteous Herfjötur, who was still upset that in the heat of battle she had broken the heel of one of her handmade Spanish pumps.

"We'll have to get the bridge cleaned up before we make port," a soft-voiced Panopolous whispered to his captain. "The stains don't look like fish blood."

"At least we have the supplies to do that." Red Larson looked and felt better than he had in a decade. The curse that was Cruz and his business had been lifted. The mysterious disappearance at sea of the smuggler and his henchmen should be enough to keep any curious fellow dealers away from the *Mary Anne.* And if it was not, Larson mused, why, his son could always put in a call for help to an escort service the likes of which was not to be found in the Providence Yellow Pages.

High overhead, the aurora borealis suddenly flashed to life, filling the night sky above the steadily chugging fishing boat with shimmering luminescence.

"You know what they say causes the light of the aurora, David?" Larson had an arm around his son's tired shoulders. "It's the flickering of light off the shields of the Valkyries."

The younger Larson nodded. "From designer-branded armor I wouldn't expect anything less."

The Killing of Bad Bull

I have been fortunate enough to have journeyed far and wide over this isolated little ball of dirt and water we call home. My travels have provided me with inspirations for entire books. East Africa for Into the Out Of; Peru, Papua New Guinea, and Australia for Interlopers; the South Pacific islands for The Howling Stones; and most recently India for Sagramanda.

I've also used memories of people I have met as the basis for characters. I have transposed and transmogrified places I've visited into alien worlds. Mamirauá in Brazil for Drowning World, Namibia for Carnivores of Light and Darkness, Peru again for Catalyst.

But sometimes—sometimes you don't have to travel very far in search of inspiration. There are days when you find it waiting for you right around the corner. That's the case with Bucky's Casino on the Yavapai-Apache Indian reservation, which is engulfed by the city limits of my hometown of Prescott, Arizona. It's much like the Nevada gambling meccas of Laughlin and Las Vegas, towns that are close enough to be neighbors. Loud and flashy neighbors, ever calling, ever enticing.

These modern-day temples of temptation are powerful enough to lure visitors from all over the globe. Are they strong enough to attract mutant powers? In such places would strange abilities be used for good or for evil? Or would they just be—used?

*   *   *

The saddest thing about it was that it was his own people who were trying to kill him. The rest of humanity didn't give a damn. Of course, the rest of humanity did not know about him. Which was the reason his own people were trying to kill him.

A quick stroll around the casino revealed nothing out of the ordinary. Here in the great tropical metropolis of Salvador, on the north coast of Brazil, the men and women sitting like sphinxes in front of the slot machines and laughing as dice ricocheted around the craps table were nearly all locals, with only a smattering of foreigners. Being Pima-Cheyenne made it easier for him to pick out strangers, since the local Indians were considerably smaller of stature than their more robust North American cousins. This was important, since strangers might be looking for more than just entertainment or the chance to make a quick dollar.

They might be looking for him.

They had chased him clear across the United States, from Vegas, to the riverboat casinos of the Mississippi, to the enclosed gambling palaces that ringed the Great Lakes, and finally to Atlantic City. Then through Europe, where he had barely managed to give them the proverbial slip. Upon reaching South America, he had begun his run in Rio before moving on to São Paulo, and now found himself here. For the well-traveled Bull Threerivers, Salvador was a comparative backwater, big city or no.

He took only one carry-on bag with him. It contained a few items of personal interest, one change of plain clothing, one of exceedingly expensive custom-tailored attire, and little else besides his passport and a dozen bankbooks held together with rubber bands. The bankbooks tallied accounts listed under half a dozen aliases in Switzerland, the Caymans, and the Cook Islands. Cumulative numbers in those books reached seven figures. When they reached eight, Threerivers would stop. That was the goal he had set for himself. That was when he felt he could safely cease working.

The people who were after him wanted him to stop *now.* He had been warned. Ignoring the warnings, he had fled eastward from his home in Los Angeles. Twice, they had almost caught up with him. Once in Connecticut, and months later in Monaco. Both times he had slipped away, though not before taking a bullet in the shoulder before leaving France. He'd had it removed and had waited for the wound to heal in a rented private residence on the borders of the souk in Casablanca. Money bought speed and silence.

He did not know if they had been able to track him to Brazil. Logic dictated a move on his part from Europe to South Africa or Australia, where the casinos and the pickings were bigger. By recrossing the Atlantic, he hoped he had finally thrown them off his trail. His confidence had been buoyed by his successes in Rio and São Paulo. From Salvador he intended to move on to other major South American cities, then to Australia, concluding his odyssey of personal financial enhancement with a visit to the fleshpots of Asia. As to where he would retire, he found his present surroundings more than congenial. Though he hailed from another continent, his Indian features allowed him to move easily among the locals, and he had discovered that both the food and climate suited him.

No one paid any attention to him as he wandered through the casino. There was no reason why they should. Though tall for a local Indian, he was not of eyecatching height or appearance. He flourished no jewelry and flaunted no evidence of the considerable wealth he had steadily accumulated in the course of his travels.

From time to time he would pause, seemingly at random, before a slot machine and drop a few coins. That was his modus. After half a day or so of aimless drifting he would zero in on a chosen machine. On the right machine. On the one with just the right scent of ripeness.

Bull Threerivers could smell electricity.

Not the way ordinary folk smell a wire that's hot and burning. Most people can do that. With a sniff and a pause, Threerivers could scent the actual flow of electrons; could detect their moods and motions, their flux and flavor. It was a talent he had not realized was unusual until he turned nine and observed that none of his playmates in the run-down LA neighborhood where he grew up could do it. Even then he had thought little of the odd aptitude and kept the knowledge to himself. No kid likes to be thought of by his peers as "weird."

It was only when he reached his teens, an age traditionally devoid of rewarding prospects for members of his ethnic faction, that he realized his ability might be useful in finding a job. He actually found two. Alternating between the auto electronics repair shop and a small local store that fixed TVs and other appliances, he demonstrated what seemed to his bosses to be an uncanny ability to find within minutes the source of any electrical problem in any device. Often, he killed time taking gadgets apart to make it look like he was working.

What he was actually doing was sniffing out the location of the defect. Short circuits, for example, had a sickly, unhealthy aroma. Dead contacts smelled not dead, but rather like burned cinnamon. Weak connections stank of damp sesame seed. Misbehaving chipsets reeked of rotten eggs. And so on, with each flaw possessing a distinctive aroma of its own: a unique identifying fragrance only he could detect. Struggling to find an explanation for his condition in the local library and on the Net, he could uncover nothing like it in the medical literature. It was then he decided that his situation was unique. Something was cross-wired in his olfactory nerves, something that enabled him to sense the ebb and flow of electrons in a current the way a master chef could taste the difference in the same kind of spice that had been grown in different locales.

From helping to fix car stereos and auto diagnostic systems on the one hand, and toasters and microwave ovens and vacuum cleaners on the other, he moved on to computers, pinpointing the location of hardware problems so intractable that the owner of the business where he had been working literally cried when Bull announced that he was leaving. Even the offer of a doubling, a tripling of his salary was not enough to induce him to remain. Because Threerivers had found a far more lucrative application for his peculiar talent.

He had started in Las Vegas. If he had confined his activities to Nevada, and perhaps New Jersey, his singular activities might have gone unremarked upon. But he made the mistake of spreading himself around, in a sensible effort not to draw attention to himself by winning too much in any one place. His travels soon led him to the many casinos that were located on individual Indian reservations throughout North America. He was observed, and then followed. For some time, security personnel sharing information were at a loss to figure out how he was managing his remarkable success.

Then, running through tape after security tape of the extraordinarily lucky Native American gambler, one particularly attentive agent with an open mind and no preconceptions happened to notice the subject of all the attention leaning forward to sniff a machine he was playing just before it paid off. Subsequent reviews of other tapes invariably captured similar moments on video. Incredible as it seemed, and without understanding how or why it was happening, casino security personnel could agree only on the incredibly obvious.

The subject, a certain Bull John Threerivers of Los Angeles, California, could somehow smell a slot machine that was about to pay off.

Tribal owners and administrators engaged in soft-voiced but quietly frantic caucus via telephone and fax and e-mail. It was not the money they were losing that set them on the knife-edge of panic. It was something much worse and of potentially far greater import.

And so the pact was made and the decision taken that as quietly as possible this one seemingly innocuous if fortunate gambler had to be stopped. A delegation from several tribes had been appointed to confront him at his discreetly lavish condominium in Los Angeles. Inviting them in, Threerivers had listened politely, even intently, to their expressions of concern. When they left, it was with his assurances that he understood the gravity of the conundrum and would take appropriate steps to see that their concerns were fully addressed.

When they came back to check on him in person, after discovering that his phone had been disconnected, it was to learn that he had moved out the day after their visit. That was when it was decided that, given what was at stake, stronger measures would have to be implemented.

Threerivers had barely escaped the first attempt on his life, which took place in the parking lot of a riverboat casino docked outside Memphis. Only the timely arrival on the scene of a bunch of semi-delirious college students on spring break had forced the three men who had pinned him against the side of a truck to let him go. Threerivers had never been so glad to see a bunch of drunken white men in his life. After that he moved quickly, erratically, staying in no one place for more than a few days. He thought he had shaken his pursuers when he shifted his activities to Europe, but soon found them on his trail once more. Fortunately the presence of several large Amerindian males in a casino in, for example, Copenhagen, was obligingly conspicuous. On such occasions he was always able to flee prior to any actual confrontation.

A distinctively sharp stench caught his attention as he patrolled the rows of gaudy, garish, insistent slots. The seat in front of the progressive poker machine was empty. His nostrils quivered. It reeked of readiness. No one else in the room, no one else in the city, and in all likelihood no one else on the planet could detect the distinctive fragrance that reminded him of sweet onions sizzling in a pan that was presently emanating from the machine. It was a scent he had come to recognize without trying: the scent of a slot machine about to pay off.

Taking the seat in front of it, he took his time arranging a handful of tokens by the side of the machine. Then it was feeding time. It ate two, four, six of the shiny base metal medallions. By the time he dropped in the eleventh coin, the perfume was so overpowering that his eyes began to water. Following the application of the twelfth, five aces lined up in the window before his eyes. Instantly lights strobed, sirens wailed, bells rang, and excited fellow players in the immediate vicinity abandoned their machines to rush over and bathe in the audiovisual display that signified someone else's great good fortune. He sat contentedly before the fireworks, trying not to look too bored, his nose wrinkling at the stench of it. Over the past year he had sat through hundreds of similarly celebratory scenarios. One more year would see him finished and done with it.

For now though, he smiled as he accepted the congratulations of the excited gamblers who crowded around him, hoping that some of the "luck" that had adhered to this undemonstrative foreigner would rub off on them.

Well-wishes in German and English in addition to the ubiquitous Portuguese filled the air around him. One well-dressed businessman had in a pocket of his suit a palm computer that was about to succumb to a particularly nasty virus. Threerivers felt bad that he could not warn the man about it.

Two smiling men in neatly pressed suits arrived very soon and led him away. At the office, he received more formal congratulations from one of the casino directors. They would want to take a picture of him holding an oversized check spelling out his winnings, he knew. That was standard casino procedure in the case of big winners. He could hardly refuse without raising unwanted suspicions. It was not a big problem. He had long since developed a procedure for dealing with the situation. He would be a thousand miles or more away from Salvador before the picture appeared in any Brazilian paper.

Those who pursued him could have put a stop to his activities by passing his curriculum vitae along to every large gaming establishment on the planet. But they would not do that, he knew. Such an incredible revelation was bound to lead to inquiries public, scientific, and commercial. Those who had especially sensitive reasons for wanting to stop him did not want inquiries—they wanted him dead. Their conundrum bought him time.

He had to convert his Brazilian reals into dollars, then find a bank that would handle the wire transfer to Zurich. That took the rest of the day. By the time evening approached his latest winnings were on their way out of the country and his fanny pack contained a newly purchased first-class ticket to Lima. There was a nice casino in the district of Miraflores, he had read. He was anxious to pay it a visit.

He had chosen a hotel on Itapuã Beach north of the city, having reserved a room for the week. It had taken only two days to find the right machine in the casino. As he exited the taxi and entered the lobby of the hotel, he located a desk clerk with some command of English and informed him that management might want to send someone to check the main transformer on the street outside. Threerivers thought he might have seen a spark, or something, he explained. Actually he had seen nothing at all, but stepping out of the cab he had smelled sage and thyme—essence of capacitor overload, as he had come to know it. He couldn't have cared less about the transformer, or the neighborhood in which it was situated, or the hotel, but he did not want to burn up in bed before he could check out the next morning.

He had inserted the plastic key into the lock to his room when he hesitated. Something on the other side of the door was tickling his nose. He always made it a point to memorize the smell of a room whenever he checked in to a new hotel. The TV, the electrical outlets, the lamps—all had their distinctive aromas. Here, now, something smelled different. The discrepancy was slight but unmistakable. Slowly he removed the key from the lock, trying not to make any noise as he did so.

Someone pushed a hard, unyielding something into his back. "Don't turn around. Walk down the hall, toward the beach." Reaching out, the man behind Threerivers rapped on the door twice, then twice again. It opened to reveal a tall Amerind who slipped a small gun into his pocket as he emerged.

"He knew you were in there," explained the man behind Threerivers. "He was starting to back away. I was afraid he might bolt."

"How?" The other man's face was a mix of concern and confusion as he stared not at his partner but at their stoic captive. "I didn't make a sound."

The other man gestured. "You wearing anything electronic?"

Shutting the door to Threerivers's room behind him, the intruder considered the question. "Only a watch. And my cell phone is off."

"But charged," replied his partner. "He probably sniffed it. Same way he does the machines." The small, hard pressure in the middle of Threerivers's back pressed sharply inward. "Didn't you?"

Threerivers shrugged indifferently as they started down the hall. It was late, and none of the other guests was around. Hopefully he and his new companions would encounter a maid or someone checking hotel security. The hotel's main building had only two floors and was situated right on the sand. Right now the beach would likely be completely deserted. That was not good.

"Cell phones stink of spoiled fruit juice," he murmured absently. "A watch hardly smells at all."

"Freak," snapped the man who had been concealing himself in Threerivers's room.

Bull replied in Cheyenne, which neither of his captors understood. "There's no need for this," he insisted as they walked him down the hall in the direction of the dark, empty beach and the wide Atlantic beyond. "Whatever they're paying you, I can add zeros to it."

"Sorry, brother," responded the one holding the pistol. "It's all been explained to us. There is too much at stake here."

"What? One guy's few winnings?"

"Few millions, is how I hear it," declared the other man. "It's not the money, though. You know that. You know what it is. The elders told you."

"Maybe I don't." Threerivers was defensive. "Why don't you explain it to me again?"

"All those hundreds of millions pouring into reservation casinos every year," the man with the gun told him. "The salvation of dozens of tribes. The basis for the preservation and the resurrection of the pride and culture of the Indian nations. Everybody's content with the arrangement: the white folks who happily gamble their money away and the tribes that gladly collect it. Then you come along. An Indian who can smell out a winning jackpot. What happens if the white media get hold of a story like that?"

"I'm the only one who can do it," Threerivers told him.

"Maybe," admitted the hired assassin. "A lot of elders and council members sure hope so. But try and tell the white man that. If they think there's one of us who can put the fix on slot machines, they'll start wondering if there are others. And if they start wondering if there are others, they're liable to stop coming to the casinos on the reservations."

"I haven't been on a rez since I left New York for London," Threerivers protested. "I haven't cost one tribe an Indian nickel in the last year and a half."

"You're too dangerous to have around," the other man pointed out. "If anyone, anywhere, finds out about what you can do, the news will get back to the States. And then we have the problem. Once the wendigo is out, you can't put him back in his hole." He gestured downward. "Mind the stairs."

Threerivers turned left instead of right. Before they could question his decision, they found themselves confronted by a waiter wheeling a hot room-service dinner for two toward a second-floor room. Threerivers had turned that way because he had smelled the electric food warmer approaching. He was counting on the fact that the assassin would not risk shooting the waiter and that the pistol he was holding was not equipped with a silencer. When he made his break, darting forward and around the startled server, he gave the food cart a hard shove sideways. Spicy Brazilian food went flying, the waiter yelled in surprise, someone stuck her head out a door to see what was happening, and Threerivers was sprinting for the service exit. Whenever he checked into a new hotel, one of the first things he did was mark the location of alternative exits.

They didn't catch him. By the time his pursuers found the service exit, he had managed to flag down a passing car. Waving a fistful of bills to persuade the startled driver, he was soon speeding away from the threatening ocean.

His pursuers went straight to the airport, but they were not sanguine about encountering their quarry there. In this they were right: Threerivers was too smart, too experienced to chance taking the first plane out of town now that his presence had been detected.

When the old bus finally rattled into Recife days later, he booked a cabin on a freighter and vanished into the Atlantic. They never caught up with him again. In the course of his travels, Threerivers had learned a lot about gambling. Despite his peculiar talent, he knew when to quit. If only his pursuers could have accepted his word that he would, his last flight would have been unnecessary. Seven figures, he decided, were of more comfort to a man alive than eight to a man permanently abed deep in the earth. He never set foot in a casino again—or, for that matter, in a city that boasted a casino.

They kept searching for him, of course, not willing to take the chance that he would keep his ability permanently under wraps. They did not find him. No one thought to look on the coast of the island-nation of Sri Lanka, a hundred miles south of its sultry capital city of Colombo. There it was that a certain expatriate Amerind lived in quiet luxury amid beautiful people who were darker than himself. He married and had four children, two of whom demonstrated the most curious propensity for fixing obstreperous computers and stereos, while the perfectly beautiful little girl spoke repeatedly of her intention to one day start her own software company. Her friends chattered instead about boys and music and movies and school, and sometimes they laughed at her behind her back.

But then, none of them could feel the Net.

Rate of Exchange

*I once shepherded to the Grand Canyon a very tal-
ented and opinionated software engineer who worked
for Symantec back in the Mesozoic era when having
four megs of RAM and a real black-on-white screen on
your home computer was considered cutting-edge technology. In the course of making conversation during the
two-hour-plus drive from my home up to the national
park, I asked him what he might like to do if he was not
deeply embedded in the software industry. I forget his
reply. (How's that for a punch line?) He then turned the
question back on me. Hoping to provoke an interesting
response, I avowed as how I might be a trader in international currency.*

"Scum of the Earth," he replied tautly.

*Marx certainly would have thought so. An ideal ex-
ample of a profession that generates income while pro-
ducing nothing in the way of real goods. Now, I confess
that I do not personally know any currency traders. I do
have a couple of friends who deal in international commodities and futures—everything from orange juice to
iron ore—and these two gentlemen happen to be quite
pleasant folk. But at least their work involves trade in
actual goods and not just the wily adjustment of figures
inside computer programs.*

*Every day, vast fortunes rise and fall on the predic-
tions, suppositions, and manipulations of currency dealers. These individuals exist in a cyberworld of their*

own, have their own arcane tribal lingo, and must perforce possess a confidence beside which that of the most prominent sports stars pales into bumbling uncertainty.

As you can see, obviously a subject gravid with humorous potential.

Speaking of worlds that exist in cyberspace, this story first appeared as a promotional tie-in for America Online. This is therefore its first appearance on a portion of the corpse of a remanufactured coniferous Terran lifeform.

Parker-Piggott's morning had proven very profitable indeed, and he fully expected the afternoon's business to go as well. While Wall Street shut down for the day and the Hang Sen went to sleep, the men and women who traded in the world's currencies never rested. It was not true, as it was sometimes rumored, that there were certain individuals in the business who never slept. A trader needed a full night's rest to function efficiently in an environment where millions upon tens of millions were wagered on value shifts as ephemeral as fractions of a yen—or baht or euro or rupee.

He was very good at what he did, was Geoffrey Parker-Piggott. His success had imbued him with a confidence that left others thinking him smug. Perhaps he was, a little. But not to the point where it affected his work. Never to the point where it affected his work. Smugness had been the ruin of many a previously victorious speculator. Parker-Piggott assiduously avoided stepping on that especially dangerous path.

By the time he had concluded lunch with three of his colleagues, including the beauteous but somewhat glacial Jennifer Lowen, the ruble had risen nearly 0.8 percent against the dollar. He smiled to himself as he watched the figures, like so many agitated insects, crawl across the screen. There were three such screens in his office, all connected to one another yet monitoring distinct sources. While he often wished for a third eye so he could keep a permanent watch on each one, he did an excellent job of monitoring them all nonetheless.

One monitor displayed figures, the other options, the third world news. Four tourists beaten up and robbed in the Masai Mara less than an hour ago. Instantly Parker-Piggott was working the lines, filching quotes, and changing one and a half million Kenyan shillings into those of its slightly more prosperous and stable neighbor, Tanzania. He was at little risk because the transaction was fully covered by a congruent forward position founded on solid South African rand. Thanks to his complex maneuvering, if the Kenyan shilling went down, then he would make money thanks to his forwards in South Africa. Conversely, if the Kenyan currency held firm, he would make money in Tanzania. Leaning back in the thickly padded and very expensive leather chair, he placed his hands behind his head and smiled contentedly. Life was good. Most people were not too bright, especially when it came to their money. This put Parker-Piggott, who was much brighter than most, especially when it came to other people's money, in an enviable position.

Seeing an opportunity to place six hundred thousand for a good customer, he proceeded to purchase a trustworthy basket of Scandinavian currencies. Little volatility there, but a safe investment he could sell off in a week or so at a slight profit. The customer would be grateful, and Parker-Piggott would chalk the humble transaction up to good public relations. Next time he would be able to take a bigger risk with the man's money. The beauty of the business was that whether the currencies traded went up or down, his commission remained the same.

Sipping a cold frappé brewed solely with rare Atiu coffee, he perused the status of the always interesting Southeast Asian exchanges. It was one of his favorite places to do business. The inherent explosive nature of the region offered potential big profits for his customers, and equivalent commissions for the company and himself. He had done particularly well in that part of the world and fully intended to do so again.

Papua New Guinea kina . . . no, that was holding steady. Nothing interesting happening there. What about the Malaysian ringgit? Already up 0.5 percent today . . . too late to jump in. The Singapore dollar he rarely played with, but the Indonesian rupee, with its wild swings, was always worth working, especially when he was in a real gambling mood. Today looked like a bad day on the Manila exchange. Possible opportunities there for him. Knowing his limits to the dollar, he whistled merrily to himself as he put in an order for 22.3 million Philippine pesos, with an eye toward unloading them by the end of the workday. The Manila bourse might be down, but his sources had been assuring him for weeks that the economy was strong and rebounding nicely from the mini-depression of two months back. If he was right, and he usually was, the swing would net the company's investors between 1 and 2 percent. Not a huge profit, but very nice indeed for one day's work.

He had authorized the buy and was in the process of plotting another when the middle screen declared, calmly and without emotion, "Purchase confirmed: twenty-two point three million *zwebagls*."

He blinked. At first he thought there was a keyboarding error. Then he realized it was a joke. There was, of course, no such unit of currency as the *zwebagl*. It did sound vaguely like an issue from one of the old Eastern European communist governments, though he knew that could not be so. Geoffrey Parker-Piggott knew the names and denominations of every currency on the planet, from Peruvian inti to Israeli shekel. The *zwebagl* did not exist. Therefore, someone was pulling an elaborate gag on him.

He ran a systems check. Expensive firewall and second-line-of-defense software assured him that neither office intranet nor his personal units had been compromised. He had not been hacked, whacked, or sacked. Who had the necessary skill to break into his private network without activating security? More importantly, who had the chutzpah? Even if the initial intent was humorous and the final goal amusement, serious damage could result.

Well, no harm done. Undoubtedly he would find out at some future date who was responsible, when the joker chose to reveal himself. Or herself, he mused, allowing himself to recall the face and figure of the exotic and lovely Jennifer Lowen. Ignoring the readout he continued with his work, reentering the order for Philippine pesos. He was gratified to see it confirmed within a few minutes.

Later that afternoon the relevant screen, as it was programmed to do, blinked for attention.

"Your recent *zwebagl* purchase is up five point two percent. Do you wish to initiate a correction or a transfer of assets? There appears to be a good opening in *gyflings*."

His software was programmed to alert him anytime a holding he had authorized rose or fell by 5 percent or more. But according to the machines, he had purchased the twenty-two million *zwebagls* less than two hours ago! The upward surge was incredible, and without knowing what was going on he had apparently made the right decision. About nothing.

Parker-Piggott licked his lower lip. A wonderful joke, yes. One so sophisticated and adept that few could enjoy its ramifications. All right—no one enjoyed a good joke more than he did. Hesitating only briefly, he entered the necessary commands to sell. Furthermore, a smile playing about his pale lips, he added additional instructions that he felt were wholly in keeping with the tone of the gag. Who said he had no sense of humor?

"Selling twenty-two million plus accumulated five point two percent profit *zwebagls*. As per request, recommend one-day forward option to purchase three hundred fifty thousand *gyflings*."

He left it at that, finishing the day with more ups than downs, and making a game as he left the office of trying to guess who was behind the goofy hoax. Whoever it was did not give themselves away in the crowded hall.

By morning of the next day he had forgotten all about it. He was deep into trying to decide what to do with half a billion new Brazilian reals when a note popped up on one screen indicating that on his authorization the computer had purchased, in addition to his slowly but steadily appreciating *gyflings*, 2.5 million worth of Posmoo *schmerkels*.

Enough was enough, he decided. But no matter how hard he tried to purge his system of the intrusion, every piece of software, including his supposedly inviolable backups, insisted that he was committed to acquiring the indicated quantity of *schmerkels*. Meanwhile, his *gyflings* continued to do well. The computer also assured him that now was the time to sell any other *zwebagls* he might be holding, and that there was a new opportunity to grab some Umutu *weesfirks* before word got out that the Umutun government was going to issue equivalent bonds at an admirable premium.

Furthermore, his commissions on all relevant transactions were substantial. The only trouble was, they were in *zwebagls*. Staring at the screen, he found himself wondering for a wild moment if he should convert his recently acquired personal profit to *schmerkels*. Then clarity returned and he wondered what the hell he was doing.

He wanted to stand up and shout, *All right—this has gone far enough!* He did not because he knew that anyone in the office within earshot of his station would look at him as if he had suddenly gone daft. For a number of good and valid reasons, he was convinced he had not. He was less certain about the sanity of his software.

Twenty minutes into negotiating a price for some Chinese yuan, screen number three, which heretofore had been acting in an entirely prudent and responsible manner, broke in with a special bulletin. War, it declared, had ceased between the Gherash Federation and the United Orb-Urbs of Frebbic, with the Gherashians conceding defeat. News would not reach the public at large for at least six minutes. If he acted quickly . . .

Parker-Piggott stared at the screen for a long time. An opportunity like this came to a currency trader maybe once or twice in a lifetime. If he moved fast, according to the information appearing on the screen he could make a monstrous killing in the market for Federation *norpits*. Of course, there was no such currency as the *norpit*, just as there were no countries named the Gherash Federation and the United Orb-Urbs of Frebbic. Still, the temptation to act swiftly was one that was ingrained in every currency trader.

It was not like him to enter figures in anything less than a crisp and competent manner. His excuse was that it took a couple of minutes to establish the correct exchange rate between the *norpit* and the *schmerkel*. If he had calculated the appreciation on the forward *schmerkel* contract correctly, then he would end up with a windfall in *norpits* without having to commit any real currency, like dollars or pounds. Not that he would have had to anyway. There is such a thing as carrying a joke too far.

The information provided by the screen turned out to be conservative. News of the Gherash Federation's defeat did not appear on the third screen for almost fifteen minutes, not six. The creature that delivered the bulletin in a flat nasal tone resembled a warty salamander with a runny nose and unsteady eyes. Watching it, Parker-Piggott reflected on how wonderful it was what creative people could do these days with a few simple wire-and-frame animation programs. Then the creature did something that made his lower jaw drop and his thoughts spin. Of one thing he was abruptly convinced: what he was watching was not the product of some clever CGI specialist's art. And if not that, then what? The possible conclusions were daunting.

Did it matter? He was beginning to wonder. Regardless, he was suddenly *norpit*-wealthy beyond the dreams of *gorplash* and decided to luxuriate in his victory. He left the office feeling absurdly triumphant, as well as slightly dizzy.

It was dawning on him that this was more than a joke. Much more. Somehow he had tapped, accidentally and unintentionally, into something important. Some *otherness*. That was cyberspace for you: full of inexplicable mathematical folds and twists not even its programmers understood. Otherworldly, elseworldly, different-dimensionally: the definitions didn't really matter. Definitions were immaterial. What *was* important was that his skills were appreciated in that other place. Why, the resources being placed at his disposal were staggering, an ongoing vote of confidence in his innate talent. That was what mattered—not the source. He drifted through dinner in a daze, wondering how he might persuade Harrods to accept *zwebagls*.

First thing the following morning, he brazenly ignored an unexpected drop in the cedi market to buy *schmerkels* like crazy. It was a reckless buying spree, consummated far more on instinct than knowledge. That it worked out to his advantage was as much a matter of luck as good timing. When something like a leprous weasel appeared in a small insert on his third screen to congratulate him, he took it in stride. The rest of the day spent dealing in bland dollars and euros was boring by comparison.

When he returned to his apartment late that night, there was a box waiting for him outside his door. It bore a peculiar and unfamiliar return address sticker but was clearly intended for him. Picking it up and carrying it inside, he removed his coat and tie, laid them neatly aside, shook the box experimentally, and then carefully opened it.

It contained the most beautiful suit he had ever seen: a lustrous, almost metallic black, fashioned of material so soft and light, it felt like woven air. A smaller box nestled within the larger contained cuff links and a tie pin sporting gemstones unlike any in his experience, including those featured in the display window at Tiffanys. They were deep violet shot through with dancing gold sparks. He wondered what they could possibly be. An accompanying card declared, "Compliments of the Öurt-Hafnook Pension Fund." As he tried on the suit, which fit him like a cool breeze on a hot Manhattan afternoon, he wondered what an Öurt-Hafnook might be besides generous.

As his work with currencies belonging to the realm of the outré progressed over the next several weeks, he found himself the recipient of half a dozen additional wondrous and inexplicable gifts. There was the toaster that materialized butter inside the bread without any visible application mechanism; the add-on stereo for his car that, while ungainly and not quite fitting the intended slot in the dash, brought in stations no one else could hear; and the special toilet seat that, while one was appropriately enthroned, quickly cured any intestinal upset, distress, or hangover while performing its other, more plebeian function. Yes, business was very good indeed.

Until the *bafferfoom* market collapsed.

Now, Parker-Piggott no more knew the nature of *bafferfooms* than he did *zwebagls*. All he knew was that it cost him nearly ten millions *quiviqaps* before he could get out. That, in turn, ruined his leverage with Kovodo *doyks*. Before he knew it he was out another million *mopulopes*. Even his beloved *schmerkel* forwards were suddenly in jeopardy.

Wait a minute, he told himself. What was he worried about? It was all done through the computer, through whatever bizarre cross-dimensional upload had infected his private system. It was all sham, the suit and toaster and other gifts notwithstanding. Prank or something more, it was time to put an end to it and get back to dealing exclusively in sound, familiar currencies, from Mexican pesos to Egyptian pounds.

Accordingly he ordered up, at his own expense, an entirely new operating system. The handling software he installed himself, layering on his own personal workware after carefully scanning each individual component for viruses, spyware, or other intrusions. Only when he was certain all was virgin did he re-power-up his office. It was with the satisfaction of the very thorough that he subsequently observed on his triple screens only figures and names that made sense. He went back to work with a vengeance. Only occasionally did he cast a quick, nervous glance in the direction of the complaisant third screen.

The only news it brought him, however, was real news. Comprehensible news, delivered by interchangeably attractive men and women. No bilious chimeras thrust their quivering proboscises in his face, announcing this or that impossible disaster or ascendancy. No scholarly worms spewing elegant elocution announced the fall of unknown deities or celebrated the arrival of some inscrutable new conjuration. He was back on solid ground, monetarily speaking.

Next week he was due to take off for ten days in the Bahamas. Sun, sand, casino glitz, good food, fine drink, and relaxation—in the company of the enchanting Jennifer Lowen, if he could persuade her to accept his invitation. He was full of happy reggae thoughts, mon, as he entered his apartment that evening and locked the door behind him.

It struck him right away, and with considerable force, that he was not alone.

One visitor was wearing a neat brown suit that might have come right off the rack at Lord & Taylor except for the four arms. The flattened oval head that barely protruded from the starched collar was neckless, hairless, and devoid of visible ears. Each hand had three fingers, and each finger ended in a long claw. These were painted cerise, which Parker-Piggott thought went decidedly poorly with the creature's coloring.

Its companion had no feet at all, sported a kind of loose-fitting dark blue turban around its middle, and was one-third oversized skull. Half a dozen bulbous eyes framed the vertical, fanged mouth, which more than anything else resembled an oozing Venus flytrap. The creature's breathing was loud, slow, and exceedingly fetid, in keeping with its air of general putridity and poor posture.

Barely visible over the collar of the brown suit, a small babyish mouth addressed him. "Time's up, Parker-Piggott. You did brilliantly there for a while. Really well, *ha-ssst*. But you stepped over the line with the Youbithian *ikkim*. What were you thinking? Don't you watch the Youbith commodities markets? Any fool should have caught that rise in Bing-wa prices!"

"Bad weather," rumbled the flytrap with the eyes. "Any fool."

"Look, I know I've had a rough couple of weeks here lately. But my basic moves have been good. Everything will come back, and more, by the end of next month. There'll be a full recovery, you'll see." Slipping out of his jacket, he loosened his tie. Another gift from gratified investors, it was impregnated with some kind of permanent perfume whose scent varied from day to day. "My instincts are still as sound as ever."

Flytrap stepped forward, advancing as if he had twice the usual number of joints.

An alarmed Parker-Piggott retreated in the general direction of the mirrored mini-bar. "Here now, my good creature! Let's control ourselves like civilized beings, shall we? This is global finance we're dealing with here. This is not a game for the nervous or faint of heart."

"Haven't got one of those," Four-arms responded, "so I wouldn't know. Your margin has been called in, Parker-Piggott. Time to forfeit." The bald half a head twisted slowly from side to side, as if mounted on a spindle. "Too bad. I made a couple of thousand *wivwuks* taking your advice on the side." Eyes that could barely see over the white collar glanced significantly kitchenward. "Drouk . . ."

"No, wait!" Parker-Piggott squeaked as Flytrap closed in on him. He quickly saw that it would be impossible to give the slip to something with six eyes. "I can fix it! I can make it all back! Just give me another couple of weeks. No, no, a week, just one week!"

Four-arms sighed and lit a cheroot. It stank alarmingly of burning flesh. "Sorry, Parker-Piggott. If it was up to me . . . But I ain't the one whose millions of *botobs* you were throwing around as if they were so much minced *spiyork*. They've run out of patience with you,

Parker-Piggott. You should've been more careful with other folks' money."

"But," Parker-Piggott screeched as Flytrap worked him into a corner from which there was no escape, "it wasn't even *money*! It wasn't real! It couldn't have been real!"

"Easy for you to say." The surreal speaker let out a porcine grunt as the shrieking Parker-Piggott was enveloped by Flytrap. Ominously Four-arms thoughtfully switched on the big-screen TV and turned up the volume to a suitably ear-numbing level. "You're not the one who lost twenty million *schmerkels* last week." With a barely visible nod from his barely visible head, he gestured tersely for his partner to proceed.

"Call in his margin, Drouk."

They did not kill Parker-Piggott. After all, only the business of the *schmerkels* constituted a truly objectionable matter. The punishment was designed to fit the crime. In consequence, he forfeited a particularly sensitive and precious 10.5 percent of himself, which could not be recalled by speculation on the relevant open market or by any other means.

As a bit of a consolation, the enchanting Jennifer Lowen agreed to accompany him to the Bahamas—until that first evening in the suite they shared. When she saw how his person had been discounted, she ran shrieking from the room and caught the first flight back to London. With a resigned sigh, he knew he really couldn't blame her.

No matter how successful in the business, a man whose gibbl has been oblately norked loses something in attractiveness . . .

Wait-a-While

In the winter of 1989 my wife and I found ourselves in a bar in a sprawling Sheraton resort in Port Douglas, Australia. Port Douglas is a tiny laid-back tourist town located on the southern fringes of the World Heritage Daintree Rainforest in northwest Queensland. In most ways the Daintree is a typical tropical rain forest: a place of enervating humidity, riotously diverse flora and fauna, oppressively sauna-like heat, and mysterious dark nooks and crannies unvisited by humankind. Atypically for a rain forest, its plant life is more threatening to human visitors than are the local animals. The exception is a giant flightless bird called the cassowary, which looks more like a dinosaur than any other avian with the possible exception of South America's hoatzin.

When my wife departed for elsewhere, I lingered awhile. I found myself listening (where do writers get their ideas?) to a conversation between a couple of local gents who had popped in out of the heat for a quick one. They rambled on about sports scores, the weather, road conditions, box jellyfish, and enough local lore to apprise me of the fact that they not only lived in the area but knew it well.

Eventually one of them started talking about two women, a mother and her grown daughter, who were known to conceal themselves in the depths of the forest, not wear clothes, and generally live off the land. In the course of the tale-teller's talk I expected to hear derision, *if not outright laughter. Instead there was more than a modicum of respect in the voices of both men. Respect for anyone, much less a couple of ladies, who would dare try to eke out an existence in a wild and inhospitable, albeit beautiful, place like the Daintree—with or without suitable attire.*

The Daintree, you see, is and always has been a special place . . .

Michael Covey had come to Queensland looking for inspiration and had found only beer. Beer and overwhelming heat, suffocating humidity, subtle bigotry, and an all-pervasive tropical dulling of the senses inconducive to cogent thought, much less the novel he hoped to write.

The bar in the hotel was solid Daintree hardwood, cut from the center of a single tree. From where he sat near the far end it looked expansive enough to handle the landing of a small plane. Dark brown veined with black, it resembled a slab of meat hacked from some dinosaurian flank. Sparkling empty glasses dangled like crystalline grapes from crazed brass piping. Spotted throughout the vast Byzantine reaches of the restaurant, potted plants squatted forlornly, as if marooned in amber. Tinted windows kept the unyielding equatorial sun at bay.

Covey sat alone at the bar. It was midday, a time when the rest of the hotel's guests were out swimming, diving, sightseeing, and shopping, their relentless desperation to enjoy themselves as remorseless as the sun. Through a vast picture window he watched a quartet of Japanese golfers putting their way through the tenth green, little mechanical windup figures in perfectly pressed slacks and shirts that somehow defied the pitiless humidity.

Lucky bastards. They don't have to think for a living.

The only thing that torments them is fear of failing to please a boss-san. He sipped cold lager.

The bartender was pale, blond, athletic, Aussie; fertile ground for skin cancer. Covey was lean, tired, non-descript; a surefire candidate for artistic anonymity. No matter where he went, no matter how often he traveled, the one thing he could not escape was the incontestable mediocrity of his talent.

"Hot," Covey muttered.

"Too right." A damp cloth shushed over the counter, slick as skis on fresh powder. Ceiling fans whirred softly overhead, agitating the cold air-conditioned atmosphere that tried to hug the tiled marble floor.

Covey shifted his butt, straightening slightly on his stool, abruptly overwhelmed with the urge to confess. "I'm a writer. I make a very nice living because I have written twenty-four novels."

"Good on ya, mate."

"No, it isn't. It isn't good on me at all. It sucks. You want to know why?" Of course the bartender wanted to know why. It was his job. "Because all twenty-four are exactly alike. The titles differ, so do some of the details, but basically I've been writing the same goddamn book over and over again for the past twenty years. Each year they sell a few more copies, and each year I get a little more in royalties and a little more disgusted with myself. Because I know I can write something else, something better." The sanctity of the confessional was interrupted by the arrival of a trio of middle-aged white men. They entered the bar cackling with midwestern twang. Covey tried to ignore them.

"That's why I came here. To find inspiration. To expose myself to new surroundings, new ideas." He held up the empty lager bottle. "So far I have found only this, and it is not worth even a novelette."

"I tell ya, they were buck naked, the both of 'em!"

"Gawann, Fred." The doubter wore plaid shorts and a white tennis shirt stretched taut over the anchored blimp of his belly.

"He's tellin' the truth, Jimmy. They weren't bad lookers, either." A dirty snigger punctuated the observation propounded by the third man. "Shoulda seen the wife's reaction to 'em. Edith like to have peed in her pants." The trio chortled as one, a Topeka chorus distinctly unmelodic. The sound grated on the smooth stone of the floor.

"We tried to get the driver to stop," said the first speaker. "Dumb Aussie ignored us. Said we were seeing things. That there wasn't nobody living in that part of the rain forest, naked or otherwise. But I seen 'em." He leaned forward, squinching the belly. "Bill did, too."

"That's right." The second man nodded solemnly. "Buck naked, they was."

An irritated Covey watched as the three traversed the length of the bar like oysters escaping a buffet. "What do you suppose that was all about?" He looked back to the bartender. "You have naked women living in your jungle?"

"Rain forest." The bartender corrected him without looking up from his work. "Maybe."

Covey chuckled, reached for his glass, hesitated. Something in the younger man's tone . . .

"It's a joke, right? You're goofing on me."

"No joke, mate. It's a woman and her daughter, fair dinkum. Eleven years they been out there. Live off the land, they do. So people say."

Covey pushed his glass aside. "Why? Why would anyone want to do that? Much less a mother and daughter."

The bartender turned away, hunkering down with the air of a man who had already said too much. "Their business. Why ask me? You're the writer."

"I'm a novelist, not a reporter." There's something

here, he found himself thinking. Something in what's not being said. Was it worth checking out? On the face of it, the story belonged near the top of the bullshit probability index. Doubtless the bartender had overheard the three clowns from Kansas as clearly as his customer and had improvised a good gag on the spot.

But the way Covey was feeling, anything was better than flying home to face the accusatory sameness of book twenty-five and the screeching inadequacy of his meager, overpaid talent.

"I don't believe you, of course, but certain of my fellow travelers whom I've been unable to avoid keep insisting I ought to see some of the jung . . . the rain forest . . . before I go home. Assuming I decide to give it a try, how might I locate these antipodean naiads?"

"You don't. They're supposed to live way up in the backside of the Daintree." As bartenders do, the young Aussie busied himself polishing a glass. "You don't 'find' anybody in the Daintree. It's a garden God planted and then forgot about and now it's all overgrown. Nobody'll take you into the back of in there."

Digging into a pocket, Covey extracted a thick wad of traveler's checks. Very slowly and deliberately he signed the one on top. "Nobody?"

Purple print caused the young bartender to waver in his better judgment.

"Maybe one larrikin. But he's mad." The traveler's check vanished. "If you're so flamin' sure it's a joke, why're you suddenly so keen on checkin' it out?"

Covey stared across at him out of eyes that could not see quite far enough. "Since my writing and I are something of a joke, I don't see the contradiction in following up on another."

* * *

Boris Schneemann didn't act crazy, but he sure as hell looked the part. Covey found himself mentally recording the man's vitals for future literary abstraction. Six-two, 210, crowned by a mat of scraggly black hair that glistened with some kind of internal ooze, Schneemann regarded the world unblinkingly while perspiring like an asphalt-layer working Phoenix streets in mid-July. Originally from a corner of Germany he declined to identify more than vaguely, he had migrated to northeast Australia fourteen years ago. Now he grew bananas and dogs when not running tourists into the Daintree.

A succession of short scars ran across his Roman bridge of a nose, fossilized evidence of some ancient battle in which an opponent had tried to remove the protuberance via amateur rhinoplasty. This and other aspects of personality and self suggested that in dear old Deutschland, Schneemann had been something other than a farmer of edible fruits and lover of dogs. Covey chose not to probe too deeply too soon into his guide's hazy history.

The battered gray Toyota Land Cruiser was to cars what a professional wrestler was to a surgeon. It did not so much drive over the road as intimidate it.

"Ninety thousand new she cost me." Schneemann railed against faceless bureaucrats as the Land Cruiser slammed contemptuously through a bottomless pothole, sending Covey's brains ricocheting off the top of his skull. *"Auschloch* import duties! Can buy nothing reasonable in this country unless it's made here." He pointed to his right.

"See that tree? Tulga. Forty thousand dollars it's worth, just standing there. Most places people poach animals. Here they try to steal trees."

"Tell me about the women." Covey's fingers were white and numb from clinging to the handgrip bolted to the Land Cruiser's frame above the passenger-side window. The so-called road they were careening down like a runaway Baja racer, the Inner Bloomfield Track, continued snaking its way through towering green walls. The roadbed was yellow-brown, the narrow strip of sky overhead shockingly blue, and the rest of the universe alternating shades of green hothouse gloom.

"Not much to tell, Mike Covey. They been back in here long time."

"So you believe in them, too?"

Schneemann was silent for a while, concentrating on the road. "Ya." He spoke softly for a change, scratching the back of his head. "Ya, I believe in them."

"Any idea how old they are?" Covey was making mental notes.

"Mother and daughter. The girl, she would be about seventeen, I'd say."

"And the local school authorities don't mind that she's not in school?"

The front end of the Land Cruiser went temporarily airborne, and the impact when it touched down stunned Covey's sacrum.

"Oh sure, they mind. Every once in a while somebody go looking for them to bring in the daughter. School nannies, state social services. They never find them."

"I was told that you could."

The burly German laughed like a demented Santa Claus. "What fool bloke guy told you that? I can track them . . . sometimes. Naked footprints in the mud, two sets. You follow them." There was a curious edge in his voice. "Over ridges, through trees, across streams. Until they disappear. Always," he muttered more to himself than to his passenger, "they disappear."

Covey began to worry that the bartender's appraisal of the guide's sanity was nearer the mark than he'd been willing to countenance when he had hired the man. He gazed out the window. One thing was already apparent.

Any inspiration to be found out here would be heavily tinged with green.

"Yeah, sure. They 'disappear.'"

Schneemann shrugged massively. "Maybe they go up in the trees, ya? Maybe they fly away."

"How can they survive in this? I mean, what do they eat?"

"Mango, pawpaw, lychee, possum, snake—plenty *für essen* in the rain forest." He gripped the wheel with both hands. "You hang on, Mike Covey. All the good road, she is behind us now."

Covey swallowed hard and wondered what the hell he was trying to prove.

They spent the night on hard beds in a tiny youth hostel situated in the absolute middle of emerald nowhere. The ramshackle clapboard-and-metal structure squatted by the side of the track like a corrugated boil engulfed in broccoli soup. It was designed to serve backpackers, which excused Covey. The only backpacking he had ever done in his life was from shopping cart to car trunk. His idea of a nature walk was crossing Central Park from the Met to the American Museum of Natural History.

Eventually they abandoned the track entirely as Schneemann turned up a shallow stream, the Land Cruiser grinding and sloshing its way over a pavement composed of water-polished pebbles and punky driftwood. Eels and crayfish scattered from beneath the crunching tires.

As the guide explained, the unpaved Inner Bloomfield Track more or less paralleled the coast. No roads led straight inland, into the heart of the mountainous rain forest. There was nowhere for any to go, and no way for them to get there.

When even the rugged, determined vehicle could advance no farther, Schneemann parked it on a rocky beach and broke out the packs. Covey struggled awkwardly with the shoulder straps and waist belt. Giant electric blue Ulysses and emerald-green Cairns Birdwing butterflies fluttered through the trees and over the stream. Each time one traversed a shaft of sunlight, a flash of unbelievable color exploded against his retinas. An effervescent column of soldier ants the color of key lime pie marched across the buttressing root of a nearby white cedar. A splotch of flaming orange skimmed the glassy surface of the stream, marking the quicksilver passage of a marauding kingfisher.

Covey could not remember when heavy sweat had coated his body. It mixed with the obligatory insect repellent to form a thin, stinking paste that clung to his hot, damp skin, smothering the pores. The German chose a direction seemingly at random and struck off, leaving the huffing, heavily perspiring Covey to follow as best he could.

The crowns of Alexandra palms burst overhead like frozen green fireworks, blotting out the sky. His hiking shoes kicked up leaf litter and mold, sending tiny black shapes with too many legs scrambling in search of fresh cover.

Schneemann paused by a patch of sunlight, his machete singling out a small, innocuous-looking plant with six-inch-wide, slightly pebbled leaves.

"Here is worst thing in the forest, my friend. Stinging tree. Those serrated leaves, they covered with glass spines. Glass! Each one is like a little hypodermic, *verstehen*? All full of a powerful alkaloid poison. Once they get in your skin, they stay there because they silicate composition, not wood. Each time you rub, or splash on cold water, or walk into an air-conditioned room, they release a little bit more poison. The pain can last six months to two years.

"I hear of one guy got a bunch all in his face. He went mad and killed himself."

The warning was wasted on Covey, who had resolved immediately upon leaving the Land Cruiser to avoid physical contact with everything in the forest, be it dead or alive.

It rained all that afternoon and through the night, a heavy warm vertical deluge that their tent shed with admirable efficiency. Sitting in a steady downpour while simultaneously perspiring heavily was an experience Covey would gladly have done without. It inspired nothing but colorful language.

They crossed two more ridges, scrambling up slick rock and mud only to stumble and slide down the far side. Covey didn't dare grab a tree or branch for support for fear it would bite back.

This constant drizzle was only a prelude to what Schneemann referred to as the Big Wet, the real rainy season. That could begin any day now, he declared jovially. His announcement failed to inspire Covey to greater effort.

When he lost his footing for the hundredth time and slid twenty feet downhill on the waterlogged, torn, butt-end of his pants, he finally cast aside the unnatural enforced stoicism under which he had been laboring for days. By the time the German reached him, Covey had removed his pack and slung it to the ground.

"Fuck this, Boris! I thought you knew where the hell you were going. I thought you knew what you were doing. You've been leading me around in circles like a prize porker so you can scam as much per diem out of my hide as you think you can get away with! I've got fungus growing between my toes, an itch in my crotch that won't go away, my clothes are starting to stink on my back, and I think all the goddamn rain's starting to affect my hearing." Bending over and breathing hard, he rested his mud-caked hands on his knees while he stared up at the impassive German.

"I've had it with this, *mein führer*. You understand? You 'versteht' or whatever the hell it is you do?"

Schneemann seemed not to hear. His thick black brows resembled mating caterpillars as he intently scanned the opposite hillside. Finally he shrugged. "We got enough supplies to go another week."

Covey inhaled deeply, straightened. "Fuck that. And fuck this country, too. It is my fervent hope that they log it to the ground." Turning to his left, he spat out an earthy mixture of soil, rainwater, and saliva. Angrily snatching his pack from the mud, he started forward.

A dark, hirsute mountain, the German blocked his path, smiling down at him.

"What the hell are you grinning at?" Covey snapped.

The guide held out an astonishingly clean hand. "You forget our contract, my friend. One-third when we start, another when we turn back, the last when I set you down, all nice and refreshed again, in your fancy hotel in Port Douglas."

Covey gaped at him, blinking painful drizzle from his eyes. "You want money *now*? Here?"

Schneemann twitched slightly. "It is the contract, yes?"

"Shit," Covey mumbled. He dragged out his shrinking packet of traveler's checks and signed several over. Schneemann fanned them like a poker hand and frowned.

"I know you are a writer, Michael Covey, and not an accountant. This is a little short. One hundred US dollars short."

Covey took a step backward. "That was going to be your bonus if we found the women. We didn't find them."

"I say I take you to where they live." He made a sweeping gesture with his free hand. "This is where they live."

Covey pursed his lower lip. "I don't see no women—mate."

The German's expression darkened. "Don't joke with me, *herr* writer. Especially about money, don't joke with me."

"Believe me, humor's the last thing on my mind. You've spent a week dragging me through God's own puke-green shithouse and you've enjoyed every minute of it." He smiled nastily. "Now it's my turn to enjoy something."

Schneemann took a step forward, halted. "I could make you sign another check, *ya*. But maybe you bring charges. All writers are crazy like that. So have it your way, my friend. Maybe I see you again in Port Douglas. Maybe not."

Without another word he whirled and started off, ascending without effort the slope they had only recently clambered down.

Covey yelled imprecations in his wake. "Yeah, that's right, go on and leave me here, jerkoff! I can find my own way back, you Teutonic asshole! You think I can't? You think I can't? Just watch me, man!"

Schneemann did not reply. In a very few minutes the forest had swallowed him up.

It began to rain harder.

Screw him, Covey thought furiously. It was more downhill than up all the way back. Just keep heading east and eventually he would hit the road and then the ocean. He had a week's worth of supplies in his pack and he wasn't sorry to see the departure of the sauna-like tent. What the hell, he was soaked through anyway. His light sleeping bag would do him. And he was ahead a hundred bucks, maybe more.

As for inspiration, he couldn't wait to get home and write down an account of his crazy experiences. His agent would be intrigued. A horror novel would be an interesting departure for his client. He could call it *A Stroll Through the Green Hell*—or had that already been used?

He had learned that when the sun went down behind the rain it got dark fast in the rain forest. Selecting a spot between the meandering roots of a massive tree, he tore down some broad pandanus leaves and improvised a roof. Highly satisfied in his righteous anger, he settled down to await the arrival of the dawn.

It took him two days to admit that he was lost. He was reasonably certain he was still traveling east, but it might have been northwest, or southwest. Or maybe not. The permanent, oppressive cloud cover and constant rain made it difficult to guess direction. Everything looked the same: every tree, every slope, every mocking, crystal-clear rivulet and stream. Sometimes he would find himself confronting a sheer drop-off or impenetrable vegetation and have to backtrack. There were no landmarks; only rocks, mud, and claustrophobic verdure.

So far he had managed to avoid the stinging trees, but between the inevitable slips and falls and the occasional inimical thorn bush he was pretty well torn up. In the dank confines of the forest, several of the cuts were already beginning to fester. There was a warm wet soreness under his heels where several blisters had popped. Yesterday he'd found a leech on his right ankle and in a paroxysm of disgust had unthinkingly and unwisely pulled it off. Despite his best efforts, the bite continued to bleed.

His hat was gone and so was much of his food. Several times exhaustion and desperation had overcome his pride and he had shouted out the guide's name. If Schneemann was secretly dogging his footsteps, waiting for his client to admit defeat, the German was taking his time about it. Surely the guide wouldn't simply abandon an outsider to fend for himself in dangerous country like this? No reasonable professional would do such a thing.

But a crazy man might.

There was a slight break in the trees ahead, barely visible through the rain. Covey angled toward it, hoping to find a stream that flowed east toward the sea. Perspiration blended with rainwater stung his eyes. His damp breathing came in long, labored wheezes now.

Someone jabbed a white-hot fishhook into his right forearm.

He howled and looked down at himself. Two narrow lengths of vine lay snugged against his bare, wet flesh. When he tried to pull away, they clung to him like green steel. Forcing himself to stand absolutely motionless, he contemplated the growth that had trapped him.

It wasn't a stinging tree, thank God. Inspecting his arm, he made out two parallel sets of backward-curving thorns running along the underside of each vine. These natural hooks were deeply embedded in his skin. Little bubbles of blood rose from the spot where each thorn had penetrated. They continued to swell until rain washed them away.

To his horror the vines seemed to contract around his arm even as he was studying the phenomenon.

"Don't move."

The voice startled him and he jerked involuntarily, sending fresh agony ripping through his flesh. Trembling slightly from the pain, he forced himself to stand motionless.

She glistened in the rain, naked and supple as a cream-colored seal. Her auburn hair was neatly combed and unmatted, though the rain made it stick to her exposed skin. She had deep, dark eyes and a slim, though mature, body. Her mouth was small and moist, and her leonine muscularity reminded him of slow-motion film he had seen of professional marathon runners.

Transfixed by both pain and surprise, he stared as she gently disengaged first one vine, then the other, from the meat of his upper arm. She offered him a half smile.

"Wait-a-while." Gripping it carefully by the edges, she held up one vine for closer inspection. He flinched away. "See? The thorns are barbed. Once you're hooked, the only way to free yourself is by backing up slowly. Move in any other direction and the barbs only dig in deeper." Her smile widened. "It's also called lawyer's cane."

A shaken Covey sat down and felt gingerly of his injured arm.

She eyed him with palpable curiosity. "What are you doing out here?"

He tried not to stare at the raindrops slithering down through her breasts and crotch. "I was looking for you."

Her smile vanished and she peered around anxiously. "Why?"

He managed a filthy grin of his own. "I'm a writer. I was looking for inspiration for a new book." When he lifted his arm, pain lanced through him and he winced. "I think I should've stuck to rewriting my old ones. My name's Covey. Mike Covey."

She was watching him closely. "No one told you my name, then?" He shook his head, momentarily too tired and too full of self-pity to care about much of anything else. "I'm Annabelle." She looked to her right. "That's my daughter, Leea. Leea, come say hello."

The girl was a slightly taller version of her mother, only blue-eyed and with hair that verged on the color of night. When her mother called to her, she was sitting in a nearby tree, her legs dangling from a thick lower branch. As an exhausted Covey looked on, she lowered herself to the ground with an effortless grace and agility that was breathtaking.

Had she been there all along? he wondered. Would she have watched in silence as he'd torn his arm to pieces trying to free himself? She slowed as she approached, while the mother regarded him with a strange mixture of curiosity and sadness.

"Where's your home?" he asked. "Do you have a lean-to or a cabin out here, or something?"

"We build shelters when and where we need them. We move around a lot. Is this how you find your inspiration, by asking questions?"

"I can't say, not having found any yet."

Shading her eyes, she tilted her head back. "Soon the afternoon rain will begin. The Big Wet is coming. If you don't get out of the forest before it starts, you'll be stuck in here till March."

As he sat and watched, the two women quickly and without a single tool cobbled together a passable shelter out of the forest material at hand. When Annabelle directed him to crawl inside, he did not object. He was too worn out to object to anything. Then they left.

Just as he had decided they didn't intend to come back and he would never see either of them again, they returned bearing armfuls of fruit. There were also large, white, fat insect grubs the taste of which, despite his hunger, he felt obliged to decline. Using fingernails and teeth, they peeled the various fruits as deftly as any monkey.

Later, with his belly full and feeling considerably better, he lay back against the gray rock that formed the rear of the shelter and gazed out at the monotonous scree of falling rain. As always there was no need for a fire. To make conversation he asked the woman about the rain forest. She had an answer or explanation for everything. Sensibly he did not try to inquire about her past or how she came to be in her present situation.

"I need to find certain plants to treat your wounds," she told him the next morning, "or you're going to develop some severe infections. A couple have already started to ulcerate." Crawling to the shelter's opening, she glanced back in at him. "Don't try to go anywhere."

"Fat chance of that," he murmured.

They had been gone less than an hour when a shape returned. The daughter entered wordlessly. In the warm confines of the shelter, he could not avoid her nor did he try to. Her nipples brushed his bare arm as she sat down next to him, folding her thighs up against her chest and clasping her arms around her knees. Outside, the early-morning drizzle obscured the rest of the world.

"Tell me," she whispered in a small voice, "about the city. Mother's told me a little, most of it bad. But I don't see how any place so interesting can be all bad." Her voice overflowed with eagerness. "I want to know."

So without a moment's thought or pause, he told her, describing life not only in the cities of his own country but in those of other lands as well. He tried to impart to her some of the excitement of Chicago, the glamour of Los Angeles, the culture of New York. She listened raptly, hanging on his every word, only occasionally interrupting with a question.

Her manner of speech was devoid of guile and long words but otherwise proper and correct. Apparently her mother had not wished her to dwell entirely in ignorance green. She had been given some home, or rather forest, schooling.

Eventually he felt secure enough in her presence to ask a few questions of his own, keeping an eye on the opening in expectation of the mother's return. "Leea, how do you come to be here, to live like this in this place?"

She replied ingenuously. "I don't exactly know. I was only seven when Mother brought us to the rain forest." Her smile was as radiant and unspoiled as the rest of her, he mused. "We've been here ever since."

"Hasn't it been lonely for you without any other children to grow up with?"

"Oh no. There was always Mother and the animals. I've had every kind of pet you can imagine. Pythons, until they got too big, and cockatoos and possums and sugar gliders. I've always had playmates."

"But you'd still like to visit a city?"

She nodded thoughtfully. "I think so. I wouldn't want to live in one, though. I don't think I could, after living in the forest."

"What about—not having any clothes?"

She shrugged. "I've seen other people. I don't understand clothes. You dry off much faster without them, and it hardly ever gets cold here."

"What about people who come looking for you? Aren't you afraid they might see you like this?"

"Well, you're looking at me right now, and I'm not afraid." Here was a directness of logic he rarely encountered and could not argue with. "Besides, if we don't want to be seen by other people, we're not."

"You can't move around all the time, Leea. You can't continue to dodge the rest of the world your whole life. People will find you, eventually."

"Not if we don't want them to." There was a certainty to her claim that puzzled and intrigued him. "We just walk off into the Dreamtime."

He frowned. "I've heard of that. It's the name for the Aborigine spirit world, isn't it?"

She nodded enthusiastically. "Something like that. There are lots of Native people around here. Mostly in the Dreamtime. They've gone there to get away from this world. Modern Aussie people did bad things to them, so they left. Those who knew how. Sometimes Mother and I talk to them, and they teach us things. Like how to live in the forest. They taught us how to find the Dreamtime. There's a lot of it in the Daintree."

He shook his head impatiently. "Leea, the Dreamtime is myth. It's the collected stories of a people. They're very beautiful stories, but they're just stories."

Her smile and her eyes were full of secrets, like pearls at the bottom of a dark, dark pool. "The deeper you go into the Daintree, the closer you get to the Dreamtime, Michael. This is one of the oldest forests that has been on the Earth, one of the very first, and the Dreamtime is the first place. They're very near to each other, the Daintree and the Dreamtime. You just have to know how to look."

Girl, I've spent my whole life trying to learn how to look. Her mother has fed her this, he realized suddenly. To keep her here, away from civilization, away from other people. But why?

"When we don't want to be seen or found, we just find a piece of the Dreamtime and go into it," she was saying. "The people who are looking for us walk right past. They don't see us. They don't know how to find the Dreamtime, so they don't see it, either."

"What's it like?" He wondered what a psychologist would make of her delusions.

She lapsed into dreamy, exquisite reminiscence. "A lot of it is forest, like this, but before the loggers and highway people came. There are no cities, no airplane tracks in the sky. No white people. Only the Aborigines, and Mother and I. It's like it was when the Earth was before people."

There was movement outside. Annabelle entered, clutching a handful of leaves and stems that were oozing sap. "This won't take long." She didn't even glance in her daughter's direction.

She's crazier than Schneemann, Covey thought, isolating herself and her daughter out here like this. Warily he eyed the vegetation she had brought back.

The poultice she fashioned lessened the fire in his wounds. He was less eager to sip the tea she brewed, but did not know how to refuse. It put him to sleep almost immediately.

When he awoke, stiff and cramped but otherwise feeling better, they had both gone.

Staggering out of the shelter, he stumbled unexpectedly into full, searing sunshine. He felt himself blinded by a thousand emerald mirrors. Thick gray mist clung to treetops where unseen lorikeets fussed. The air had the clarity of a sudden vision.

"Annabelle!" He turned a slow circle as he shouted. "Leea!" Within his limited range of vision, nothing moved. There was no reply.

"Leea!"

He thought he heard a voice. Most probably it was some kind of animal, but he pursued it anyway. It was all there was.

The voices grew louder, contentious. Among them was one deeper than any he had heard in days. Eyes widening, he increased his pace, suddenly heedless of the possibility of encountering stinging trees, or worse.

He came up short, breathing hard, on the steep bank of a deep gully. Leea was there, her hands cupped over her mouth, eyes wide and staring. He could hear her muffled screams clearly.

Boris Schneemann, his agonized face framed by his wild black mane, knelt by the drop-off. His thick, callused hands clutched the edge and he was sobbing and screaming in a berserk, unintelligible mix of German, French, and English.

Not far below him the twisted, naked form of Anna-belle hung crucified in a tangled mat of wait-a-while. Where the unrelenting vines had torn her flesh, blood flowed freely in thin, viscous streamlets. Her head was bent back so far that Covey could not see her face. It rested at an angle unnatural to her shoulders.

One large vine was wrapped tightly around her neck.

The anguish that welled up unexpectedly in his throat far exceeded anything he felt in his arm or feet. Anger glazed his eyes as he rushed forward.

Leea turned to him, her ethereally beautiful unblem-ished face wide-eyed with shock. Schneemann rose slowly. Then he threw back his head and shook his clenched fists at whatever gods hid behind the mist-shrouded sky, screaming in guttural, uncontrollable, wretched German.

"You rotten, rotten bastard." Covey eyed the other man carefully as he approached. "What the fuck hap pened?"

Schneemann suddenly became aware of his presence. "It was an accident. She would not listen. I only wanted to talk and she would not listen. She ran from me. Toward the Dreamtime, she said. Where she would be safe. Crazy, crazy! *Gott in himmel*. She ran and she fell." He looked down. "There." He inhaled massively then turned and, before she could retreat, grabbed Leea's wrist.

"You. Leea. You are all that is left. You come back with me now."

The girl stared at him, half mad with terror and despair. "N-no. I don't want to go with you. I don't want to."

"You must. Now."

"No!" She dug her heels into the mud, sliding forward as he dragged her, beating at him with her free hand. He took no notice of the feeble resistance.

The air went out of him when Covey tackled him around both legs.

They went down in a damp, muddy heap. Covey struck out blindly, furiously, slamming fist after fist into the German's face. With a roar like a wounded rhino, Schneemann threw him off.

Rolling over, Covey saw the guide grinning insanely back at him. The big man was back on his feet, tense as a panther, a knife clutched in his right fist. In Covey's eyes the short, thick blade loomed as large as a ceremonial sword. Reaching up, he felt blood streaming from his nose.

"So little writer wants to fight, eh?" Covey scrambled to his feet, only to find himself caught between the drop-off and his opponent. "You *verdampt* swine, you niggly little son-of-a-bitch. Ten years I spend looking for these two. Ten years of my life hacking and sweating at this stinking jungle, and you, city man, *you* find them. And then she don't listen to me." His face contorted and he began to sob anew.

"No more Anna. No more Anna! She wouldn't listen to me," he bawled. "I just wanted to talk!" The sobbing snapped like a worn tape. A rictus of gut-seated pain, the kind that twists bowels and haunts eyes, made a horrible, inhuman mask of his face. "Ten years, little writer. Ten long, terrible years tearing me to tiny pieces. Ten years in which to think too much."

"She's dead." Covey's gaze hung on the point of the knife as intently as if he were tracking the movements of a weaving cobra. "What do you want from the girl? Leave her alone!"

Schneemann stared at him out of eyes that were dull and empty, like a shark's. "What do I want from her? *What do I want from her?* You stupid brainless American shit, *she's my daughter*!" With a rasping cry of inhuman rage and frustration, he threw himself forward, a black-maned juggernaut wielding a knife that gleamed like death itself in the hazy light.

Covey tried to block the thrust. As he did so he lost his footing in the mud and fell. The knife sliced air above his head as the onrushing German tried to redirect his bull-like charge. His legs struck Covey's sprawling form, and the bigger man tripped over him.

He went over the drop without a sound.

"Christ." Covey scrambled to the edge on hands and knees. Schneemann lay on his back on a barbed pillow of wait-a-while, the knife protruding from his chest like fresh new rain forest growth. His eyes stared sightlessly at the sky. Drizzle filled the sockets, masking the pupils, spilling over both sides of his face in tiny twin waterfalls. The naked woman who had given birth to his daughter lay nearby, in death enshrouded by the rain forest she had loved: the greenery that had sheltered her, fed her, and ultimately protected her from her abusive, enraged lover for ten long years of hiding and wandering.

The wait-a-while would hold them close even as it kept them apart.

Fighting to catch his breath, Covey rose slowly and turned. Leea was nowhere to be seen.

He ran to the edge of the dense undergrowth. "Leea! Leea!" Ignoring the thorns and vines that tore at him, restrained him, deliberately held him back, he searched for her all the rest of that dreadful day and all the next, screaming her name at the silent, uncaring trees.

"Leea! Leea, I love you! *Le-aaaaa!*"

Two days later his food ran out. He kept going, eating what fruits he could scavenge, trying and failing to kill small animals. Eventually he was reduced to scrabbling for lizards and insects, until they, too, were insufficient to replenish his strength.

He lasted three more days before he collapsed, half

blind and utterly spent, on the soft, moist leaf litter that carpeted the forest floor.

"Leea . . . ," he sobbed. Something crawled onto his neck and bit, testing him. He did not have strength enough remaining to swat it away. The rain started; the warm, omnipresent rain, running into his ears and eyes. At least, he thought wearily, he would not die of thirst. He had heard that it was a bad way to die.

He slept then. Later, he dreamed that something touched him, and he struggled one final time to open his eyes.

For a local eccentric to vanish without warning was sufficient to raise a knowing alarm, but the disappearance of a foreign tourist was enough to bring out the police and forest rangers in full strength.

They found a collapsed, temporary shelter of sticks and leaves. Then they found the bodies of Boris Schneemann and his long-missing paramour. Carefully they hacked the bodies free from the tangle of wait-a-while, which even when severed seemed reluctant to let the dead couple go.

Of the American writer of modest reputation and desperate desire they found no sign. No tracks, no broken branches to show that he had once passed this way, no blood or bone. Then the Big Wet arrived with a vengeance and the search had to be called off. Nothing could move in the Daintree until it ended, hopefully sometime in March.

The consensus among the rain-forest-wise citizens of Mossman and Port Douglas was that with luck they might find his body come next year, perhaps washed down from the hills by the rains. He'd gone troppo for sure, stumbling madly off into the forest without direction or knowledge, searching for his hoped-for inspiration.

What they did not, could not know, was that Michael Covey found it, though it was not of a kind he had ever imagined. It lay just a little farther on, just a shade deeper back in the dark green depths of the Daintrec. If one looked long and hard enough, one could find anything in the Daintree. Even the Dreamtime. Even inspiration.

Even innocence.

The Short, Labored
Breath of Time

The fantasy oeuvre is replete with stories of heroes who die and then return to save the day. Or the empire or the critical battle or the important righteous marriage. Tolkien's Gandalf is just one example. The great majority of these fictional heroes are resurrected for some great or noble purpose. Often their return to life forms the turning point of the novel.

Yet there is nothing extraordinary about death. It comes to all of us. It's coming for you and it's coming for me. Death is a common, ordinary, everyday occurrence. Despite this, only a small percentage of those facing their demise are adequately prepared for it either mentally or spiritually—never mind physically.

What if for one individual death was not only a common, ordinary occurrence—but a daily one? Subject to all the discomfort and trauma that dying brings with it?

And you think you have trouble getting up in the morning just to make it to work or school on time . . .

Farrell was dying. It was something of a surprise. He usually died between ten twenty and eleven thirty PM, though he had died as early as nine forty and once as late as ten minutes to midnight. Each time he thought he was ready for it, and every night he discovered anew that he never was.

As the familiar pain, the little preliminary warning

electrical shocks, began to splinter his breathing, he grasped at his chest with one hand and raised the other to check the time. Seven fifty-five. A new record. He regretted it for several reasons, not the least of which was that he would miss his favorite news program. Not many began before nine. Of far more importance, he was still several blocks from home.

The pain abated, and he felt a little better. The couple that had hesitated to look in his direction tucked themselves tighter beneath their black umbrella when he smiled in their direction. Good. The last thing he wanted was help. Dying he was used to, and knew how to deal with. Help could prove fatal.

Lengthening his stride, he turned the corner and headed up the last sloping sidewalk. Below, the lights of the city beaconed through the steady rain. Though no downpour, it was heavy enough to discourage casual strollers. Not Farrell, though. Dying every day, a man learned to appreciate every component of existence, every smidgen of reality. That was a belief that had grown stronger over time, ever since he had begun dying.

He was twenty-six when he died for the first time. Back then, the sharp, unexpected pain in his chest had been terrifying. Frantic co-workers had rushed him to the nearest emergency room, but the doctors were unable to save him. Full cardiac arrest, they had proclaimed solemnly to weeping friends and family. Despite his youth, he never had a chance.

When he awoke or was raised or however one chose to designate the phenomenon, in the hospital morgue at five thirty the following morning, it was pronounced a miracle. Unable to find anything wrong with his heart or lungs or general systemic health, the astonished but delighted physicians had no choice but to consent to his wishes and allow him to return home. He felt fine all the rest of that day, even when running his customary three miles before dinner.

That night he died about ten minutes earlier, in his own bed.

There was no mistaking it. Some things a man can get wrong, like the fullness of his stomach or the nature of a new dog, but dying is not one of them. When he came to at seven fifteen the next morning, long after his alarm had sung out the hour and subsequently gone silent, he knew that something was very, very wrong. He moved cautiously at work, doing nothing strenuous, taking it as easy as possible. That evening he skipped his run through the park and had an American Heart Association–approved heart-safe meal for supper.

In spite of all his caution and preparedness, at ten forty-three exactly he experienced a profound cardiac seizure, then died.

That was twelve years ago. Nothing had changed since then. His life had settled into a daily routine of frenetic, satisfying living followed by nightly expiration. Seeking anonymity for himself and his condition, he had moved from the heartland of Des Moines to the enchanting indifference of San Francisco, a city where a man could dwell every day in beauty and die every night in peace. By its very nature his was a tentative existence, but not a particularly fragile one. Every night he died, and every morning arose strong and eager to contemplate a new day.

Periodic checkups revealed the presence in his chest of a normal heart. Only he knew the singular difference. He bought home-care monitoring equipment and assiduously checked the readings on following mornings. Each time the indications were the same. His heart stopped, followed by his breathing, and the little lines on the compact screen of the electrocardiogram flattened out like the waters of the lower bay on a July evening. Each morning without prompting it all started up again: brain waves first, then heart, then lungs.

If there was reason behind the recurring phenomenon, a scientific or religious explanation, he was unable to determine it. If some inimical deity had it in for him, it chose not to reveal itself. The exact moment of death varied from day to day, but never the ultimate consequence. Each night he died. Each morning he lived again.

He had no social life, but other than that, managed something akin to a normal existence. Another individual might have spent his daylight hours brooding on his misfortune, bewailing his strange fate while losing himself in drugs or strong drink. Not Farrell. There was too much in the world to take pleasure in: the sunlight on the bay, the fog that smothered the Golden Gate, the manic musical babble of many tongues that filled the streets of the great cosmopolitan city, dinners in Chinatown, paper cups of cold crab with horseradish sauce consumed at the Wharf, the springy sight of laughing young women enjoying their lunch breaks. Women he could never know because to do so would be unfair to them. All that, and so much more. All the small ingredients of life that filled up existence like slices of apple in a pie, from the sight of a house sparrow with a newly scavenged nest-twig in its mouth to the smell of freshly laundered sheets hanging outside a neighborhood window. He accounted himself a rich man with a full life, because his plight had taught him how to fully enjoy that which everyone around him seemed to ignore.

But tonight was different. Tonight was bad. At the age of thirty-eight, he had been dying daily for more than twelve years and had learned how to manage it as well as anyone *could* learn how to manage such a situation. His one horror, the only circumstance he truly feared, had him dying in a bed controlled by strangers. His own apartment was safe, a secure hotel room was safe, even a locked rented car was adequate. If he died out here on the street, though, someone, some well-meaning Samaritan, would *find* him. Find him and call 911. Paramedics would rush him to a hospital, where with luck he would be placed in a morgue by sorrowful doctors to await final treatment and identification.

But what if they did not wait? What if he was given immediate preparation for burial, the blood siphoned from his veins and arteries to be replaced by embalming fluid trickling from long plastic tubes? Would he still wake the next morning, and if so, how would his body react to the absence of that life-sustaining red fluid? Would it put him in a nether state, neither dead nor awake? What if apathetic authorities signed off on an expedited cremation? Or worse, a quick interment, leaving him to wake each morning in the inescapable confines of a sealed coffin, gasping for air, unable to die until that night, unable to live until death overcame him?

The pains surged afresh, worse than before, bending him double as if he had been kicked in the stomach. Gritting his teeth and clutching his chest, he staggered onward. Another couple of blocks, just a couple of blocks, and he would be at the locked door of his building. Another few minutes and he could stumble, safe and secure for one more day, into his apartment, there to expire on the floor if need be. All he asked was to be allowed to make it inside the door. The rain hammered dank cold against his bare head and neck. He wore only black jeans, expensive running shoes, a cotton-wool pullover, and a lightweight coat. It did not matter that he was soaked through. In more than a decade of dying he had never had a sick day. A tiny, ironic smile creased his mouth. Pneumonia would be a novelty.

The next spasm hit behind his sternum like a sledgehammer, knocking him to his knees. He just did manage to grab one of the city's ubiquitous free newspapers racks to break his fall. Sprawling out on the sidewalk, unable to move, with the rain splashing on his upturned face, he wondered dazedly who would find him. Despite the crushing, familiar agony he found he could still smile. He had one hope. This *was* San Francisco. With luck, no one would come near him until morning, by which time he would be fully recovered from the terminal nocturnal episode. Then he could pick himself up and go on with his life. His only other fear was that he might have torn his jacket.

"Hey. Hey, mister, what's wrong?"

Blinking away melting raindrops, he slowly turned his head and found himself staring up into a hooded face. Not Death itself, unless Death had chosen a guise utterly deviant from that described in the traditional literature. She could have been twenty-five or forty. It was hard to tell through the pain and the night and the rain. He settled on a guess of not quite thirty. Curls of black hair had been plastered against her forehead by the downpour the rain hood could not entirely keep at bay. As she bent tentatively over him she reached up to brush one strand out of her eyes.

"Go away." It took most of his remaining strength to gasp out the admonition. From experience he knew he had very little time.

She started to straighten. Looking around and seeing no one else, she hesitated, then bent over him once again. "You don't look so good."

"I—I'm fine. I'll just lie here for a while until I get my strength back. Go away. *Please*." Within his chest his heart was beating only intermittently. It would not be long. In a very few minutes it would stop altogether. He would be dead.

"I'll call for help. My apartment's in this building right here."

"*No!*" Alarmed, he forced himself to raise an arm. Panic gave him the strength to reach out and grasp the hem of her raincoat. "No ambulance. No paramedics, no hospital. I just need—to rest."

Honest concern racked her face as she chewed on her lower lip. "You really look bad." Something within her came to a decision she knew was wrong. As it so often did, it rolled up against her identity and stopped there. Crouching, she worked an arm beneath his shoulders and strained to lift.

"Leave me—leave me alone," he whispered tightly.

"Sorry. My mother didn't raise me to be that kind of a person. My friends keep saying that one day it's gonna get me killed. Not by you, I don't think. Right now you don't look like you could kill an ant." She grunted softly as she heaved against his body weight. "Come on, use your legs. Help me, if you won't help yourself. Otherwise I'm calling nine-one-one."

What else could he do? He did not want to die there in the street, to be whisked away by listless sirens in the night. Summoning forth a tremendous effort of will, he accepted the offer of her strong, willing arms and body to leverage himself erect. With her help he managed to stumble into her ground-floor elevator. It carried them up several flights. When the door slid aside, she half carried, half shoved him down the hall to her apartment. As she locked the door behind them and started to take off her raincoat, he felt his vision going. In his immediate line of sight stood a couch, a table, three chairs all of different manufacture. The table was closer but the couch worth the extra effort. Only the upper half of his body made it.

"Okay now, if you won't let me call anybody, maybe I can—hey, you asleep?" Approaching tentatively, knowing that she had already broken every rule for sensible behavior by a single young female living alone in San

Francisco, she touched the man's back. He did not move. Drunk, stoned, or . . . ?

Rolling him over, she saw the shuttered eyes, the motionless mouth. First she put a hand over his lips and then she put an ear to his chest and then she stood right back away from him and put both hands to her face. A little squeak of a smothered scream filtered out between her fingers.

"Omigod. Omigod. You said you'd be all right. You said there was nothing wrong." As much as the thought of doing so terrified her, she knew she had to make sure. She couldn't do anything more unless she was sure. Advancing as hesitantly as a lizard patrolling a branch, she approached the immobile form a second time, forcing herself to bend down to listen to the stranger's silent chest, putting an ear close to his unmoving lips. What she found was unequivocal. No heartbeat, no movement of air.

A strange man was dead in her apartment. And she had only been trying to help. She ought to have ignored him, lying there gasping in the street. Turned away to pick up her mail. Why didn't she? Why, why, *why*?

How could she cope with what had happened? How did *anyone* cope with something like this? She thought he had just been sick, just needed a few minutes of respite from the cold and indifference of the street. Now . . .

Whirling, looking around wildly, she snatched up her purse and fled from the apartment. Carol was out of town. She had a key, could use her friend's place to get herself together. In the morning she could call to have someone come and take the body away. What could she have been *thinking*? But she hadn't expected him to die.

She did not sleep much, and not very well. When she awoke she took a long, hot shower in Carol's sunlight-washed, plant-filled bathroom. Dressing, she moved to pick up the phone, and hesitated.

No. She ought to be in her place when the ambulance and the police came. They would want to ask questions. There was no avoiding it.

As she gingerly pushed open the still-unlocked door to her apartment, a strange sound greeted her. No, not strange, she corrected herself. Unexpected. A distinctive crackling, popping noise. It came from the vicinity of the kitchen. Automatically she looked in that direction, but could see nothing. Her gaze swiveled left.

The couch was empty.

Carol, she decided, her head pounding. Carol had come home in the night, found the door to her friend's place standing ajar, gone inside, discovered everything, and in her firm, efficient way had Taken Care of Things, leaving Marjorie to sleep off the misadventure in her good friend's bed. Carol was in the kitchen now, making breakfast, waiting for an explanation. Deserving one, too. Feeling better, Marjorie headed purposefully toward the kitchen, with its reinvigorating view over the rooftops of the city, already preparing in her mind the rationalization she intended to offer to her friend.

A man was standing there, frying bacon and eggs. A half-familiar face. A dead man, wearing one of her bathrobes. Crazily, she noted that it was too short for him.

"Oh, good morning." He smiled at her. He had a very agreeable smile, set in a passably handsome face. She fainted.

When she regained consciousness, the first thing she did was apologize. She did so without thinking, because concern for the feelings of others was such an integral part of her. "I'm sorry. I've never done that before." The second thing she did, as soon as she realized where she was lying, was to get off the couch. "You're dead."

Keeping well away from him, she walked slowly over to the den table and sat down heavily in one of the chairs. "No. You *were* dead."

He nodded casually, still smiling. "Yes, I was. Would you like some bacon and eggs? I made some toast, too." He glanced back toward the kitchen. "They're not cold yet. You weren't gone very long."

"I'm not hungry, thanks. Marjorie Parker."

"Joel Farrell. If you don't want anything, I hope you don't mind if I eat. I'm always famished in the morning. I'll pay you for the food."

"Sure. Whatever. Go ahead." She tracked him with her eyes as he walked back into the compact kitchen. After sitting for several moments to make sure she was in control of herself, she rose and followed him as far as the portal between the two rooms. "Farrell. Not Jesus Christ?"

Sitting down at the two-chair kitchenette set, he heavily salted and peppered his eggs before digging in with knife and fork. "I don't think so. At least, I've never been given any reason to think so. Just Joel Farrell. From Iowa, originally. And you're Marjorie. Thank you, Marjorie, for helping me and for not calling an ambulance."

Moving to the refrigerator, she opened it and took out a half gallon of skim milk. Sipping straight from the carton, she watched him eat, her eyes never straying from his face. "So. You do this sort of thing often?" To her mind it sounded incredibly inane. She had, of course, no idea she was being accurate.

His smile faded and his expression turned solemn as a saint's. Holding a slice of buttered whole wheat toast in one hand, he paused with it halfway to his mouth. Something in her manner, or maybe it was something about the moment, or maybe just a bad attack of no longer caring, compelled his answer.

"Yes, actually. I do it every day." He bit into the toast,

chewed. It was delicious. Everything was delicious in the morning, when the day was new and death was still fourteen or fifteen hours away. "Every night, really."

She blinked. A thin white mustache of lingering cow juice clung to her upper lip. The sight was delicious, he decided. It made her look like a little girl trying to look like a woman. "Do what every night?" she asked him.

His shrug was almost imperceptible. "Die." The bacon was particularly good, he mused. Slab-thick and pungent.

"Oh right, sure." Leaning against the scored white enamel of the old fridge, she crossed one leg over the other below the knee and clung to the carton of milk as if it represented all the security in the world. "You mean you pass out or something."

"No." He chose his words deliberately. "I die. My heart stops, then my breathing, and every electrical impulse in my brain fizzles like a socket in the process of shorting out. I know. I've checked it all many times, studied the alternatives. It's not narcolepsy, it's not a recurring fragmentary coma, it's not a voodoo stasis. It's death. Usually happens later at night, and then I'm alive again by sunrise. Last night was an exception. I'm not usually caught by surprise, much less outside my place." He gestured with the half-eaten toast. "I live two blocks up the street and one over."

"You know what you are?" Her nervousness translated as excitement. "You're a *nut,* that's what you are. A crazie. One of San Francisco's finest. I should've listened to you. I should've left you lying there in the street."

For the first time he looked directly into her eyes. She drew in an involuntary little breath, staggered by a sense of sorrow and compassion the likes of which she had never experienced before. It was as if something had squeezed her insides. As well as being bottomless, she noted that his eyes were a very deep shade of blue. Corn-fed midwestern blondness, she thought.

"Why didn't you?"

She found herself having to look away as she sputtered a reply. "I—I don't know, not really. I'm always doing stuff like that. Stupid stuff. Usually it's animals, but sometimes it's people. I just can't . . ." She made herself look back and meet his eyes again. "I can't stand to see anything suffer."

He nodded slowly, as if he understood. "You're a good person, Marjorie Parker. I wish I could say that you saved my life, but I would've come around this morning anyway. What you did was save my death."

"Please." She turned back to him. "I wish you'd stop talking like that. I'm having a hard enough time with this as it is."

Contemplating the remnants of his wonderful breakfast—all breakfasts being inherently wonderful because they came at the start of a new day—he took a deep breath and then fixed her with an impenetrable mournful contented happy stare.

"Okay. I'll prove it to you."

She was instantly on guard, standing away from the hard cool humming reality of the refrigerator. "What do you mean, you'll 'prove' it to me?"

He gestured toward the window and the bright summer sunshine outside. "You can come over to my place tonight and watch me die."

With great deliberation she set the half-empty carton of milk aside. "First of all, watching somebody die isn't my idea of an agreeable evening. Second, that's the damnedest pickup line I ever heard."

He chuckled softly as he mopped yolk with the last of the toast. Every bite, every swallow, was a mixture of joy and delight, of taste and smell and the delicious tactile sensation of simply swallowing. A small miracle.

"I'm sitting here in your bathrobe, eating breakfast in your kitchen, after having spent the night, in a manner of speaking, in your apartment. If you prefer, I can come back this evening and die on your couch again."

Her expression was rock solid. "Still not my idea of a hot date."

Rising to carry his dishes to the sink, he nodded sagely. "I understand. Do you think it's easy for me? How about dinner, then, and maybe a movie?" Running the hot water over the dishes, he offered her a wan smile. "It'll have to be the early show."

Lowering her defenses, which largely consisted of trying to be funny at serious moments, she eyed him evenly. "This is for real, isn't it? You're not kidding about this?"

"No, Marjorie." He applied soap to his juice glass and used a sponge to scrub it out. "I'm not kidding." As he set the dripping tumbler into the rubber rack to drain, he flicked its rim with a fingernail. A single musical note hung in the air, perfect and immutable. "Don't worry. Whatever I am, whatever I've got, it's not contagious. Like I told you, I've done a lot of research on my—condition. As far as I've been able to determine, it's unique."

A part of her shouted warnings, but she could not keep herself from moving a little closer. He cooked, he washed dishes. What other special traits did he possess?—besides the single small drawback of being crazy. "What do the doctors say?"

His glance fell. "The doctors don't say anything. I don't have to consult with them. I *know* what's wrong with me. I die. Every night, seven nights a week, three hundred and sixty-five days a year and an extra day during leap years. There's no fancy Latin term for that in the medical literature, although I'm sure some surgeon with half a dozen degrees could come up with one. Officially my condition doesn't exist, so there can't be any

cure for it. I'm a walking, waking, dying impossibility—
except, I'm still here."

She wasn't sure what impelled her to reach out and
put a hand on his shoulder. Probably the same impulse
that led her to rescue stray cats and give spare change to
the winos who slept in the alleys off Union Square.

"Maybe if they studied you, tried to—"

He whirled on her, but the look on his face was so
piteous it wholly mitigated the sharpness of his gesture
and she was not afraid, did not pull away. "Studied me?
And prodded and probed and poked and analyzed and
took tissue samples to culture?" He made scissoring motions with the middle and index finger of his right hand.
"Snip, snip—another nip for the lab. Think they'd ever
let me go? No. Too 'valuable' to medical science, they'd
label it. 'Matter of national security,' the spin would
say." Angrily he pushed the washcloth over his plate.
"No thanks. I'll live with it," he finished sardonically.

Her hand fell from his shoulder. "It can't be much of
a life, Joel."

This time when he looked up it was to stare out the
window. "See that?" He nodded at the view, sun-
washed but uninspired. "Ever take the time to notice
how beautiful it is? Cracked paint, sunlight, blue sky,
the fog trying to push its way through the Gate. Kids
playing on the street, houseplants flourishing on window-
sills, sticks and stones and unbroken bones and words
can never hurt me because I've got nothing to lose. Ordinary stuff. Trite things. You know, there is wonder in
triteness. I remember reading an old aphorism, 'Live
each day as if it was your last.'" He turned around to
meet her gaze. "That's no aphorism, Marjorie. That's
me. Joel Farrell. That's my life."

Motion caught her eye. A pigeon was settling on the
projecting brick of the condominium building next to
hers. Pigeons did that all the time. She just never really

noticed. Leaning back against the sink counter, she impacted his field of view. He was almost finished with the dishes anyway.

"Dinner and a movie sounds great." She hesitated, then decided it was foolish to try to dance around the issue that had and would continue to dominate their relationship. "You'll have—enough time?"

His grin was brighter than the June sunshine that was steadily intensifying outside. "I have all the time in the world."

She'd never met anyone like him. Sure, it was a cliché. In the case of Joel Farrell, it just happened to be true. He was warm and funny and considerate and thoughtful. The computer search service he ran out of his home marked him as a man of intelligence, and his taste in day trips—museums, exhibitions, wildlife cruises, concerts of every imaginable type of music—marked him as an intellect. He was well, even widely, read, and could quote poetry, plays, and film with equal facility. Every time she thought he had revealed all of himself, he surprised her with something new. Joel Farrell had more sides than a hexagon, something he explained to her at the Exploratorium. Each of them shone, each was polished to a high sheen. He was wonderful to be around, and since he had deliberately chosen to cultivate many casual but no close friends, she had him mostly to herself.

Except late at night and early in the morning, when death claimed him for its own.

"Doesn't it hurt?" After several weeks of dating she had finally screwed up enough courage to spend the night at his place and observe the inevitable. She had lain there in bed next to him, her head propped up on one hand and elbow, and had watched as he twitched and grimaced until his eyes closed, his voice stilled, and his heart stopped. The last thing he had said before dying was "Marjorie—don't worry.

"Don't worry. I'll see you in the morning. Nothing to concern yourself about. I'm only going to die." And he did.

She was sure she would not be able to sleep. But he looked so peaceful lying there, not moving, not breathing. Astonishing herself, she drifted off around two thirty. The emotional tension must have exhausted her, she decided later. How else to explain enjoying a good if brief night's sleep alongside a dead man?

When she awoke, startling herself awake with remembrance, he was making breakfast for her again. Not bacon and eggs this time. Unlike her own provincial cupboard, his larder gave birth to eggs Savoyard and chive hash browns with sour cream. She was sure she had gained at least five pounds since she had started going out with him, and that despite having to eat early every night. As for Joel, he never put on an ounce. Nothing like being dead, he had joked darkly, to keep off the extra weight.

"Sure it hurts." He was checking on the poached eggs. "Whoever said dying doesn't hurt never tried it themselves." He shrugged, working beater and pan, concocting sauces. "Sometimes I feel like the guys who handle poisonous snakes for a living. After a couple dozen, or a hundred, bites you acquire some immunity to the toxins. The bite itself still hurts, but you don't die. Lucky bastards." The two sauces were almost ready.

She nodded, and decided to wait until after they had finished eating to tell him that she was in love with him. He did not take it well.

"You can't be in love with me, Marjorie."

It was Saturday and they lay out on his porch, soaking up both the sun and the spectacular view of the bay from his apartment. Across the water eclectic houseboats gleamed Tom Sawyer white in the treed crotch of Sausalito. Alcatraz was a rough gray diamond set in a diadem of gray-green, and cargo container ships piled high with the amputated abdomens of eighteen-wheelers plied the watery boulevard between Oakland and Manila, Richmond and Seoul, San Francisco and Hong Kong.

"Tell that to my heart." Reaching over from her lounger, she put her hand on his bare arm.

"Your hormones, you mean."

The hand twitched but stayed. "That was cruel, Joel."

He turned over to face her, and the desperation in his eyes was underlined by the raw emotion in his voice. "Oh God, I'm sorry, Marjorie! I didn't mean that. I wouldn't hurt you for the world." His fingers stroked her cheek, her neck, the sweat-beaded hollow between her breasts. They were trembling. "I—I can't love you back. You know that. I can't fall in love with anybody. It wouldn't be right. It wouldn't be *fair*."

She smiled hopefully at him, not sure how to proceed or what road to take or where to go: only knowing that go there she must. "Why don't you let me be the judge of that? I love you, Joel."

He rolled back onto the other lounger. "Don't you think I've thought about having a woman say that to me? Much less someone as beautiful and sweet as you. I'm almost forty and I've done everything possible to avoid it."

She kept her tone as gentle and reassuring as possible. "Then you shouldn't have died on my couch."

Lips pressed tightly together, he was shaking his head. "It just wouldn't be fair. What kind of a life would we have, me dying every night, you not knowing if the next morning would be the one when I didn't wake up? How would we explain it to our kids? What if my condition has something to do with some freak genetic mutation?

What if it can be passed on?" A hand came down hard and angry on the white plastic of the lounge. "Whatever the damn thing is, when I die for the last time, when I don't wake up, I want to be sure it dies with me."

Unfolding herself from her lounge, she lay down next to him, hearing the metal and plastic complain, feeling the sun-sweat of their bodies mingle and flow together. Her arm fell lazily across his chest to lie there reassuringly. "Joel Farrell, you're a better man dead than most of the men I know who are alive. If I'm willing to take a chance on a life together, why can't you?"

She didn't know if he sustained the kiss that followed out of pure passion or a need to give himself time to think of an appropriate response. Frankly she didn't care.

"I'll think about it, Marjorie. That's all I can promise."

"Then that's enough—for now." Turning in his strong, tanned arms, she gazed out and down at the glorious bay. Though she had lived in San Francisco all her life, it had always been just "the bay." Now it was much more, so very much more, thanks to him. Just as everything was so much more. She sighed and closed her eyes, thinking and feeling and hearing as she never had before in her life.

When she found the note in her mailbox the next week, her screams brought Carol running from down the hall. When pounding on her friend's door failed to elicit a response from within, the other woman swiftly used her copy of the key.

Bursting in, she saw Marjorie sitting on the old couch, clutching a crumpled piece of paper in one hand and holding the other over her mouth. It did not come close to stifling her uncontrollable sobs.

"Marjorie—Christ, what's the matter?"

"He's gone! Joel's gone!"

Sitting down alongside her friend, Carol put an arm

around her shoulders and drew her close. "The guy you've been telling me about for months? What do you mean, 'he's gone'? Did something happen? Was he called away on work? Did he—is he—dead?"

'Marjorie's sob froze in mid-rack as she gaped abruptly at her friend. When she began to laugh, that's when Carol grew really worried.

"Right, that's it," she said in clipped tones. "Come on, I'm taking you to a doctor."

"No, no!" Forcing herself to mute the wailing mixture of laughter and sobs, Marjorie used both hands to gently but firmly draw her friend back down onto the couch. "You don't understand. What you said—" She broke off, choking slightly, afraid the laughter would become uncontrollable and might degenerate into hysteria. She held out the crumpled, handwritten note. Carol took it and glanced down.

"He has beautiful handwriting, this guy."

"I know." Marjorie did not try to wipe her face, preferring to let the tears dry on her cheeks, a thin crust of salt. "Everything about him is beautiful."

Carol read. "He says he loves you more than any woman, more than any person he's ever known. That you mean more to him than anything in this or any other world. That he wants nothing more than to hold you in his arms and whisper his love to you forever. And that's why he's leaving San Francisco, and you." She put the note down. Carol was not hard, but she was a woman who brooked no nonsense. "This is a crock, Marj. A typical Dear Jenny letter if I ever heard one. I think you're well rid of the guy."

"No, you don't understand!" Reaching out, Marjorie took the note in shaky fingers. "Nobody understands."

"All right." Sitting back on the couch, the other

woman crossed her arms and waited patiently. "Explain it to me."

Her friend looked down at her lap. "I—I can't. You wouldn't believe me. And Joel wouldn't want me to."

Carol was not shy of gestures. "The son-of-a-bitch walks out on you without so much as a good-bye kiss, and you're worried about what *he* wants?" She shook her head, disgust plain on her face. "What's with this guy? I thought you said he was perfect."

"No." Finding a tissue, Marjorie reluctantly began to dab at her eyes. "I never said he was perfect. He'd be the last person on Earth to think that about himself."

"I would hope so. Ah, shit." Reaching out with both arms, she pulled Marjorie to her and let her cry herself out. Later, much later, they were finally able to talk.

"What are you going to do about it?" Carol was missing work, but she didn't care. Her friend came first. "Me, I'd forget about him. Starting right now."

"I can't." Marjorie's reply was barely audible. She looked miserable.

"What is this guy, the only man in the world? Is he rich?"

"No."

Carol persisted. "Movie-star handsome? Gigolo-great in bed? Nobel Prize material?"

"No."

"Then what? What makes him so special?"

Marjorie looked up at her friend. "I know it sounds corny, Carol, but he was alive. More than alive. He knew, like nobody else I ever met, maybe like nobody else who ever was, what being alive means. It was something special, and he shared it with me, every time, every day, every minute we were together. He showed me what life is really about."

Her friend pondered, then sipped from her cup. "I'm alive. You're alive. So what. It's nothing special."

Marjorie's reply was unintentionally condescending. "I told you you wouldn't understand. Don't feel bad. Neither would anyone else. Not without knowing Joel."

"Okay, okay." Carol put her cup down on the burl-wood coffee table, careful to set it on a coaster. "What are you going to do now? Any idea where he's gone to?"

Marjorie shook her head. "He wouldn't leave hints or clues. If he wants to lose himself, he knows how to do it. I thought about hiring a detective agency to look for him, or reporting him as missing to the police, or telling the Red Cross that I had to contact him because of an emergency, but it would just be a waste of time. I know Joel. If he wants to be gone, then he's gone."

Carol's tone was thick with concern for her friend. "I hate seeing you like this, Marjorie."

She shrugged. "I hate being like this. It's kind of like—like dying a little."

Now her friend was more than concerned; she was alarmed. "You're not thinking of doing anything crazy, are you? Because if you are, I'm not leaving this apart-ment. Work can go take a flying—"

"No, Carol." Marjorie mustered a forced smile. "I'd never do that. No matter what. That's something else Joel taught me." She inhaled deeply. "Doesn't it smell wonderful?"

Carol frowned. "What, the coffee? It's okay, but . . ."

"No, not the coffee. Life."

The other woman sighed tiredly. "Life doesn't 'smell.'"

Her friend looked her straight in the eye. "You didn't know Joel Farrell."

Five months went by, and then he was there. Just like that. At her door one Thursday evening, when he was sure she would be home. They didn't say anything for a very long time. Then she threw herself at him hard, with deliberate force, so that he would have to either put his arms around her or be knocked to the ground. Eventually they went inside.

"You rotten bastard," she muttered lovingly. "Why'd you come back?"

He shrugged, his expression half-irresistible boyish grin, half barely contained inner torment. "I needed a place to die."

"Funny man. Oh, what a funny, funny man you are." She didn't know whether to smile or slap him.

He saved her the trouble of deciding. Putting his arm around her, he walked her toward the tiny kitchen where once he had methodically washed cheap dishes. "When I died, it was thinking of you. Since that happens every night, I finally decided I had no choice but to come back." His tone was serious. Dead serious. "If you still want me back, after what I did."

She tried to make light of it. That was her nature. Inside she was joy and jelly. "So you went away for a while, to think things over. You took a vacation. I can handle that. I guess if I want you back, I have to." Her fingers played on his chest as he opened the door to the tiny porch and they walked outside. The autumn night was cold and brittle, invigorating and full of new life. "I mean, it's not like you died or something." She put her hand on his face, caressing the stubbly skin. "I guess nothing—has changed?"

He shook his head slowly. "Nothing has changed. I didn't tell you—one of the reasons I left was because I was afraid, after that night when you found me in the street, that I might start dying sooner. Earlier. That it might become a regular thing or even become worse. That I might start dying at six o'clock or five or three in the afternoon. I needed to check that out before I could even think of doing anything about—us."

Her heart was pounding. "And did you? Do you?"

His smile was a recurrent miracle that she had never thought to see again. "No. I had a couple more seven o'clock episodes, but other than that I'm still usually good until after ten. Nine thirty at the worst."

She nodded. "I can live with that, too. If you can." Tears were streaming down her face, completely soaking her good blue blouse. She didn't care. About that or anything else.

"Then you'll take me back?" The sense of hope rising in his voice pierced her heart like a long needle. "You still want me? If you do, if you will—Marjorie, I swear to God I'll never leave you again, ever. I'll do anything for you. Anything and everything. Please, let me do everything for you. Money, travel, cooking, laundry, I'll give you everything if you'll just take me back. I'll do anything. Just name it." He put a hand on either side of her face, cupping her cheeks, framing her smile and her tears. They were glorious, phenomenal, astonishing. As was everything about her, and the world they found themselves in. "I'll even die for you."

She was crying uncontrollably as she threw her arms around his neck and drew him close. Crying and laughing at the same time.

"You'll have to do better than that," she sobbed.

A Fatal Exception
Has Occurred at . . .

As I have mentioned previously, the first story I ever sold (though not the first one to appear in print) was "Some Notes Concerning a Green Box." This was a Lovecraftian pastiche done in the style of a letter to Arkham House's founder and editor, August Derleth. I never expected it to see print as a story, yet that's what happened. Its purchase by Derleth taught me a valuable lesson. Write for yourself, write what pleases you, and do not write simply to appeal to a perceived market.

I never stopped loving Lovecraft. When I was young, his leavening of gothic horror with a soupçon of science was the only fiction that caused me to cast furtive glances at night in the direction of darkened windows. I even taught at UCLA a graduate literature seminar in Lovecraft's works. Many years went by, and many words, during which time I wrote only one other very early tale set in Lovecraft's Cthulhu Mythos.

Then editor John Pelan came calling with an invitation to compose a new Mythos story for an anthology of same that he was putting together for Del Rey Books. The Children of Cthulhu, *it was called. Aside from the obvious opportunity to write about unnamable cephalopodian offspring (the title "Cthulhu's Nursery" sprang to mind— and was as swiftly discarded), I wondered how to bring the Mythos out of the dark alleys of towns like Dunwich and Innsmouth and into the present day. Besides, I've never been to either malevolent community (does the new eminent domain–urban renewal law apply to Inns-mouth?) and would not be able to describe them (or even Boston) with proper justice.*

I was becoming more and more familiar with another aspect of contemporary culture, however, and thought its own arcane argot and evolving mythology might make a nice fit with the Mythos, if only I could figure out a way to make it work as a story.

The answer lay in the mutual mouthing of horrific curses. Both Lovecraft's Mythos and that of Microsoft possess, and are possessed by, their own singular liturgy of eldritch moans and eerie execrations. Believe me, if I thought lifting my bloodstained arms to the skies and thrice chanting "Ia, Ia, Shub-Niggurath, ftaghn!" would keep MS Word from crashing before automatic save engaged to protect heartfelt work otherwise lost, I would readily do so . . .

"He's going to post *what*?"

Hayes looked up from his handheld. He had known from the beginning that this was going to be tough to explain. Now that he actually found himself in the conference room with the others, the true difficulty of it was more apparent than ever. Nonetheless he not only had to try, he had to convince them of the seriousness of the situation.

Outside, the sun was shining through a dusky scrim of clouds: a perfect Virginia autumn day. The trees were as saturated with color as high-priced film, the creeks were meandering rather than running, and he would have preferred to be anywhere other than in the room. Unfortunately there was the minor matter of a job. It was a good job, his was, and he wanted to keep it. Even if it meant commuting to Quantico from the woodsy homestead he shared with his wife and two kids.

The men and women seated at the table were sensible folk. Practical, rational, intelligent. How was he going to explain the situation to them? Aware that the silence that had followed Morrison's query was gathering size and strength like a quiet thunderhead, he decided he might as well plunge onward.

"The Necronomicon," he explained. "Online. All of it. Unless the government of the United States agrees to pay ten million dollars into a specified Swiss bank account by midnight tomorrow."

"That's not much time." Marion Tiffin fiddled with her glasses, which irrespective of the style of the day always seemed to be sliding off her nose.

Voice low and threatening, Morrison leaned forward over the table. "What, pray tell, is this 'Necronomicon,' and why should we give one of the hundreds of nutso hackers this Section deals with every month ten dollars not to post it online, much less ten million?"

Hayes fought to hold his ground, intellectual as well as physical. He might as well, he knew. There was no place else to go. "It's a legendary volume of esoteric lore, thought for many years to be the fictional invention of a writer from Providence."

"Providence as in Heaven or Providence as in Rhode Island?" Spitzer wanted to know. Spitzer was the biggest man in the room. By the physical conditioning standards of the Bureau, he ought to have been let go twenty years ago. That had not happened because he was recogniz ably smarter than almost everyone else. It was Spitzer who had solved the White River murders six years ago, and Spitzer who had deduced the psychological pattern that had allowed the Bureau to claim credit for catching the Cleveland serial child killer Frank Coleman. So his girth was conveniently ignored when the time came, as it inevitably did, to update personnel files.

"The state," Hayes replied flatly. It was no good getting into a battle of wits with Spitzer. You'd lose.

Chief Agent Morrison leaned back in his chair and put his hands behind his head. His bristly blond hair looked stiff enough to remove paint. "I'm surprised at you, Hayes. Unless you're doing this to try to lighten the mood. Otherwise I think your story makes a good item for the tabloid files."

"No." This was even harder than Hayes had imagined it was going to be. "It's a genuine threat, not a crank call. Don't you think I'd check it out before bringing it up here for discussion? Give me five minutes."

Morrison glanced absently at his watch. "Okay—but only if you make it fun."

Hayes wanted to say that it was anything but fun, but suspected that if he did so, he would lose his precious five minutes. And he could not afford to. "The hacker calls himself Wilbur. Don't ask me why. Maybe it's even his real name. He says he gained access to the restricted section of the Special Collections Department at the Widener Library at Harvard, snuck in a portable wide-angle scanner, and spent the better part of a day copying out as much of this venerable if not venerated book as he could manage."

Morrison frowned. "I thought you said it was fictional."

"No. I said it was *thought* to be fictional. Just for the hell of it, I checked with Harvard. Routine follow-up to this sort of thing. I had to go through four different people until I could find someone who'd admit to the library even possessing the volume in question. As soon as I did so, they went off to recheck my identification and credentials.

"I finally got to speak to a Professor Fitchburn. When I told him the reason for my call, he got downright frantic. First he sent someone to check the records of recent visitors to the restricted shelves of the Widener. They were able to identify only three people in the past year who had been granted access to see the book. All three were well known to the staff, either academically, personally, or both. Then someone—apparently people were gathering in this Fitchburn's office all the time we were talking—remembered that a renovation crew had been in the Special Collections area for less than a week back in April, updating the fire suppression system. That must have been how this Wilbur guy gained access."

"He would have to have known the book is there, what to look for," Tiffin pointed out.

"Even if all of this is true, so what?" Morrison reached for the glass of ice water that always stood ready exactly six inches to the northeast of his notepad. "What does Harvard want us to do about it? Perform an exorcism? Tell this Fitchburn to contact the local Catholic parish." Under his breath he growled, "Damn academics."

"It's not that kind of esoterica." Hayes's fingers kept twisting together, like small snakes seeking holes in which to hide. "The information in it has nothing to do with any of the major religions. It's—Professor Fitchburn was reluctant to go into details. I got the feeling he didn't want to tell me any more about it than he felt I needed to know."

"This discussion is also woefully short on details." Morrison checked his watch again. "Your five minutes are about up, Hayes, and we have real work to do this morning. Sorry that all these kidnappings and murders and terrorist threats have to take up our valuable time."

"You remember the sinking of the *Paradise Four*?" Hayes asked him.

It was Van Wert who responded. "The cruise ship that sank off Pohnpei in that typhoon six months ago?"

Hayes nodded. "This Wilbur claims he's responsible

for that. Claims he was trying out a couple of pages from the scanned book."

Morrison guffawed. "Typical nutcase. Next he'll be claiming credit for last week's earthquake in Denver."

"As a matter of fact . . . ," Hayes began.

"Five minutes are up." The Chief Agent shuffled the neat pile of papers in front of him, preparatory to changing the subject.

At that point it was doubtful he would have listened to anyone—except Spitzer. "A seven point one. Lots of property damage, forty-six killed, hundreds injured."

"I know the stats," Morrison growled, but let the big man continue.

Spitzer scratched at his impregnable five o'clock shadow. "Denver doesn't have earthquakes. It's situated in a tectonically stable region. The geologists said it was a freak occurrence. They still can't find the fault responsible for the geological shift."

"So?" Morrison groused. Time was fleeting.

"What," Spitzer continued softly, "if there is no fault?"

"Are you actually suggesting that it was somehow this Wilbur person's fault?" Tiffin was gaping at the big man. "Sorry."

Spitzer was looking at Hayes. "All I'm saying is that while gaining admittance to the restricted section of the Special Collections Department of the Harvard Library may not be a federal crime, and therefore not fall under our purview, making threats against and attempting to extort money from the government is another matter entirely. Bob, I presume you've tried to trace this Wilbur person and without success, or you wouldn't be here discussing the matter with us."

Hayes nodded, more grateful than he could say for Spitzer's support. "Wilbur says that if we don't comply with his demands, he'll post to the Net everything he's scanned from this book. According to him, that will let anyone from third-world dictators to role-playing teens have an equal shot at destroying the world."

Van Wert pursued his lips. "Wouldn't that kind of render his ten million worthless?"

"I had the impression he's pretty desperate. Or pretty crazy. You know how hard it is to deduce personality types from e-mail." He went silent, watching Morrison.

The Chief Agent sipped from his glass, then set it back down in precisely the same place where it had been resting. "This is ridiculous, and I can't believe I'm wasting the Bureau's time on it." His gaze narrowed suspiciously as he stared across the table at Spitzer. "If I find out that you two have conspired on this, to try to put one over on me and get a couple of days off, I'll see you both spending the rest of your respective careers tracking retirees' bank transfers in South Florida."

Spitzer folded his hands over his imposing belly. "I swear to God I never heard anything of it until Hayes started talking ten minutes ago."

Morrison grunted, mumbling something under his breath. "This 'Wilbur' isn't the only crazy person around. I ought to be committed myself for even listening to this. If any word of this leaks beyond this room, I won't be able to buy a burger in this town without people pointing at me and cracking up." His glare at that moment could have melted manhole covers.

"All right—do a quick follow-up. A harmless ranting nut can turn into a dangerous nut. See if you can find him. We'll stop him from making threats, anyway. Hollow or otherwise." He picked up his papers. "Now then, about this new militia site on the Web. We know it's being routed through a server in Madison, Wisconsin, but after that . . ."

An hour later, puffing slightly, Spitzer caught up to Hayes in the hallway. "He doesn't buy it, does he?"

"Morrison? No." Hayes didn't know whether to feel half justified or half disappointed. "What about you? And thanks for sticking up for me back there."

"You're welcome. Let's say I have an open mind on the subject. What do you intend to do now?"

"We don't have much time. In between talking to Harvard and trying to calm them down, I asked them what I should do. One of their people suggested I contact a Herman Rumford in New York. Gave me his number."

"By the brevity of your response I take it you have already done so."

Hayes nodded as they strolled together down the corridor. "If anything, he sounds even weirder than this Wilbur character. But he said to come on up, bring what information I had with me, and he would see what he could do." For the first time that morning, he smiled. "Morrison as much as said you could come along on this with me. Be nice to spend a day in the city."

Spitzer nodded indifferently. "You think this guy can do anything?"

"Well, I put the usual technical people on the trace, and they haven't been able to run any surreptitious Wilburs to ground. So we might as well take a few of the citizenry's tax dollars and head on up to the Big Wormhome. Either that or find a way to winkle ten million bucks out of the discretionary terrorism fund."

Spitzer looked thoughtful. "I think we'd better try talking to this Rumford first." They walked a little farther. "That was very strange, the Denver earthquake. And before that, the cruise ship going down. Of course, it was caught in a typhoon. A very sudden typhoon, but not unusual for that time of year in the Pacific. Or so I've read."

"The ship was less than two years old. They're not supposed to sink," Hayes pointed out.

"No, they're not." Spitzer suddenly smiled. He had a charming, disarming smile. "We can take the eight PM express to Grand Central. Better not wait until morning."

"That's what I was thinking" were Hayes's last words to his fellow agent.

Somewhat to the surprise of both men, Herman Rumford lived in a fine old brownstone in a notable Upper East Side neighborhood, among which were sprinkled elegant shops, overpriced restaurants the size of shoe closets, and a smattering of celebrities. Rumford admitted them not to a slovenly garret, but to a pleasant living room decorated with contemporary furniture and thick Chinese woolen rugs. The art on the walls, however, instantly notified both agents they were not in the presence of one of New York's ubiquitous brokers, bankers, or political mavens.

Some of the subject matter was unapologetically horrific. Some was in appallingly bad taste. Some reflected views of the world and of existence that would have seriously distressed even the most tolerant priest. Some was authentically old. And somehow it was all of a piece, as one seemingly unrelated composition flowed unexpectedly into another.

"My collection." Rumford was a short, thickset, fortyish fellow with shoulder-length hair tied back in a ponytail, dull blue eyes, and biceps that were more than blips beneath his shirt. He looked like a human grenade and reminded Hayes of a renegade cherub. "Not to everyone's taste, I'm afraid. It's part of my hobby. And my hobby is my life. I spend most of my time studying its ramifications and variations."

"What is it that you study?" Spitzer loomed over their host like a sumo grand champion alongside a new student.

"Evil. I've made quite a study of it, with a view toward battling it wherever and whenever possible. You might say that we're sort of in the same business, although for me it's not a job." He gestured for them to follow. "Of course, I don't have access to the breadth of resources that you gentlemen do, but it's astonishing what you can find on the Net these days. But then, that's why you're here, isn't it?"

Leaving the pleasant living room and its disturbing art collection behind, the two agents followed their host into a small, book-filled study. Potted plants, some of them reaching to the ceiling, brought a touch of tropical rain forest into the city. They had been well looked after. Two tall, narrow windows looked out onto the street. Queer sculptures and eccentric whatnots lay scattered about the dark mahogany shelves as if consulting the books neatly cataloged there. It was a reassuring contrast with the painted threats of the room they had just left.

"Not your usual hobby," Hayes told Rumford, making conversation.

"It does demand a certain devotion." Settling himself into a comfortable office chair, their host confronted an enormous LCD monitor. Not one, but several computers were arrayed against the wall beside the Spartan desk. It was more of a workbench, actually, Hayes thought. There were two other monitors, both presently displaying wallpaper that could only be described as eclectic, a tangle of cables, and a host of winking, humming ancillary electronics.

"As I said, it's a hobby, not my business. I don't have a business, really. My grandfather left me a trust, you see. I live comfortably, but not to excess. I would rather do good deeds with my money than live to excess."

"Righteous of you." Spitzer lumbered forward until he was standing behind the seated Rumford's left shoulder.

Hayes took the right side. "Have you been able to find anything on our insistent and avaricious friend Wilbur, with the information we provided to you last night?"

"Oh, I caught up with him this morning. About an hour ago. We've been chatting." He indicated the miniature video camera sitting atop one of the nearby server boxes. "Not face-to-face. He's adamant, not stupid." Rumford chuckled as he did things to the ergonomic keyboard in front of him. Screens flashed and on went the huge monitor, the images large enough for both agents to scrutinize without straining. "He has no objection to talking. He just wants his ten million dollars."

"We can't give it to him. No government agency would approve it." Spitzer wanted to ask what several enigmatic metal boxes connected to the main server were for, but decided he could inquire later. All of them were black instead of the usual bland ivory white. One appeared badly scarred and scorched, as if by fire.

"I suspected as much, but I hardly have the authority to tell him that. After all," Rumford added modestly, "I'm only helping you gentlemen out. I have no real clout here at all." Though naturally soft, his voice could take on a certain firmness when he wished it to. "I might mention that he's already threatened me."

Hayes looked alarmed. "Threatened you? But he doesn't know where you live—does he?" Glancing back through the front room, he eyed the front door uneasily.

"I seriously doubt it. I know how to cover my ass online. And I don't know where he is, either. Not physically. We only know where the other person is on the Net. Still," he added as he tapped a fistful of keys, "there are a few things we can try. Ah!" He indicated the screen. "Say hello, gentlemen."

The image on the monitor was a mass of writhing tentacles, bulging cephalopodan eyeballs, and slavering ichorous maws. Well-done for an applet, Hayes decided, but not especially well-animated. Words began to appear beneath the image.

When do I get my money . . . ?

Rumford glanced expectantly at his visitors. "What do you want me to tell him?"

Spitzer and Hayes exchanged a glance. Coming up on the train the previous night, they had already rehearsed a number of possible scenarios. Two-way audio would have made things easier, Hayes knew, just as he knew that unless he was dumber than he seemed, their quarry would not risk committing even a disguised voice to storage that could be studied later. Speech patterns were too easily divined and applied to future suspects.

"Tell him it's in the works. He'll have his money before ten tonight, well ahead of his deadline. Provided we can assure ourselves of his sincerity and that his threat is real."

Rumford typed in the response. Moments later a reply was forthcoming.

Actually, I'm surprised. The government usually isn't this sensible. Of course, this may be a stall on your part, but I don't care. You can't find me, certainly not by tonight, if at all. As for further proof of the seriousness of my intentions, turn on CNN and keep watching.

Spitzer shrugged. A somber-faced Rumford directed them back to the living room and to the TV sequestered there. The big agent switched it on, found the requisite cable channel, and returned to the study. Two hours slipped by before the National Aquarium in Baltimore, an exceptionally sturdy and well-designed building, collapsed into the harbor amid much screaming and panic and death by drowning. Collapsed—or was pulled.

An ashen-faced Hayes relayed a response via their host.

"Enough! We get your point."

Back came the reply.

I thought you would. There are quite a few passages in the Necronomicon dealing with a certain Cthulhu, his minions, and other really unpleasant ocean dwellers. Next time, I thought I might try to call up the servants of Ithaqua. The East Coast hasn't had a really serious blow in five years.

"You've done enough," Spitzer had Rumford type back. "Give us till ten."

You'd better come through. This stuff is almost too easy. Those Columbine guys could've blown away their whole state with it. Imagine al-Qaeda's people scrolling through the file, or some of those murderous tribal types in Central Africa.

At the end of the message, the onscreen cursor winked patiently back at the three men, awaiting commands.

Spitzer and Hayes caucused. "There's no way the Bureau is going to cough up ten million for this weirdo on our say-so alone. No way." Despite the fact that it was very comfortable in the study, sweat was beading on Hayes's forehead. "We've got to find a way to get to him before he starts posting."

"We don't even know if he's in this country," Spitzer reminded his partner somberly. "He could have come in just to pay his visit to the library."

"I know, I know!"

"I said there were one or two things I could try." In the room, with the sun beginning to set outside, only their host remained relatively composed. "I can't go ahead—I won't go ahead—without your authorization, though."

Turning, Hayes frowned down at their host. "Why not?"

Rumford's expression did not change. "There could be ancillary consequences that I can't predict."

"What, online? Go ahead. If there's something you can try, try it."

Rumford was very precise. "Then I have your authorization?"

"Sure, go ahead," Spitzer told him. "If a router goes down somewhere or you crash an ISP, we'll take responsibility. We have to try something. Maybe you can find out where this guy is. If you can do that, and if it's on this continent, we can have people there within the hour. Overseas, within a day."

Their host nodded. "That's not really what I intend to try, but I'll keep it in mind." Swiveling in his seat, he turned back to his monitor.

It took less than thirty minutes. There was no shout of triumph from their host. He clearly wasn't the type. But there was quiet satisfaction in his voice. "Got him."

Both agents were more than a little impressed. "That's impossible," Hayes insisted tersely. "Our technical people at the Bureau have been working on this since yesterday, and all through the night, and we haven't been beeped. Which means they couldn't locate squat." He eyed their stocky, intense host closely. "How come you could do it?"

Beady blue eyes flicked in the agent's direction. "I've been dealing with individuals of this type for some time. Let's just say I have access to a search engine or two even your people don't know about." He smiled thinly. "The Net's a big place, you know."

Spitzer loomed over both of them. "It doesn't matter. Where is he? Physically, I mean." He already had his phone in his hand, ready to transmit the vital information back to Virginia.

"Let me try something first." Without waiting for a

response, Rumford returned to his typing. "If he thinks you're on to him, he can still post a lot of dangerous material before your people can restrain him physically." Both agents read over their host's shoulder.

Wilbur: Do not post the Necronomicon or any part of it online. By doing so you're making it available to children and to people unaware of what they are dealing with. The Necronomicon is not a video game.

The response was immediate.

Don't lecture me, Rumford. I know all about the Necronomicon and I know what I'm doing. I want my ten million! Tell the Bureau people that.

"He doesn't know you're here," their host murmured. "Probably thinks I have and am on a phone connection to you." He typed.

If you persist in going ahead with this, steps will have to be taken.

The reply was prompt.

I'm not afraid of the government. I know how fast they don't move. By the time they find out where I buy my groceries, I can post the entire contents of The Book. They'd better not try anything. Tell them that.

Rumford didn't have to. Hayes could see it for himself.

Their host looked up at the agent. His expression was set. "Hand me that box of flash drives, will you?" He pointed. "The one in the open cabinet, over there."

Hayes fetched the indicated container. For a box full of flash drives, it seemed excessive. Solid steel, with a tiny combination lock. Returning, he tripped on a roll in the throw rug and nearly fell. Their host's reaction was instructive.

"For God's sake, don't drop that!" Rumford's round pink face had turned white.

Hayes frowned at the metal box, infinitely sturdier than the usual plastic container. "Flash drives can handle shock. What's the problem?"

"Just don't drop it." Carefully taking the container from the bemused agent, their host opened it slowly. Spitzer was surprised to see that it contained only one silvery KeyDrive. Mumbling something under his breath, Rumford slipped this into the appropriate socket on his main machine. The drive did not, Hayes observed, automatically identify itself.

A couple of clicks and a macro or two later, and the monitor filled with a jumble of symbols and words that were unintelligible to the two agents. Working with grim-faced determination, their host began to use his mouse to methodically highlight specific sections. These were then cut and copied to another page, where he proceeded to carefully position them over an intricate template of symbols. After some twenty minutes of this, he sat back and double-clicked. Immediately the monitor began to pulse with a rich red glow.

Spitzer observed the vivid visual activity with interest. "Java applet?" he wondered aloud. "ActiveX?"

Rumford shook his head. "Not exactly."

"Nice animation," the agent continued, watching without understanding what was going on. "Bryce or something from SG?"

"My own code. I correspond with people with similar interests. There's a guy in Germany, and interestingly, a woman in R'yleh—sorry, Riyadh. We play around with our own software. Closed-source. It's kind of a hobby within a hobby."

Hayes indicated the monitor. The intense, swirling, necrotic colors had given way to the more familiar instant-messaging screen format.

What do you think you're doing? You think you can trouble me with this?

"What did you do?" Spitzer leaned even closer, dominating his surroundings. "Send him a virus?"

"Something like that," Rumford replied noncommittally. In his server, the flash drive continued to blink softly even though no eldritch colors or patterns were visible any longer on the monitor.

Wait—what's going on?

A pause, then,

Stop it . . . stop it now! You can't block me. I'm not waiting any longer. Just for this, I'm going to post the first chapter *right now*!

Hayes tensed, but their host did not appear overly concerned. He just sat staring, Buddha-like, at the screen.

What is this? Make it stop—stop it now, I'm warning you! Rumford, make it stop! You sonofabitch bastard, do something!

A chill trickled down Spitzer's broad back as the words appeared on the screen. The flash drive, he noted, had stopped blinking.

Make it go away! Rumford, do something now! I won't post—I'll do anything you want. Make it go away! Rumford, please, don't let it—oh god, stop it now—please, do someth

No more words appeared on the screen.

Sighing softly, Rumford leaned back in his chair and rubbed his forehead. He looked and sounded like a man who had just driven several fast laps around an especially bumpy track. "That's it."

Hayes made a face. "That's it? What do you mean, 'that's it'?"

Turning away from the monitor, their host looked up at him. "It's over. He's not going to post anything. Not now. Not ever."

The chill Spitzer had been experiencing deepened. "What did you do? Where is he? *What did you send him?*"

Rumford rose. "Something to drink? No? Well, I'm thirsty. Nasty business, this. You need to tell those people at Harvard to be more careful. They really ought to burn the damn thing, but I know they won't." He shook his head dolefully. "Book people! They're more dangerous than you can imagine." He eyed Spitzer.

"It doesn't matter where he is or was. I took care of the problem. He can't post a 'you've got mail' note, much less an entire book. Much less the Necronomicon."

Realization dawned on Hayes's face. "You got into his machine! You wiped the copy!"

Rumford nodded. "In a manner of speaking, yes."

Spitzer was not impressed. "Unless this Wilbur was a complete idiot, he made at least one duplicate and stored it somewhere safe."

"It doesn't matter," Rumford reiterated. "He can't make use of it. Just take my word for it."

"That's asking a lot." Spitzer studied the smaller man. "How can we be sure?" He indicated his partner. "We have responsibilities, too, you know. This isn't a hobby for us."

Their host considered. Then he pulled a KeyDrive from a box in a drawer. An ordinary box full of ordinary drives. Slipping it into an open socket, he entered a series of commands. In response, the computer's hard drive began to hum efficiently. Moments later the flash drive ejected. Carefully, very carefully, Rumford removed it, slipped it into a protective case, and handed it to Hayes.

"Here's a copy of the program I used." His eyes burned, and for an instant he seemed rather larger than he was in person. "You might think of it as an anti-virus program, but it's not intended for general use. It's very case-specific. You'd be surprised what can be digitized these days. If someone like this Wilbur surfaces again, you can utilize it without having to come to me."

Hayes accepted the drive and slipped it into an inside coat pocket. "Thanks, but I couldn't make sense of anything you put up on screen."

Rumford smiled humorlessly. "Just press F-one for help. There's an intuitive guide built in. I had it translated from the German." He brightened. "Now, let's have something cold to drink!"

Later, in the cab on the way back to Grand Central to catch the express back to Washington, while their Nigerian driver cursed steadily in Yoruba and battled midtown traffic, Hayes pulled the KeyDrive from his pocket. It was a perfectly ordinary-looking drive, rainbow-reflective and silvery. Their host had hastily added a few explanatory words to a piece of notepaper he had passed to Hayes just before the two agents had departed.

"You really think he dealt satisfactorily with that Wilbur person?" Spitzer asked his partner and friend.

Hayes shrugged. "Unless this was all some kind of elaborate hoax."

The other agent grunted, and his belly heaved. "Better not let Morrison hear you say that. Not after we pressed for the time and expense money to come up here and do the follow-through."

Hayes nodded, absently scanning the notepaper. "If it wasn't a hoax, at least we won't have to come up here again. The instructions for making use of this are pretty straightforward." He had no trouble deciphering Rumford's precise, prominent handwriting, which he proceeded to quote to his partner.

"'To download Shoggoth,'" he began thoughtfully . . .

Basted

Theme anthologies force a writer to think about subjects that are often, at most, of passing interest. For example, it's hard to imagine writers of fantasy who have not at one time or another in their lives gone through a spell of fascination with ancient Egypt. There is simply so much of that great civilization that inspires, from its art to its technological developments to its incredibly long lineage. It is a fascination that persists to this day in films like the modern Mummy and its sequel and humankind's continuing obsession with the afterlife. Not to mention the alien science that helped to raised the pyramids— though one would think that any civilization with the knowledge to shortcut such massive construction would prefer a more modern building material than rock.

Ah well. Some of the mysteries of the Pharaohs must remain forever as inscrutable to us as their preferred hairstyles and their penchant for being portrayed in profile. They have even given us a word for it: sphinxlike.

And now, a word about cats. I love cats. I adore cats. I like to think that this affection is reciprocated. Certainly it is among the six cats who sleep on the bed with us. Sleep with six cats, and you will never be cold— though morning will often find you extricating stray cat hairs from the oddest places.

Cheetahs are an especial favorite of mine (no, one of those six cats is not a cheetah). Once in Namibia in 1993, at a private wildlife preserve called Mount Etjo that lies about halfway between the capital of Windhoek and the great national park Etosha, I was allowed to spend more than an hour interacting in an open environment in excessive midday heat with a local resident named Felix. A full-grown male cheetah, Felix was content to sit quietly while I scratched him on his head and behind his ears. He did not, however, like to be scratched between his front legs, a fact that the local guide in attendance declared was something new to him.

I was grateful to Felix for apprising me of this fact in a forthright and unmistakable manner while not simultaneously removing my face. I also discovered that cheetahs not only purr like oversized house cats, but occasionally go "meow," just like a cartoon cat's meow in a dialogue balloon.

So, out of ancient Egypt and modern Namibia comes the following story . . .

It was Harima who drove Ali into the desert that night. Harima was his wife. There had been a time in the not-so-distant past when Ali had thought Harima a great beauty, as had a number of his friends. When, exactly, had that time been? He tried to remember. How long ago? He could not recall.

Now his wife was rather larger than he remembered from their time of courtship. In fact, the joke around the village was that she was as big as the pyramids at Giza— and her voice shrill and loud enough to wake every mummy in the City of the Dead. Whatever she had become, she was no longer the sweet and alluring woman he had married. Her voice, old Mustapha Kalem was fond of saying over strong coffee in the village café, was harsh enough to drown out the morning call to prayer.

Ali was sick of that voice, just as he was sick of what his life had become.

Once, long ago, he was a bright and promising student who had done well in school. Well enough to be considered for attending the university, in Cairo. But his hardworking family, Allah's blessings be upon them, had been dirt poor—which in soil-poor Egypt is a description to be taken literally. Even with Ali being an only child, there had been barely enough money for food, let alone higher schooling. As for the university, it was made clear to Ali that such a notion was out of the question.

Forced to look for a job to help support himself and his increasingly feeble parents, the ever-resourceful Ali had seen how rich tourists paid incredible amounts of money to visit and view the fabled ancient wonders of his country. The guides who escorted such people through temples and tombs not only received substantial salaries from the tour companies, but were also the recipients of frequent tips, sometimes in hard currency, from the grateful visitors. Espying an opportunity where there seemed to be none—something Ali had always been good at—he proceeded to apprentice himself to one of the best-known and most successful of the local guide groups.

Alas, many years had passed, and he was still carrying heavy luggage and fetching cold drinks and doing only the most menial of tasks for the guide service. They guarded their privileges jealously, did the guides. Many times, Ali had seen less qualified apprentices promoted over him, only because they had connections: this one was somebody's cousin or that one, wealthy Aunt Aamal's son. A poor boy like himself was kept down.

This sorry state of affairs continued despite his excellent and ever-improving command of English, as well as his knowledge of many things ancient that he had acquired from listening to the other guides, reading guidebooks, and humbly asking questions of the more knowledgeable tourists themselves. In truth, it had to be admitted that the visitors from overseas encouraged him in his efforts to better himself more than did his own countrymen.

Especially more than Harima. He was not good enough for her, she was fond of telling anyone who would listen. He was too short, too dark, he didn't make enough money, he was a lousy lover—ah, Harima, he mused! Wild-haired, lovely, full-lipped Harima—who once was the love of his life and he, he had thought, of hers. No longer. Black visions of drooling jackals and squawking buzzards helping themselves to hearty hunks of the hefty Harima filled his head. Unworthy thoughts, he knew. But he could not help them.

To get away from her he had taken Suhar, his favorite camel (truth be told, his only camel) for a nocturnal jaunt into the desert in the direction of the canal. A piece of the desert, the real desert, was very near to Ali's village. It was not hard to get away from contemporary civilization and back to those of the great Pharaohs and kings of ancient Egypt. It was their temples that brought the tourists to his town and kept them coming back. Neither Ali nor the guides for whom he worked were ashamed to admit that the best thing about the temples was the money they continued to bring in, thousands of years after their builders had vanished.

The moon that floated high in the star-flecked sky was nearly full. Ali enjoyed the ride, as did Suhar. The farther from the village they rode, the more a calming peace settled on both man and camel, and the farther the lights of the city of Zagazig faded into the distance. He took a different track than usual. As his mount's wide, splayed feet shushed over the sands, away from the roads and trails that led to the main tourist sites, the steady yammering of televisions and of boom boxes and, yes, of Harima faded from memory as well as from earshot.

It was well past midnight when Suhar suddenly stopped. Ali frowned. Nothing lay in front of them but flat desert and the still-distant canal. Giving her a firm nudge in the ribs, he yelled "Hut, hut!" Still she refused to move.

What ails the beast? he wondered. Dismounting, he strode out in front of her. If he failed to return before sunrise, Harima would lay into him even more than usual. She would accuse him of spending their money, her money, on illegal liquor or women or khat. He winced as he envisioned the knowing smiles that would appear on the faces of his neighbors, and the disapproving expressions he would encounter the next time he went into town for coffee.

Taking the reins, he began tugging. Gently at first, then more forcefully. But neither sharp gesture nor angry words could persuade the camel to budge so much as a foot.

"Spawn of the devil! Spewer of sour milk! Why do I waste good money on food for you? If not for the tourists who like to have their picture taken with you, I would sell you for steaks and chops!" Unimpressed, in the manner of camels, Suhar stood and chewed and said nothing.

"Come *on*," Ali snapped. Leaning back, he put his full weight into the reins. As he took a step, Suhar emitted an outraged bawl. This was overridden by the sound of a loud crack beneath his feet. With a yelp and a shout, he felt himself plunge downward and out of sight.

Above, Suhar stood quietly masticating her cud. She did not move forward toward the yawning cavity that had appeared in the desert.

Spitting out dust and grit while mustering several suitable curses, a groaning Ali rolled over and climbed slowly to his feet. Though his backside throbbed where he had landed, the fall had wounded his dignity more than his body. Feeling carefully of himself, he decided that nothing was broken. Looking up, he saw that the hole through which he had fallen was no more than a meter wide. Sand continued to spill from the edges of the opening, the trickling grains illuminated by the moon that was still high in the night sky.

What had he tumbled into? An old well, perhaps. But a well would have been deeper. Turning as he continued to dust himself off, he let his eyes adjust to the subdued moonlight.

And sucked in his breath.

Surrounding him were beautifully painted walls. Fourth or Fifth Dynasty, he decided, drawing upon his years of accumulated knowledge about his ancestors' works. The elaborate murals were intact and completely undamaged. At the four corners of the chamber stood four massive diorite statues of Bastet, the cat god of the ancient Egyptians. Except for them the tomb—for such it had to be with a stone sarcophagus in its center—was empty. His heart, which had leaped so high the instant he had recognized his surroundings, now fell. No golden chariots blinded his gaze, no metal chests of precious stones stood waiting to be opened. The tomb was in excellent condition, but it either had been looted or else was the resting place of some poor man.

And yet—the quality of the murals was exceptional. That did not square with the apparent emptiness of the chamber. And then there was the single sarcophagus, resting in isolated majesty in the exact center of the room. It was not large, indicating that this was perhaps the final resting place of a juvenile. Or maybe an intended resting place, given the barrenness of the chamber.

He consoled himself with the knowledge that while there might not be any great riches present, the four massive and well-made statues of Bastet would surely be worth something. Even mummies themselves could be sold. He hesitated. That was provided there was a mummy here, of course, and that the sarcophagus was not empty.

It took him nearly an hour to shift the heavy stone cover far enough to one side to let him get at the inner sarcophagus. For a second time, his heart jumped, this time at the flash of gold within. Sadly, the inner container was only of gilded wood. It opened far more easily than had the upper cover. Another person might have been frightened, working there alone beneath the desert in a previously undiscovered tomb, opening ancient sarcophagi. Not Ali. The desert, the nearby ancient city of Bubastis, were his home. He had spent all his life among such relics of the distant past. The only danger in doing what he was doing, he knew, came from inhaling too much dust and mold or being discovered by the antiquities authorities.

The inner cover was muscled aside, allowing him to see within. His brows furrowed uncertainly. The inner sarcophagus contained a mummy, all right—but a mummy unlike any he had ever seen. It was too big to be a child, and the wrong shape for a man or woman. What could it be? From local excavations in and around Tell Basta, Ali knew that the rulers of Bubastis had sometimes caused selected holy cats to be interred beside them along with human members of their household. The statues of Bastet pointed the way to the answer, helping him to finally recognize the shape.

It was indeed a mummified feline, not unlike those from the famous graveyard of mummified holy cats— but this was no house cat. This was big, much bigger. Was it unusual or unique enough to be particularly valuable? There was no way of telling without calling on expert help. It did not look particularly heavy—certainly no heavier than had been the stone lid of the main sarcophagus. He knew a man who, for a reasonable price, could identify such things and who would ask no awkward questions.

Ali was very strong in the arms and shoulders from years of carrying tourists' overfilled luggage. Suhar could manage the dual burden of man and mummy easily. Reaching into the inner container, he carefully slipped both hands under the wrappings that had lain undisturbed for thousands of years, preparatory to lifting it out.

Something moved against his fingers. And coughed.

"Inshallah!" he exclaimed involuntarily as he dropped the weight and stumbled backward. Eyes wide, his back pressed against the far wall, he gaped in wide-eyed fear and wonder at the sarcophagus.

The mummy was getting up.

It rose slowly on all four feet, a lean and lithe bundle of unimaginably ancient linen and encrusted, desiccated preservatives. Trembling violently, Ali scuttled to his right. But there was no stairway that led to freedom, no ladder with which to climb out of the chamber. Come to think of it, how had he intended to get the mummy out of the tomb, much less himself? Excited by his accidental discovery, he had not thought that far ahead. Now he looked at the circle of moonlight overhead as if it represented the route to Heaven. He would have screamed, but there was no one to hear him.

An odor reached his nostrils: the smell of something incredibly ancient but rapidly reviving. Suhar caught a whiff of it, too. He heard her snort once, in fear, before the clomp-clomp of her big, oversized, suddenly lovable feet commenced to recede rapidly into the distance.

Now he was well and truly alone. Alone with—something.

Oh God, he thought. *It's looking at me.*

Indeed, the bandage-swathed head had turned toward him. Behind the rapidly disintegrating wrappings, a pair of intense yellow eyes were gazing directly back into his own. They seemed to burn into his soul, to squeeze his very heart. And yet, and yet—there was no murder in them, but something else. Curiosity, perhaps. Curiosity, and—intelligence.

That was impossible, he knew. But then, to have a millennia-old mummy suddenly stand up and stare back at you was not exactly possible, either, and that was happening before his very eyes.

The feline shape coughed again. Louder, this time. Then it seemed to stretch, to expand, as if taking a deep breath. It shook furiously. Before his terrified eyes, desiccated, ancient linens snapped and crumbled. Chewing hard enough on the knuckles of his left hand to bring blood to the surface, Ali could only stare and pray.

In the full flush of vibrant, new life, the cheetah concluded its yawning stretch. When it turned toward him again, there was no mistaking what it was. When it started toward him, he closed his eyes. Mummy or magic, anything this old with teeth like that was bound to be hungry.

Shivering, Ali felt a powerful paw reach out to touch his thigh. He could smell the creature clearly now, much as Suhar had smelled it—and fled. He waited for the sharp caress of claw against his throat. It would all be over in an instant, he knew. His friends in the village would never know what had happened to him. Maybe someday someone would find his gnawed, whitened bones. At least, he reflected, he would no longer have to listen to Harima's shrill, shrewish insults. There were some small good things to be said even for a premature death.

"Open your eyes, man. I'm not going to kill you."

Somehow the idea of a talking cheetah struck him as even more absurd than that of a revivified mummy. But since there was no one else in the tomb with him, the words had to be coming from the revived cat. Opening his eyes, still shaking with fear, Ali found himself looking down at the creature. A truly magnificent specimen it was, too, he thought.

"Thank you," the cheetah responded politely, which was when Ali realized that they were not speaking aloud, but speaking athink, as it were. Whether he was reading the cat's mind or it his, he did not know. Nor did it seem to matter much.

"It doesn't," the cat thought at him. Slowly, deliberately, it looked around the chamber before its eyes settled on him once more. Some of his trembling having ceased, Ali could not keep from thinking half-sensible thoughts.

"Who are you, peace be unto him?"

"I do not know who 'him' may be, but I am Unarhotep, Pharaoh of Egypt, son of Arenatem the Fourth, grandson of Arenatem the Third, Lord of the Upper and Lower Kingdoms, Ruler of the Nile. Who are *you*?"

"Just Ali. Ali Kedal. That's all. I'm a guide. I show to visitors the wonders of this part of my country." He took a chance. He had always been a bit of a gambler. "Our country."

"I see. Then you are not a servant of Osiris, and this is not the Underworld." The cheetah paced thoughtfully for a moment before looking up again. "What year is this, Ali Kedal?"

Ali considered. The modern calendar would mean nothing to someone from so ancient a time. Unarhotep would have no reference for it. "As near as I can tell, it has been some four thousand eight hundred years since your entombment, my lord."

"So long! The mere thinking of it makes me tired. If this is the truth, then I cannot be your lord. You may call me Unar. My mother did. The kingdom of Egypt still exists, then?"

"As it ever has been, Egypt remains a wonder of the world. Its history and its monuments are still revered by all mankind." He hesitated briefly. "Might I ask, oh lor—Unar, how you came to be in this . . . form?"

The Pharaonic feline began to pace restlessly; back and forth, back and forth. "I was Pharaoh only for a very short time. I contracted a wasting illness with which my court physicians were, sadly, unfamiliar. There was at that time a certain mystic working in Thebes. A sorcerer named, if I remember correctly, Horexx. A venerable man. Nubian, I believe. He claimed to be able to oversee the transfer of a soul from one body to another. But not to that of another human person. To do that would require chasing the soul from that other person's body. This feat was beyond Horexx's powers.

"But he felt certain that, if given the opportunity, he could shift a person's soul into any other kind of body. As it rapidly became clear that the disease that was consuming my person would leave me with nothing in which to dwell in the other world, it was left to me to choose the vessel for my soul's life after death. Following much discussion among my most learned advisers, it was decided to put me in this body, of my beloved pet Musat, and consecrate the result to the cat god Bastet." Raising up on hind legs—a thing Ali had never before seen or heard of—the cheetah pawed gently at the air in the direction of the open sarcophagus.

"Though the procedure was both torturous and painful, in the end Musat's body welcomed me. It is a powerful form, handsome, swift, and elegant. A fitting container for the soul of a Pharaoh. Unfortunately so shocking was the transfer that it resulted in the death of Musat's body as well as mine." The big cat dropped back down onto all fours. "It was declared by Horexx that the first person who should touch my preserved form would have the ability to think 'with' me, and that

that person alone should be my guide through the Underworld for all eternity." A paw gestured, taking in the modest chamber.

"I determined to be interred here, in this simple place, so that my person would not be disturbed by those low-born ones who live by pillaging the tombs of better men who went before them."

"I am sorry, Unar." Ali was genuinely apologetic. "I have disturbed your sleep of thousands of years only to have to welcome you yet again to the real world, and not that of Osiris and Horus, of Bastet and Anubis." Privately he knew that such imaginary beings did not exist, nor did the Underworld they were supposed to rule. But he could hardly venture that opinion to one who believed in them as deeply and personally as did Unarhotep. One man's superstitious nonsense is another man's true religion.

But the revived Pharaoh surprised him.

"Perhaps it is just as well. I was never so certain of the existence of Osiris's realm myself. To the unending frustration of my scholars, I was always a freethinking sort of man. Such beliefs could be discussed freely only on rare, private occasions." The cat's head came up proudly. "A Pharaoh must be strong for his people.

"If I am to live again, perhaps this real world is not such a bad place or time in which to do so. Is Egypt still the ruler of the known world?"

Emboldened by both his knowledge and the continued friendliness of the most ancient one, Ali stepped a little bit away from the beautifully painted wall.

"The world has changed in ways you cannot imagine, Unar. There are many more countries and lands than when you reigned. Science has changed the way the world runs. There are great things about it that even I do not understand. Computers, atomic energy, the Internet . . ."

The cat raised a paw to forestall him. "Do men still lie with women, and thus make children?"

"Yes." Ali could not keep from smiling. "That, at least, has not changed."

"And what of riches, of the material wealth of men? Do they still value such things as gold and silver, and precious stones?" Once again, Ali nodded. "Then it may be," the cheetah thought clearly, "that it is only the superficial things that have changed as much as you say, and that at heart and at base, men are still much the same. Do they still choose others to rule over them?"

"It is, indeed. If I may say so, Unar, you are handling this very well."

"Though I did not rule long, I ruled well. To do so, one must learn to adapt to new things very quickly, be they an unexpected war, foreign alliances, or something as small as a new way of raising building stones. Even for a Pharaoh, a living god, life is a constant battle to learn and to retain mastery over others." He looked down at himself. "Yet I confess that for all my experience and knowledge, I cannot see how I can make myself again even a little bit of what once I was: a lord over men, wealthy and admired, with a host of concubines at my side and great men trembling and waiting at my every utterance. Because for as long as I may live again, I will have to live in this form and no other."

It was then that Ali had the idea. He was, after all, sophisticated from extensive contact with foreign tourists. And while his village was poor, it was not isolated. There were things about the world that Ali had learned and remembered. Things that anyone who lives in the real world learns very quickly.

"I think, my lo—Unar—that I may be able to help you to regain some of what you once had. Some of your stature, some of the effect you had on other people. Maybe even the company of beautiful concubines."

"This is a true thing? You do not lie?" The cheetah grinned, which, unfortunately, had the opposite effect on Ali than what was intended. "If you can do such a thing, Ali, then you will truly be my friend for the remainder of my life in this world, as well as in the next."

"We can but try," Ali confessed. Turning, he looked up at the circle of moonlight overhead. "Hopefully someone will come along and find us before the desert overtakes us." He gestured helplessly. "I found this place by accident, by falling in, and have no way out."

"Is that all?" Unarlotep asked. And with a single bound, he leaped upward and through the opening.

It does not matter how Unarhotep helped Ali to get out of the tomb. It only matters that he did. Nor need it be dwelled upon how the two got themselves out of Egypt. Only that they did.

So it was that one day, camel guide and resurrected cat found themselves in another country far, far from the dehydrated delights of Thebes and that haranguing harridan Harima. A tall man was standing next to Ali. He wore a very fine shirt and pants along with sunglasses that themselves would have cost Ali six months' earnings as a guide's assistant. The tall man was nervous, and made no effort to hide it.

"You're sure about your animal, now, Ali? We can't take any chances here. I'm not using a double for Tiffany. She really wants to do this shot herself, and I want her to do it. But if anything goes wrong, the studio, the insurance company, and the ASPCA will have my ass in a grinder for it."

Ali waved off the concerns. "I assure you, Carl, that my cat will do exactly as I instruct it. You have nothing to worry about. Nothing whatsoever."

The director still looked uncertain. "Yeah, well, you'd

better be right. I mean, when the time came to do the animal casting for this picture, your name was at the top of the list. I'm told you're the best big cat trainer in the business, even if you only work with the one animal."

"I only need one," Ali replied loftily. "Do your shot, Carl. I'll be right here, watching in case I am needed."

But he would not be needed, he knew, as he watched the final touches being put on the elaborate setup for the next sequence. He wouldn't be needed because Unar, the wonder cheetah, the best-trained and by far the most famous big cat in Hollywood, who was now known and admired all over the world, had demonstrated again and again an astonishing ability to carry out the most complex series of owner commands in response to hand and eye gestures even the most experienced animal trainers were unable to detect.

So it was that Ali was able to relax and watch the action unfold as the director called for action, the cameras rolled, and the snarling cheetah, guardian of the mysterious lost temple of Unak-Pathon, approached the two nearly naked heroines. It proceeding to paw and lick them threateningly and thoroughly, but yet with the most astonishing self-control . . .

Serenade

When, after years of writing science fiction, I decided to try my hand at novel-length fantasy, I determined not to write anything that included sweeping pseudo-medieval empires, all-knowing wizards with long white beards (if they possess such deep and unfathomable knowledge, why can't they keep their hair from turning white?), noble elves, evil dragons, and all the other all-too-familiar-paraphernalia of traditional European-derived fantasy.

So the Spellsinger books include references to drug-taking and much fooling around, fairies too fat to get off the ground (aerobics are in order), flying horses afraid of heights, a Marxist dragon who only wants to organize the masses (except that the masses are terrified of dragons and run like hell at the sight of him), misplaced stage magicians, a unicorn who cannot be lured to his death by a virgin because he's gay, and much, much more. For better or verse, Tolkien and Rowling it is not.

Of those who have read the series, one of their favorite characters is a five-foot-tall talking otter named Mudge. Mudge is a consumer of mind-altering substances, a drunk, a thief, an irrepressible lech (irrespective of species), a coward at heart, and a luster after money obtained through any means possible. He is also a great deal of fun to be around and a true friend (most of the time) to the nominal hero of the stories, a displaced university law student and would-be rock gui-

tarist named Jon-Tom Meriweather who can make (usually bad) magic with the aid of a unique instrument called a duar.

"Serenade" eventuated as the result of a request by an editor in England who was planning a series of extended graphic novels and wished to include a Spellsinger story among them. Sadly, his financing for the series fell through, but the story remained. Here it is—alas, sans graphics—though Mudge's antics may be sufficiently graphic for most . . .

I

The young woman was beautiful, her male companion was shy, and the hat was surreptitious. This feathered chapeau of uncertain parentage bobbed along innocently enough behind the stone wall on which the two young paramours sat whispering sweet nothings to each other. The hat dipped out of sight an instant before the girl's lips parted in shock. Reacting swiftly to the perceived offense, she whirled and struck the startled young man seated beside her hard enough to knock him backward off the wall. But by that time the intruding hat had hastened beyond sight, sound, and probable indictment.

Occupying the space beneath the hat and having happily strewn amorous chaos in his wake was a five-foot-tall otter, clad (in addition to the aforementioned feathered cap) in short pants, long vest, and a self-satisfied smirk. Ignoring the occasional glances that came his way, the hirsute, bewhiskered, and thoroughly disreputable Mudge continued wending his way through the busy streets of downtown Timswitty. Eventually his sharp eyes caught sight of his friend, companion, and frequent irritant from another world leaning against the wall of a dry-goods shop while soaking up the sun. Dodging a single lizard-drawn wagon festooned with clanging pots and pans for sale, he hailed his companion with a cheery early-morning obscenity.

Arms crossed over his chest, duar slung across his back, scabbard flanking his right leg, Jon-Tom Meriweather opened one eye to regard his much shorter friend. In this world of undersized humans and loquacious animals, the six-foot-tall involuntary visitor stood out in any crowd. Except for his unusual height, however, he was not an especially impressive specimen of his species.

"Back already? Let me guess—you've been making mischief again."

"Wot, me, guv'nor? You strike me to the quick! Why, I didn't even know the lass."

Jon-Tom frowned. "What lass?"

The otter mustered a look of innocence, at which self-defense mechanism he had enjoyed extensive practice. "Why, Miss Chief, o' course."

"One of these days I'll strike you for real." Pushing away from the wall, Jon-Tom nearly stepped into the path of a goat hauling firewood. Apologizing to the annoyed billy, he started up Pikk Street, only to find his path blocked by a lean human little taller than Mudge. Of an age greater than that of the two travelers combined, the well-dressed graybeard wore a colorful cloak, and trousers woven of some soft red and blue material. The cloak's cowl covered his head, and he carried a simple wooden staff finialed with a polished globe. Mudge eyed the sphere with cursory interest. This flagged the instant he identified the opaque vitriosity as ordinary glass not worth pilfering

"Excuse me, good sirs." Though he addressed them both, it was Jon-Tom's face that drew the bulk of the visitor's interest. Jon-Tom had spent enough time in this world to be wary of strangers. Even those who were elderly, polite, well-dressed, and to all intents and purposes harmless.

"Is there something we can do for you, esteemed sir?"

"I am called Wolfram. I am in need of assistance of an uncommon kind." With a nod he indicated a nearby doorway. Swaying from an iron rod above the portal was a sign that identified the establishment as the WILD BOAR INN. "Perhaps it would be better to discuss matters of business somewhere other than in the street."

Mudge, who had been tracking the progress of an attractive lady mink, responded without taking his eyes from the passing tail. "Me friend an' me don't interrupt our day to shoot the scat with just anyone who accosts us in public." As the mink tail vanished, so, too, did the otter's interest in its slinky owner. He sighed. "You buyin'?" The stranger nodded again. Mudge's whiskers quivered appreciatively. "Then I guess we're shootin'." He preceded the two humans into the establishment, his short tail twitching expectantly from side to side.

Like most such Bellwoods establishments, the Wild Boar Inn was already crowded with drinkers and natterers, characters unsavory and tasteful, trolling wenches and amenable marks. The owner, a husky but amiable wild boar name of Focgren, paused in the careful ladling out of questionable libations long enough to grunt in the direction of an unoccupied booth near the back. Their order was taken by an obviously bored but nonetheless attractive vixen whose agility as she avoided Mudge's wandering fingers was admirable to behold. Spangles and beads jangled against the back of her dress and upraised, carefully coiffed tail. The booth's battered, thick wooden walls served to mute the convivial chaos that swirled around the newly seated trio.

"You were saying something about assistance of an uncommon kind?" Jon-Tom sipped politely at his tankard while Mudge made a conscious effort to bury his snout in the one that had been set before him.

Having set his walking staff carefully aside, Wolfram indicated the duar that now rested alongside the tall young human. "Your instrument is as conspicuous as your height, and not the sort to be carried by just any wandering minstrel. You are, perchance, a spellsinger?"

Jon-Tom's interest in the stranger rose appreciably. Recognizing a duar for what it was marked the older man as more sophisticated than originally supposed. There might be real business to be done here.

"While lacking in experience, I assure you I try every day to improve my art."

Wolfram nodded appreciatively. "Excellent! I am most of all in need simply of your musical talents, but I will not deny that a touch of wizardry would also prove useful."

Suds foaming on his whiskers, a suddenly wary Mudge extracted his face from the tankard. His bright brown eyes flicked rapidly from friend to benefactor and back again. "Wizardry? Spellsingin'-type magic-making?" He pushed the tankard aside. "Oh no, mate. Count me out! I've 'ad enough o' your so-called singin' o' spells to last me a lifetime!" Rising from the table, he moved to leave.

While continuing his conversation with Wolfram, Jon-Tom kept the fingers of one hand wrapped around the otter's belt, thus preventing the frantic Mudge from fleeing. Short legs fought for purchase on the liquor-slick stone floor.

Jon-Tom smiled reassuringly at their host. "Don't mind Mudge. He's just anxious to get started."

"I'm anxious, all right, you bloody great stick-twit!" To no avail, the otter continued his furious struggle to free himself from his friend's grasp. "Let loose o' me pants!"

The three-way conversation was interrupted by a violent crash from the center of the floor. Peering out from the booth, their attention was drawn to a singularly unwholesome-looking human and his puma companion. Breathing hard, both were staring down at something on the floor. The human held the shattered remnants of a wooden mace, his snarling companion a club that had been broken in half. The upper, knobbed end of the mace hung from the handle by a splinter. As Jon-Tom tried to see what it was they were concentrating on, their expressions changed markedly.

An enormous dark mass was rising slowly from the ground. As it blotted out a wide section of inn, human and feline began to back away from it. Whirling abruptly, the man dropped his broken weapon and tried to run. A leather-wrapped wrist bigger around than his head reached out and enormous brown-furred fingers closed around his neck, lifting him off the floor. As he ascended he clawed frantically at the grasping digits while his legs kicked uselessly at empty air. Waving the human over his head like a limp flag, the now fully upright armor-clad grizzly reached out for the panicked puma. As he did so, a chair slammed into his back and shattered into kindling. When someone in the crowd took physical as well as verbal objection to this cowardly blow from behind, the inn's population descended—not entirely unwillingly—into instant and complete pandemonium.

Above it all the immense ursine could be seen clearly, still waving his now unconscious human assailant while bellowing above the increasingly thunderous fray, *"Stromagg stomp!"*

Mudge was already heading for the back exit, ducking flying utensils and other debris, some of it obnoxiously organic. Their elderly host stayed close to him, equally anxious to be clear of the rapidly escalating skirmish.

But Jon-Tom hung back. The otter bawled imploringly at his friend.

"Quickly, guv, quickly! The coppers'll be 'ere any minute! An' you know wot that'll mean."

Jon-Tom did, but lingered still. "You two go on. I'll be right there." So saying, he plunged back into the affray. Shaking his head in disbelief and venting a whistle of disgust, Mudge concentrated on chaperoning their erstwhile benefactor away from the intensifying chaos.

The tall human with sword and duar was largely ignored by the combatants, actively engaged as they were in forcibly removing one another's appendages and resolving old scores. Jon-Tom had to strike out only occasionally to remain above the fray as he worked his way toward its nucleus. When the enormous bear leaned in his direction, all monolithic chest and pungent fur and glistening teeth, he found himself wondering if this was such a good idea after all. Despite his sudden apprehension, he managed to call out, "Come with me! The police are on their way."

Absently crushing to the floor with one massive fist an onrushing, sword-wielding wombat, the grizzly's heavy brows drew together as he considered the offer. "Why should I go with you? I don't know you."

There was a commotion near the entrance to the inn. Timswitty's deservedly feared finest were arriving. "Because I'm offering you a job—I think."

Whirling about, the sextet of uniformed skunks prepared to put an end to the fighting in a manner only they could manage, by means not even the strongest berserker could defy. Jon-Tom broke into a cold sweat. Still, the bear was reluctant.

"You help Stromagg?"

"My word on it." Instinctively Jon-Tom found himself starting to edge toward the rear exit, wondering as he did so if there would be enough time to vacate the room before it was too late.

Fishing into the mob, the bear came up with the battered, bleeding body of the puma who had first attacked him. When smacking the sagging feline across its limp face failed to produce any reaction, Stromagg let out a grunt and casually tossed the cat into the roiling crowd.

"Hurry!" Jon-Tom pulled on the bear's forearm to urge haste. He might as well have been tugging on a sequoia. But the ursine moved.

They did make it out just before the police tactical squad let loose, so to speak. An cacophonous chorus of mass retching filled the air behind the escapees as they fled down a rear alley.

As soon as they were safely clear of all noxious olfactory intrusions, they slowed to a walk. Mudge guardedly eyed the mountainous newcomer in their midst. Stromagg endured the inspection thoughtfully. Or perhaps, Jon-Tom mused, "thoughtfully" was not the appropriate description. The bear's attitude hinted at a combative nature, but one that only infrequently strayed into the alien realm of higher cogitation.

"Wot's with the meat-mountain, mate?"

His breathing at last beginning to ease, Jon-Tom beamed and put a reassuring hand on the grizzly's immense arm. "I've just taken on a little extra muscle."

"Wot for?" the otter snapped. "The job we ain't goin' to take?"

Ignoring his friend, Jon-Tom turned to the somewhat bedraggled Wolfram. "Now then, good sir. What was the nature of the task for which you desired to employ my services?" He steeled himself for the reply.

It was not anything like what he expected.

Pulling his gaze away from the looming immensity of the bear, their benefactor gathered his wits. "I wish you to serenade a lady with whom I am deeply and hopelessly in love."

Jon-Tom and Mudge exchanged a glance. The graybeard's request fell somewhat short of requiring them to slay bad-breathed dragons, save the world, or some equally life-threatening exercise. The stunned otter was too relieved to offer his usual ill-mannered comment.

"That's all?" Jon-Tom wondered aloud.

Wolfram nodded slowly. "That's all. And for that I will pay you well. You see, I am a very wise man, but a terrible singer."

Mudge jerked a furry thumb in Jon-Tom's direction. "Then this be a good fit, guv, as me mate 'ere is an improving singer, but terrible stupid."

Ignoring the slur, Jon-Tom proved the otter wrong by asking, "If all that's needed is an amorous song, why not hire any wandering troubadour? Why seek out a spellsinger like myself?"

Wolfram nodded approvingly. "A song to Larinda is all that is required. It is the reaching her that may require the application of some magic in concert with the music."

"Oi, I knew it were too good to be true," Mudge muttered under his breath.

"Calmness be upon you, my peripatetic friend," Wolfram tried to reassure the otter. "A simple spellsong should suffice. Nothing too elaborate. I would attempt it myself except that I, as previously stated, cannot carry a tune in a bucket."

"'Ow simple a spellsong, guv'nor?" the otter inquired warily.

"That is for the singer to decide. I shall provide you with directions. I will also pay your expenses and hand over half your fee in advance." Extracting a heavy purse from within the depths of his cloak, he proceeded to spill a clinking pile of gold coins into Jon-Tom's cupped hands. Mudge's eyes widened while Stromagg looked on appreciatively.

"'*Alf*, you say, guv'nor?" The otter eyed the golden flood greedily.

Wolfram nodded as he slipped the now empty purse back into his cloak. "The other half when the object of my affection responds." Turning, he gestured with his staff. "Do you know the lands of the Agu Canyon, which lies between here and Hygria?"

Jon-Tom's expression wrinkled with concentration. "I know the direction, though I've never been there."

"Nor I," Mudge added. "I 'ave 'eard 'tis a dry and homey place."

"There is an unclimbable cliff," Wolfram explained. "I will give you specific directions that will enable you to find it. On the far side lies Namur Castle, wherein dwells the beauteous Larinda. Serenade her on my behalf. Sing to her of my undying affection, then return to collect the rest of your well-earned due."

"'Scuse me 'ere a minim, guv." The otter squinted skeptically at the graybeard. "'Ow now are we supposed to get up an unclimbable cliff?"

Wolfram smiled from beneath the cowl of his blue-and-red cloak. "That, my energetic friend, is why I have sought out a spellsinger to do the singing. How you surmount the barrier is your problem. Or did you think I was paying you only to deliver a love song?"

Jon-Tom was not discouraged "I'm a pretty decent climber. No ascent is 'unclimbable.'" He looked down at Mudge. "If necessary, I'll just sing us up the appropriate climbing gear. Or perhaps a great bird to ferry us over."

Mudge winced. "You forget, guv, that I've seen 'ow all too much o' your spellsingin' 'as a way o' turnin' out."

"We'll cope." Jon-Tom stood a little straighter. "After all, I've had plenty of practice by now. I'm far more in command of my skills than I was when I first picked up this duar." He patted the instrument confidently, then turned his gaze to the looming grizzly. "How about it, Stromagg? It's always useful to have someone like yourself along on a journey such as this. Are you with us?"

The bear's great brows furrowed. "Will there be beer?"

II

The granite cliffs and buttes that rose around them were streaked with gray and black, ivory and umber, and lightning-like streaks of olivine green. Stromagg strode tirelessly forward on his hind legs, Jon-Tom riding on one shoulder and Mudge on the other. The twice-burdened bear seemed not to notice the weight at all. In any event, he did not complain. Not even when Mudge would rise to a standing position for a better view. Jon-Tom did not venture criticism of his companion's unstable stance. For one thing, it would do no good. The otter held advice in the same regard as teetotaling. For another, otters have superb natural balance—and very low centers of gravity.

Overhead, vultures circled, gossiping like black-cloaked old women. They were as civilized as any bird that inhabited the Warmlands, exceedingly polite, and fastidious in their table manners.

"There are the twin buttes." Jon-Tom consulted the map their employer had provided to them. There was no mistaking the distinctive geological formations. From a distance, the spellsinger saw, the eroded massif known as Mouravi resembled a horned skull. "The cliff wall should lie just to the left of them."

Hiking down the arroyo to the left of the nearest butte, they suddenly and unexpectedly encountered proof of his observation in the form of a solid wall of rock. Slipping down from Stromagg's shoulder, Jon-Tom tilted his head back, back, until his neck began to ache. The cliff wall was at least five hundred feet high and as smooth as a marble slab. Close inspection revealed that the featureless schist would make for a treacherous ascent even with the best of available climbing equipment.

Examining the obstacle, Mudge let out a short, derisive whistle. "Ain't no problem, guv. I say we keep the 'alf payment that old geezer gave us and 'ightail it up to Malderpot. Nice taverns there be in Malderpot. By the time the old man can track us down, we'll bloody well 'ave drunk away the last of 'is gold."

"Now, Mudge." The spellsinger studied the seemingly impassable obstacle. "That would hardly be honorable."

"*Honorable, honorable.*" The otter scratched under his chin, his whiskers quivering slightly. "From wot foreign tongue arises that strange word, wot I am sure I never 'eard before and ain't conversant with?"

Stromagg frowned at the wall and promptly sat down, dust rising from the fringes of his enormous brown behind. His armor hung loose against the vastness of his immense frame. "Stromagg not built for climbing."

"That's all right." Jon-Tom unlimbered his duar. "When Wolfram described this to us, actually having to climb it was something I only half expected would be possible. That's what he, and anyone else, would think." Slipping the unique instrument across his front, he gently strummed the intersecting set of dual strings. Accompanying the first notes, a soft pulse of light appeared at the nexus. "We're not going over this barrier. We're going through it."

"Through it?" Mudge squinted at the solid rock, glanced meaningfully at Stromagg. "Through wot, mate? Am I missin' somethin' 'ere?"

"Why, through that tunnel." Jon-Tom pointed. "The one right there."

Once again Mudge eyed the stone. Then he made the connection with the duar, the position of his friend's hovering hands, and his eyes widened slightly. "Now, mate, are you sure this is a better idea than wastin' away old Wolfprick's money in temptingly lubricious Malderpot? You know wot 'appens when you open your mouth and some strange caterwaulin' vaguely like a song comes out."

"Just like I told Wolfram, Mudge. My skill has improved greatly with time and practice."

The otter grunted. "As opposed to the odds improvin', I suppose." He moved to stand closer to, or rather behind, the curious Stromagg as Jon-Tom walked up to the solid rock face. The bear frowned down at the infinitely smaller otter.

"What happens now?"

Mudge put his hands over his ears. "If you've any sensitivity at all, large brother, you'll 'ave a care to cover your bloomin' ears."

Stromagg hesitated, then raised his enormous paws. "There will be pain from the wizardry?"

"Not from the wizardry, guv." Mudge winced. "Trust me on this. You ain't 'eard ol' Jonnny-Tom sing. I 'ave. All too many times."

His fingers quickening on the duar, Jon-Tom launched into the song he had selected, a lengthy ditty of penetrating power that dated from early Zeppelin. The grizzly immediately clapped his great paws over his ears, bending them down forcefully against the top of his head.

Usually the eldritch mists that rose from the junction of the duar's intersecting sets of enchanted strings were pastel in hue: light blue or lavender, bright pink or pale green. This time they were black and ominous. Mudge edged farther behind Stromagg, peering warily out from

behind the grizzly's protective bulk. So peculiar, so en-
thralling was the coil of darkness that emerged from
Jon-Tom's song that the fascinated otter could not take
his eyes from it.

Detaching itself from the interdimensional wherever
of the duar, an orb of ebon vapor drifted slowly toward
the rock wall. It hesitated there and began to reverse direction. That shift prompted a redoubling of power
chords by a suddenly anxious Jon-Tom. What might
happen if the blackness fell back *into* the duar, he could
not imagine, except to believe it could not possibly be
good. The orb wavered, seeming to be considering something known only to eldritch orbs, and then resumed its
drift toward the cliff face. Jon-Tom allowed himself to
relax ever so slightly.

Upon making contact with the rock the dark sphere
expanded across the smooth vertical surface like a giant
droplet of spreading oil. When the last of it had seeped
into the stone, Jon-Tom brought the vibrant song he was
playing to a rousing if dissonant conclusion that made
both his furry companions cringe.

Wiping sweat from his brow, the spellsinger gestured
proudly at the cliff face. "There! I told you I could do it."

Emerging from Stromagg's shadow, Mudge warily approached the dark blot in the rock and peered—inward.
"'Tis a tunnel, all right." Pushing his feathered cap back
on his forehead, he eyed his friend warily. "So I suppose
all we 'ave to do now is stroll right on through the solid
mountain?"

Jon-Tom nodded. "If everything has worked as it
should, Namur Castle will lie on the other side." He
drew himself up proudly. "And I'd say it's worked,
wouldn't you?"

"Well now," Mudge muttered, argumentative to the
last, "there's right enough a big whackin' 'ole in this 'ere

'ill. Anyone can see that. But as to whether it leads to a castle or somethin' else remains to be seen, wot?"

"Only one way to find out." Striding confidently past his friend, Jon-Tom started forward.

The spellsung tunnel was wide and high enough for Stromagg to enter without bending. Its floor was composed of smooth, clean sand. There was only one problem with the music-magicked passageway.

It was already occupied.

Drawing his short sword, a growling, whistling Mudge started to back up. Next to him, Stromagg drew the huge mace that he carried slung across his broad back. "Oi, you've done it again, all right, mate. Quick, sing it closed!"

His expression falling, Jon-Tom strummed lightly on the duar as he backpedaled. "I only wanted the tunnel," he muttered to himself. "Just the tunnel."

The things that crawled and crept and slithered from the depths of the darkness had glowing red eyes and manifold sharp teeth. Multi-legged shapes with fangs, they resembled nothing in this world. Which made perfect sense, since Jon-Tom had sung them up from an entirely different world. While Mudge and Stromagg hacked and sliced, Jon-Tom tried to think of an appropriate song to send the fanged horde back to the Hell from which they had sprung.

Slashing wildly at something sporting tentacles and razor-lined suckers, the otter spared a frantic glance for his friend. The tunnel continued to vomit forth more and more of the sinister, red-eyed assassins. "Sing 'em away, mate! Sing 'em gone. Sing the bloody tunnel *closed*!"

"Strange." Refusing to be distracted by the conflict, Jon-Tom was preoccupied with trying to remember lyrics appropriate to resolving their suddenly desperate situation. "I could try singing the same song backward,

I suppose." He did so, to no effect other than to further outrage Mudge's ears.

Using a kick to fend off something with long incisors and three eyes, he finally did begin a second song. Mudge recognized the tune immediately. It was the same one his friend had sung moments earlier to create the tunnel.

"Are you mad, mate? We don't need twice as many of these 'orrors. We need less of 'em!" Ducking with astonishing speed, he cut the legs out from an onrushing assailant that had plenty of spares.

A second surging blackness emerged from the duar, drifted past the combatants, and struck the stone barrier. A second tunnel appeared. Fending off assailants, Jon-Tom raced toward it. "Come on! This is the right one, for sure. I was just a bit off tempo the first time."

"A bit off? You've always been a bit off, mate!" Fighting a ferocious rear-guard action, the otter and the grizzly followed the spellsinger into the new tunnel.

Unlike the first, this one was filled with a dim, indistinct light. Floor and walls were much smoother than those of their predecessor, devoid of sand, and firmer underfoot. The walls of the tunnel looked to be made of cut instead of untouched stone: an excellent sign, Jon-Tom decided. It was exactly the sort of passage that might lead to a hidden underground entrance underneath a castle. Certainly its dimensions were impressive.

Then they heard the roaring, growing steadily louder and coming toward them. "There!" A frantic Mudge pointed. A burning yellow eye was visible in the distance. As the roaring intensified, the fiery illumination grew brighter, washing over them.

"I think I liked the other critters better," an awed Mudge murmured.

Jon-Tom was looking around wildly. "Here, this

way!" Turning to his right, he dashed up the stairs that had suddenly appeared in a side passageway. As they climbed, they could hear the monster approaching rapidly behind them. To everyone's great relief, it rushed past without taking notice of the intruders, keeping to the main tunnel.

"The castle must be right above us." Shifting his duar around into carrying position on his back, Jon-Tom slowed as new light appeared above them. Light, and a familiar, unthreatening noise. The sound of rain on pavement. "Probably the courtyard. Keep alert."

"Keep alert, 'e says." Gripping his sword tightly, Mudge strove to peer through the brighter gloom above.

They emerged into a light rain that was falling, not on a castle courtyard, but on a narrow street. Storefronts, darkened and shuttered, were visible on the opposite side. There was no one in sight.

The otter's sensitive nose appraised their surroundings as his sharp eyes continued to scan the darkness. "No castle this, mate. Smells bleedin' nasty, it does." He looked up at his friend. "Where the bloody 'ell are we?"

"I don't know." Thoroughly bemused, Jon-Tom walked out onto a sidewalk and turned a slow circle. "This should be Namur Castle, or at least its immediate vicinity." His eyes fell on a pair of rain-swept signs. Across the street, one hanging from an iron rod proclaimed the location of the CORK & CASTLE—PUB. Light from within reached out into the street, as did muted sounds of polite revelry. The second sign hung above the entrance to the stairway from which they had emerged. It was a softly illuminated red-and-white circle with a single red bar running horizontally through it. The hairs on the back of his neck began to stiffen.

They had stumbled into an unsuspected path back into his own world.

III

Sounds of casual conversation reached the three stunned travelers. Retreating to the top of the gum-spotted, urine-stained stairway, he peered back down. Two young couples were mounting the steps from the Underground, chatting and laughing about the casual inconsequentialities of a life he himself had long ago been forced to relinquish. He looked around worriedly.

"We can't go back down this way. We've got to hide."

Stromagg looked baffled. "Why? More monsters come?"

"No, no. Somehow the song has opened an entrance through into my world. You and Mudge can't be seen here. Only humans talk and make sense here."

Unimpressed, Mudge let out a snort. "Who says 'umans make sense anywhere?" His nose twitched. "I *thought* this place stank."

"Hurry!" Espying an alley off the main street, Jon-Tom led his friends away from the subway entrance.

It was dark in the rain-washed passageway, but not so dark as to hide the overcoated sot standing with his bottle amid the daily deposit of debris expelled by the establishments that lined the more respectable street on the other side. Leaning up against the damp brick, he waved the nearly empty container at the new arrivals. Jon-Tom froze.

"Evenin' t'you, friends." The drunk extended the bottle. "Share a swig?"

Stromagg immediately started forward, forcing Jon-Tom to put out an arm to restrain the bear. "You two stay here!" he whispered urgently. Approaching the idling imbiber, he adopted a wide smile, hoping the man was too far gone to notice Jon-Tom's strange attire.

"Excuse me, sir. Can you tell us exactly where we are? We're kind of lost."

Squinting through the rain, the inebriated reveler frowned at him. His breath, Jon-Tom decided, was no worse than what he had experienced numerous times in the company of Mudge and his furry drinking buddies.

"What are you, tourists?" The drinker levered himself away from the wall. "Bloody ignorant tourists! You're in Knightsbridge, friend."

"Knightsbridge?" Jon-Tom thought hard. The name sounded sufficiently castle-like to jibe with his spellsong, but it did not square with what he had just seen. "Where is that?"

"'Where is that?'" the drunk echoed in disbelief. "London, man! Where did you think you were?" Squinting harder, he finally caught sight of the very large otter and far larger armored grizzly standing silently behind his questioner. His bloodshot eyes went wide enough for the small veins to flare. "Oh, gawd." Letting the nearly empty bottle fall from his suddenly limp fingers, he whirled, stumbled and almost fell, and vanished down the alley. They heard him banging and crashing through assorted trash receptacles and boxes for several minutes.

Picking up the bottle, Mudge sniffed the contents, made a disgusted face, shrugged, and promptly downed the remaining contents before Jon-Tom could stop him. Wiping his lips, he eyed his friend meaningfully.

"You spellsang us 'ere, mate. Now you bleedin' well better sing us a way back."

Jon-Tom looked helpless. "We could try the way we came. Maybe the creatures in the other tunnel have gone. I don't know what else to do." Discouraged and tentative, he started back toward the street. The rain was beginning to let up, turning to a heavy mist.

The exit back onto the street was blocked.

"A minute of your time, friend."

There were three of them. All younger than Jon-Tom, all more confident, two clearly high on something stronger than liquor. The speaker held a switchblade, open. The larger boy flashed a small handgun. The girl between them wielded a disdainful smirk.

Jon-Tom scrutinized them all and did not much like what he saw or what he sensed. "We don't want any trouble. We're just on our way home."

The boy with the blade nodded contentedly. "American, is it? Good. I knew I heard American accents at the party. You'll have traveler's checks. Americans always carry traveler's checks." He extended the hand that was not holding the switchblade. "Hand 'em over. Also any cash. Also your watch, if you're wearing one. Your friends, too. Then you can go safely back to the stupid costume ball that your snooty friends wouldn't let us into."

Jon-Tom tensed. "I haven't got any traveler's checks on me. Or any cash, either. At least, not any you could use here."

"American dollars suit me just fine, friend." The kid gestured agitatedly with the open hand. "Hurry it up. We ain't got time for talk." His gaze flicked sideways. "Maybe you'll get it if I cut the kid, here." He lunged toward Mudge.

Effortlessly, the otter bent the middle of his body out of the way. As the switchblade passed harmlessly to his left, he drew his short sword. Steel flashed in the dim light of the street.

Alarmed, the bigger boy raised his pistol. Emerging from the mist behind him, an enormous paw clamped over both weapon and hand. Stromagg squeezed. Bones popped. Startled, the big kid let out a subdued, girlish scream. Bared teeth dripping saliva, the grizzly put another paw around the punk's neck, lifted him bodily off the ground, and turned him. As he got his first glimpse of what had picked him up, the street kid's eyes bugged out and frantic gurgling sounds emerged from his throat.

The bear drew the boy's face closer to his own. Low and dangerous, it was a voice that reeked of imminent death.

"You make trouble for Stromagg?" the grizzly growled.

"Urk . . . ulk . . ." Straining with both hands, legs flailing at empty air, the punk fought to disengage that huge paw from around his neck. Looking like white grapes, his eyes threatened to pop out of his head.

Holding his sword, Mudge easily danced around each swipe and cut of the switchblade that was thrust in his direction, not even bothering to riposte. Once, he ducked clear of a wild swing and in the same motion, bowed elegantly to the now incredulous and dazed girl, chivalrously doffing his peaked cap in the process. Furious, the boy threw himself in the unstrikable otter's direction. Still bowing to the girl, Mudge brought the flat of his sword up between his young assailant's legs. All thought of continuing combat immediately forgotten, the kid collapsed on the alley pavement and curled into a tight ball, moaning.

Still holding the bigger boy by his neck, Stromagg frowned and turned to Jon-Tom. "Uh, this one don't talk no more."

"Put him down." Jon-Tom approached the now apprehensive girl.

"Please, don't hurt me!" She gestured unevenly in the direction of the moaning coil of boy lying on the ground. "It was all Marko's idea. He said we could make some easy money. He said American tourists never fight back."

Mudge eyed her with interest. "Wot's an American?"

"We're not going to hurt you," Jon-Tom assured her. "We just need some help getting home." He looked past her. "Your friend said something about a costume ball?"

"A-around the corner. In the hotel."

Thinking hard, Jon-Tom nodded at nothing in particular. "Might work. For a little while. I need some time to

think. Thanks," he told her absently. He started off in
the indicated direction. With a wink at the girl that left
her feeling decidedly confused, Mudge jogged after his
friend. Gently lowering to the wet pavement the unconscious youth he was holding, Stromagg proceeded to follow. The girl stared after them. Then she began to shake.

The hotel was an older establishment, nonchain, and
not particularly large. Motioning for his friends to remain behind, quiet and in shadow, Jon-Tom performed a
hasty survey until he found what he was looking for: a
side entrance that would allow them entry without the
necessity of passing through the main lobby. He was further relieved when he saw two couples emerge. One pair
were dressed in medieval garb, a third individual was
clad in the guise of a large alien insect with a latex head,
and the fourth was wearing the silken body stocking and
pale gossamer wings of an oversized pixie. Having met
real pixies, he almost paused to offer a critique of the latter costume, but settled for asking directions to the party.
Returning to his companions and explaining the situation, he then boldly led them across the street.

Mudge remained wary. "'Ere now, mate. Are you sure
this is goin' to work?"

As they approached the ancillary entrance, Jon-Tom
replied with growing confidence, "I've heard about
these fantasy convention masquerades, Mudge. For
tonight, many of those attending are in full costume.
They'll think you and Stromagg are fellow participants." He glanced back at the bear. "Try and make
yourself look a little smaller, Stromagg." The grizzly
obediently hunched his shoulders and lowered his head.
"Also, there will probably be food."

The bear's interest picked up noticeably. "Food?"

No one challenged them as they entered through the
side lobby. After asking directions of a pair of over-
weight warriors who would have cut a laughable figure

in Lynchbany Towne, they proceeded to a large auditorium. It was packed with milling, chatting participants, more than half of whom were in costume. A few glanced up at the arrival of the newcomers, but no one appeared startled or otherwise alerted that they were anything other than fellow costumers. While Mudge and Stromagg surveyed the scene with varying degrees of incredulity, Jon-Tom led them toward a line of tables piled high with snack foods. Sniffing the air, the grizzly's expression brightened perceptibly.

"Beer! Stromagg smell beer." Whereupon the bear, despite Jon-Tom's entreaties, promptly angled off on a course of his own.

"Let the bleedin' oversized 'ulk 'ave 'imself a drink," Mudge advised his concerned companion. "'E deserves it, after the bloody 'elp 'e rendered back at the first tunnel. I wish I could—oi there! Watch where you're goin'!"

The girl who had bumped into him was dressed as a butterfly. There was not much to her costume, and she was considerably more svelte than the erstwhile warriors the travelers had encountered in the hallway outside the auditorium. Mudge's anger dissipated as rapidly as it had surged.

She gazed admiringly from him to Jon-Tom. "Hey, *love* your costumes. Did you make them yourselves?"

Seeking to terminate the conversation as quickly as possible, a hungry Jon-Tom eyed the long table. Food was vanishing rapidly from the stained white tablecloths. "Uh, pretty much, yeah."

She eyed him with increasing interest, her wire-supported wings and other things bobbing with her movements. "You're not writers or artists, because you don't have name tags on." She indicated the duar slung across Jon-Tom's back. "That's a neat lute or whatever. It looks too functional to be just a prop." She gestured in the direction of the busy stage at the far end of the auditorium. "There's filksinging going on right now. I'm getting this vibe that you're pretty good at it. I'm kind of psychic, you see, and I have a feel for other people." Her smile widened. "I bet you're a—computer programmer!"

"Not exac—" he tried to explain as she grabbed his hand and pulled him forward. Mudge watched with amusement as his friend found himself dragged helplessly in the direction of the stage. Then he turned and headed for the food-laden tables.

Welcoming Jon-Tom, the flute player currently holding court on stage cast his own admiring glance at the duar. "Cool strings. You need a cord and an amp?"

Aware that others in the crowd had turned to face him, Jon-Tom played—but only for time. "Uh, no. Strictly acoustic."

The flute player stepped aside. "Right. Let's see what you can do." Conscious that the butterfly was still watching him intently, Jon-Tom decided that a quick, straightforward song would be the easiest, and safest, way to escape the unwelcome attention now being directed toward him. As his fingers started to slide across the strings of the duar, a familiar multihued mist began to congeal at the interdimensional nexus.

Someone in the forefront of the crowd pointed excitedly. "Hey, look—light show!" Responding with a lame grin, Jon-Tom tried to strum as simple and unaffecting a melody as possible. Gritting his teeth, he forced himself to remember the chords to the Barry Manilow tune. At least, he told himself, he would not have to worry about making any inadvertent magic.

Following his nose, Stromagg found himself confronting a pay bar near the far side of the auditorium. As he approached, someone thrust a tankard in his direction.

"Here you go, big guy. Have one on me." The man

dressed as Henry VIII pressed a full container into the grizzly's paw. Accepting the offer, Stromagg took a suspicious sniff of the contents. His face lit up and he proceeded to drain the container in one long swallow. Looking on admiringly, the fan who would be king beckoned his friends to meet the new arrival.

Scarfing finger food as fast as he could evaluate it with eyes and nostrils, Mudge was distracted from his gorging by the tapping of a furry forefinger on his shoulder. A ready retort on his lips, he turned—only to find himself struck dumb by the sight that confronted him.

The girl's otter costume was not only superbly rendered; it was, in a word, compelling.

Twirling a whisker, he slowly put aside the piled-high plate of goodies he had commandeered from the table. "Well now. And wot might your name be, darlin'?"

Peering through the eye cutouts in the papier-mâché head, the girl's gaze reflected a mix of admiration and disbelief. "And I thought I had the best giant otter costume in England!" Her eyes inspected every inch of him, scrutinizing thoroughly. "I've never seen such good seamstress work. I can't even see the stitches or where you've hidden the zipper." Her eyes met his. "Costumers are good about sharing their secrets. Could you spare a couple of minutes to maybe give me some pointers?"

Mudge considered his platter. Food, girl. Food, girl. Cookies . . .

IV

On stage Jon-Tom found himself, despite his reservations, slipping into the freewheeling spirit of the occasion. Participants were dancing in front of him, twirling in costume, reveling in his music-making. So self-absorbed were they that they failed to see the small black ball of vapor that emerged from the center of the duar to flash offstage and vanish in the direction of the farthest doorway. Judging from its angle of departure, Jon-Tom guessed it to be heading fast in the direction of the Underground stairway from which he and his companions had emerged earlier that same evening. Raising his voice excitedly while continuing to strum, Jon-Tom sought to alert his companions.

"Mudge, Stromagg! I think I've done it!" Ignoring the applause of the flute player, who took up the refrain, and the admiring stare of butterfly girl, Jon-Tom leaped off the stage and plunged into the crowd. There was no telling how long the revitalized, recharged tunnel would last. He and his friends had to make use of it before the thaumaturgic alteration was accidentally discovered by some unknowing late-night pedestrians.

Stromagg was not hard to locate. The bear had by now gathered a small army of awed acolytes around him. They looked on in jaw-dropping astonishment as the grizzly continued to chugalug inhuman quantities of beer with no apparent ill effects.

Well, maybe a few.

Arriving breathlessly from the stage, Jon-Tom looked around uncertainly. "Stromagg, it's time to leave. We have to go—now. Where's Mudge?"

Weaving slightly, the more than modestly zonkered ursine frowned down at him and replied, in the tone of one only slightly interested, "Duhhh?"

"Oh great!" Latching on to the grizzly's arm, Jon-Tom struggled to drag him away from the crowd. Behind him, tankards and glasses and Styrofoam cups rose in admiring salute. "We've got to get out of here while we have the chance."

There was no sign of Mudge on the auditorium floor, nor out in the hallway, nor in an annex costume room. Confronting a participant made up as an exceedingly stocky, slime-dripping alien, Jon-Tom fought to keep Stromagg from keeling over.

"This may sound funny, but have you seen a five-foot-tall otter come this way?"

"Nothing funny about it," the gray-green alien replied in an incongruously high-pitched voice. It jerked a thumb down the hall. "Matter of fact, I just saw two of 'em."

"Two?" Jon-Tom's confusion was sincere. Then realization dawned, and he broke into a desperate sprint. *"Mudge!"*

He found his friend in the third room he tried: an empty office. Bursting in, he and Stromagg discovered Mudge and the otter other in a position that had nothing to do with passing along the finer points of advanced amateur costuming. Jon-Tom's outrage was palpable.

"Mudge!"

Rising from the couch, his friend looked back over his shoulder, not in the least at a loss.

"'Ello, mate." He indicated the figure beneath him. "This 'ere is Althea. She's psychic. We been discussin' matters of the moment, you might say."

Stark naked except for otter mask and furry feet, the girl struggled to cover herself as best she could. Though surprised by the unexpected intrusion, she did not appear particularly distressed. Rather the contrary. Ignoring her, an angry Jon-Tom confronted his companion.

"What the hell do you think you're doing? Aren't matters complicated enough as it is?"

Hopping off the long couch and into his short pants, the otter proceeded to defend himself. "Back off, mate. Me and Althea 'ere weren't 'avin' no problems. It were all perfectly consentable, it were."

"That's right." Rising in all her admirable suppleness, she reached out with one hand to grab hold of Mudge's right ear. "And now that I've fulfilled my half of the bargain, it's time to see how your outfit is put together, like you promised." She pulled hard.

Yelping, Mudge twisted around as his ear was yanked. "Owch! 'Ave a care there, darlin'. I need that."

Looking puzzled, the girl's gaze descended. Grabbing a fistful of fur in the otter's nether regions, she pulled again. Once more the otter let out a hurt bark. A look of confusion crossed her countenance, to be replaced by one of revelation, followed by one of shock. As this panoply of expression transformed her lovely face, Jon-Tom was half carrying Mudge, who was engaged in trying to buckle the belt of his shorts, toward the doorway where Stromagg kept tipsy watch.

"Omigod!" the girl suddenly screamed, one hand rising to her mouth, *"it's not a special effect!"*

Wearing a hurt look as he was hauled out the door, an offended Mudge called back, "I resent that, luv!"

Hearing the girl's screams, a group of heavily armed attendees had begun to gather at the far end of the hallway. While any band of professionals from Lynchbany would have made short work of the lot, several of the costumed cluster did appear to be more than a little competent at arms. Certainly there was nothing slipshod or fragile about the assortment of swords and axes they carried.

"This way!" With the increasingly outraged costumers following, Jon-Tom led his friends around the corner of the hallway that encircled the auditorium, searching for an exit that led back out onto the rain-washed side street.

"Here, you three." Up ahead, a hotel security guard in a freshly pressed suit and tie had materialized to block their path. "What's this I hear about you freaks causing trouble wi—" His slightly pompous accusation was cut off in midsentence as Stromagg stiff-armed him into the nearest wall, cracking plaster directly beside a painting of a skinny lord seated astride a decidedly astringent thoroughbred.

Bursting back out into the street, Jon-Tom led the way back toward the Underground station. It was darker than ever outside, but at least the rain had let up. An oncoming car had to screech to a halt to avoid slamming into the fleeing trio.

Within the vehicle, a well-dressed middle-aged couple stared as the tall, medievally clad spellsinger; giant otter in feathered cap, vest, and short pants; and rapidly sobering, heavily armored grizzly bear thundered past. They were followed soon after by an enraged mob of weapon-waving fans dressed as everything from a giant spider to a female Mr. Spock missing one ear. Peering through the windshield in the wake of this singular procession, the husband slowly shook his head before commenting knowingly to his equally bewildered spouse. Pressing gently on the accelerator, he urged the car forward.

"I'm telling you, dear. There's no question about it. The city gets worse every year."

Looking back over his shoulder, Mudge began to make insulting faces at their pursuers. He would have dropped his pants except that Jon-Tom threatened to brain him with the flat of his own sword. As usual, the otter reflected, the often dour spellsinger simply did not know how to have fun.

"There!" Jon-Tom pointed in the direction of the softly glowing split circle. A sphere of black mist was just visible plunging down the portal.

Racing past a brace of startled subway travelers, he and Stromagg hurtled down the stairs in pursuit of the ebony globe. Mudge chose to slide gleefully down the central banister, looking back up the stairwell to flash obscene gestures in the direction of their pursuers. The outraged

howl these sparked were unarguable proof that his intricate scatological gesticulations transcended species.

Alongside the automatic gates that led to the boarding
platform, a startled security officer looked up in the direction of the approaching commotion.

"See here, you lot need to slow down and—"

Accelerating to pass Jon-Tom, Stromagg shoved the
officer aside. Grabbing one in each paw, he ripped two
of the barriers out of the floor and flung them ceiling-
ward. From one, old-style subway tokens rained down
on the fleeing trio.

Lying off to one side amid the rubble, cap and uni-
form askew, the unlucky guard looked up dazedly. "Of
course, if it's an emergency . . ."

Slowing as they reached the subway platform, a pant-
ing Jon-Tom looked back to see that pursuit had slowed
as the angry fans were slowed by the debris. Meanwhile
Mudge was fairly dancing with belligerence.

"Pulin' 'umans! Shrew-pricked candy lobbers!" He
had his short sword out and was stabbing repeatedly at
empty air. "I'll skewer the bleedin' lot o' them!"

"You aren't going to skewer anyone." Climbing down
off the platform onto the tunnel track, Jon-Tom started
north, in the direction taken by the floating ball of black
mist-magic. His companions followed. Unlimbering his
duar as they plunged into the feebly illuminated tunnel,
he began to play softly. The steadily intensifying glow
from the instrument served to show the way.

Sword rescabbarded, hands jammed in pockets, Mudge
kicked angrily at the occasional rock or empty soda can
underfoot. "'Tis an unaccommodatin' world yours is,
mate. Unfriendly an' worse—no sense o' fellowship."
Then he remembered the other otter, and a small smile
played across his mouth.

As if recalling a fond and distant thought, Stromagg
peered into the darkness ahead. "Beer?"

A light appeared, growing brighter as it came toward them. A light, and a roaring they had heard once before. Startled, Jon-Tom began to backtrack. Literally.

"Oh shit."

Mudge made a face. "More incomprehensible spell-singer lyrics?"

"Run!" Turning, Jon-Tom broke into a desperate sprint. How far up the tunnel had they come? How far was it back to the passenger platform?

As the light of the oncoming train bore down on them, he fumbled with the duar and with memories of train-related songs. There was the theme from the film *Trainspotting*—no, that probably wouldn't work. He could not remember the words to "A Train a-Comin'." Heavy metal, punk, ska, even industrial had little use for trains.

He was frantically seeking efficacious lyrics as the train bore down on them. The engineer saw the wide-eyed trio running in front of his engine and threw on the brakes. An ear-piercing *screeee!* echoed from the walls of the tunnel. Too little, too late.

Jon-Tom found himself stumbling, going down. As he fell, he saw something directly beneath him. It was not the empty candy wrappers or stubbed cigarettes or torn, useless lotto tickets that drew his attention. It was a flat circle of softly seething black mist, lying neatly between but not touching the tracks or the center rail. He let himself fall, hoping his companions would see what was happening to him, hoping they would follow.

Of course, it might simply be a lingering patch of black fog, rising from the heat of the tracks.

He felt himself thankfully, blissfully, continuing to fall long after he should have struck the ground.

Seeming to pass directly over his head, barely inches from his ear, the roar of the train faded. He hit the ground, rolled, and opened his eyes. They were still in his head, which was in turn still attached to his shoulders. These were good signs. Sitting up, he rubbed the back of his neck and winced. Reaching around behind him, he found that the precious duar had taken a battering from the fall but was still intact.

Nearby, Mudge cast a pain-racked eye at his friend. "That's it, mate. I've bleedin' 'ad it, I 'ave. Gimme me share o' old Wolfham's gold and I'll be quietly on me way." Behind him a groaning Stromagg was just starting to regain consciousness.

Looking away from the angry otter, Jon-Tom found himself staring. "Don't you think you ought to have a look around, first?"

"Why? Wot the bloody 'ell should I . . ." The otter broke off, joined his friend in gawking silently.

Namur Castle rose from a narrow ridge of rock surrounded on all sides by sheer precipices. A wooden bridge crossed from the mountainside on which man and otter found themselves to a small intervening pinnacle, from where a second, slightly narrower bridge arched upward to meet a high wooden doorway. Towering granite spires rose on all sides, while a tree-lined flat-topped plateau dominated the distant horizon. Jon-Tom and his companions were enthralled. It was an impressive setting.

The London Underground, bemused pedestrians, and wild-eyed pursuing costumers were nowhere to be seen.

Starting across the first bridge, a cautious Mudge glanced over the single railing. Like a bright blue ribbon dropped from a giant's hand, a small river wound and twisted its way through the deep canyon beneath. They reached the intervening pinnacle and crossed the second bridge, whereupon they found themselves confronting a massive, iron-bound door.

Tilting back his head, Mudge rested hands on low hips and muttered to his friend and companion. "Wot now, Mr. Spelltwit, sor? You goin' to sing us up a key, or wot?"

An annoyed Jon-Tom contemplated the barrier. "Give me a minute, Mudge. I got us here, didn't I?"

The otter snorted softly. "Oi, that you did—though one might complain about the roundaboutness o' the route you chose. 'London,' it were called?" He shook his head dolefully. "Give me Lynchbany any day."

While man and otter argued, the silent Stromagg approached the impediment, spent a moment contemplating the wood and iron, then balled both paws into fists the size of cannonballs. Raising them high over his head and rising on tiptoes—a sight in itself to behold—he brought both fists down and forward with all his considerable weight behind them. The center of the door promptly imploded in a cloud of shattered slats and splinters. Dust rose from the apex of the destruction.

Approaching cautiously, Mudge peered through the newly made opening. "So much for a bloomin' key."

The interior of the foyer was dim, illuminated only by light shining through high windows. Nothing moved within, not even a piebald rat. Mudge's sensitive nose was working overtime, his long whiskers twitching.

"Sure you got the right towerin', forebodin' castle 'ere, mate?"

Jon-Tom continued through the high vestibule, eyed the sweeping double stairway at the far end of the great room. "I sang for one and one only. This has to be the right place."

Still, he found himself wondering and worrying until their explorations eventually brought them to an expansive, exquisitely decorated bedchamber. Rainbow-hued light poured in through stained-glass windows, burnishing the furnishings with gold and turning the canopied, lace-netted bed at the far end to filigreed sunshine.

The woman who slept thereon might or might not be

a princess, but she was certainly of ravishing beauty. She was sleeping peacefully on her back, her hands folded across her chest, a soft smile on her full lips. Slapping away Mudge's fingers, Jon-Tom considered the somnifacient figure thoughtfully.

"Something familiar about this . . ."

V

"Not to mention somethin' irregular." Mudge contemplated the unconscious female with mixed emotions. "That Wolfsheep didn't say anythin' about 'is beloved bein' in a coma. 'Ow are you supposed to sing 'er a song o' love if she can't bleedin' 'ear you?"

The soft shussh of leather on stone made the trio turn as one. Standing in the doorway was their erstwhile employer, but it was a Wolfram transformed. No longer the supplicating elder, he seemed to have grown taller in stature and broader of frame. His formerly simple cloth cloak glistened in the stained-glass light, and the vitreous globe atop his staff flickered with caged lightning. His entire being and bearing radiated barely restrained power.

"So you have done that which I could not." Stepping into the room, he ignored them to focus his attention on the figure lying supine in the bed. "Ignorant sots. Did you really think that I, Wolfram the Magnificent, the All-Consuming, Master of the Warmlands, would consign the future of the Mistress of the Namur to your puerile attentions?"

As he replied, Jon-Tom slowly edged his duar around in front of him. "Somehow I knew you'd say something like that."

A belligerent Mudge stepped forward. "If you're so

bloody all-whatever, guv'nor, then wot did you need us poor souls for?"

The sorcerer gazed down contemptuously. "Isn't it obvious? The bonds that conceal this place are such as I cannot penetrate. It needs the attention of a kind of magic entirely different from what I propound, powerful as that may be. It required someone such as an innocent spellsinger to blaze a path here and divert any dangers that might lie along the way. This so that I could follow safely in your wake—as I have done."

"Then," Jon-Tom said, indicating the exquisite figure reposing serenely in the bed, "this isn't your beloved?"

"Oh, but she is." Wolfram smiled thinly from behind his narrow, pointed beard. "It is just that she does not know it yet. You see, whoever touches the princess in such a way as to rouse her from her sleep shall make of her a perfect match to the one who does the touching, and shall have her to wife, thus acquiring dominion over this portion of an important realm and its concurrent significant interdimensionality."

"Is that all?" Mudge was studying his fingernails. " 'Tis okay by me, guv."

"Oh no it isn't." Jon-Tom advanced to stand alongside the otter. "If an interdimensionality is involved here, it means that this piece of whiskery double-crossing scum might be able to make trouble in my world as well."

The otter shrugged. "Not me problem. Mayhap 'is meddlin's might improve that revoltin' London place."

The sorcerer nodded knowingly. "I thought I would have no trouble with you three."

His fingers creeping across the strings of the duar, Jon-Tom mentally considered and discarded a dozen different songs. Which would be the most effective against a powerful, malign personality like Wolfram? Knowing little about the man, it was hard to conjure something specific. Then he recalled the sorcerer's words, and knew what he needed to do.

Whirling, he made a dive for the bed.

"Hassone!" Raising his staff, Wolfram thrust it in the spellsinger's direction. Gray vapor shot from the globe at its terminus to coalesce directly between the diving Jon-Tom and the bed. Slamming into the abruptly materialized wall of solid rock, Jon-Tom stumbled once, staggered slightly, and then crumpled to the floor.

Gathering anxiously around their fallen comrade, Mudge and Stromagg exchanged a look, then turned their rising ire on the serene figure of Wolfram. Raising their weapons, they rushed the sorcerer, each screaming his own battle cry.

"BEEER!" The grizzly's bellow echoed off the walls and rattled the stained-glass windows.

"No refunds!" the otter howled in tandem.

"Parimazzo!" Wolfram countered, bringing his glowing staff around in a sweeping arc parallel to the floor.

Rising from the stone underfoot, all manner of fetid, armed horrors confronted the onrushing duo, swinging weapons made of the same stone as that from which they had been called forth. Mildly amused, Wolfram leaned on his staff and coolly observed the battle that ensued.

Behind the fracas, a groggy Jon-Tom slowly came around. Seeing what was taking place, he reached cautiously for his duar. Still lying on the floor, trying to avoid Wolfram's notice, he began to play, and started to sing.

"Once there was an—urrrp!"

The unexpected belch did more than put a crimp in the chosen spellsong. The visible, tangible result was a solid, softly glowing jet-black musical quarter note that hovered in the air a foot or so in front of the astonished Jon-Tom's face.

"Well what do you know," he murmured to himself. "Music really *does* look like that."

Reaching up he grabbed the note, rose, whirled it over his head, and flung it in Wolfram's direction. Seeing it coming, the startled sorcerer raised his staff to defend himself. The note passed right through the protective glow to smack the startled mage on the forehead and send him staggering backward.

Emboldened, avoiding the nearby swordplay, Jon-Tom strode determinedly toward the stunned sorcerer, playing, singing, and belching as never before.

"And ever the drink—*urp*—shall flow freely—*breep*— to the sea—*burk* . . ."

Each belch produced a fresh glowing note, which he heaved one after another in the direction of the now panicking Wolfram. Desperate, the wizard executed a small motion in the air with his staff.

"*Immunitago!*" A pair of large earmuffs appeared before him, drifted backward to settle themselves against his ears. Slowly his confident smile returned. Staff upraised, he started toward Jon-Tom. Now the notes thrown by the spellsinger burst harmlessly in the air before reaching their target.

It was a newly anxious Jon-Tom's turn to retreat. Changing tactics as he backpedaled, he also changed music. The roar of Rammstein thundered through the chaotic chamber. The duar glowed angrily, fiery with *bist* mist.

Shaken by the heavy-metal chords, Wolfram halted and clutched at his stricken ears. Trying to keep the earmuffs from vibrating off his head, he flung a wild blast from his staff. Ducking, Jon-Tom watched as the flare of malevolent energy shot over his head.

To strike the grizzly, who was busy turning his stony, stone-faced assailants into gravel.

"Stromagg!" a pained Jon-Tom yelled.

The force of the blast blew the bear backward into, and through, the stone wall that Wolfram had conjured earlier to encircle the sleeping princess. Rock went flying as the barely conscious bear landed on the bed. Groaning, he rolled to his right. His arm rose, arced, and fell feebly—to land on the waist of the slumbering princess.

Aghast, a horrified Wolfram let out a shriek of despair. *"Nooo!"* Jon-Tom remembered the sorcerer's words.

Whoever touches the princess in such a way as to rouse her from her sleep shall make of her a perfect match to the one who does the touching, and shall have her to wife.

A delicate, swirling haze now rose about and enveloped the Princess Larinda. Her outline shimmered, shifted, flowed. She was changing, metamorphosing, into . . .

When the mist finally cleared, not one but two grizzlies lay recumbent on the bed. One was clad in armor, the other in attire most elegant and comely. Rubbing at her eyes, the princess sat up and turned to gaze at her savior. Blinking, holding one hand to his bleeding head, Stromagg looked back. Instantly the pain of the sorcerer's perfidious blow was forgotten.

"Duhh—*wow!*"

"No, no, no!" Shrouded in tantrum sorceral, a despairing Wolfram was jumping up and down, swinging his deadly staff indiscriminately.

Sitting up on the bed, which now creaked alarmingly beneath the unexpected weight, Stromagg took both of the princess's hands—or rather, paws—in his own and gazed deeply into dark brown eyes that mirrored his.

"Duh, hiya."

Long lashes fluttered as she met his unflinching, if somewhat overwhelmed, gaze. "I always did like the strong, silent type."

"This shall not last! By my oath, I swear it!" Numinous cape swirling about him, Wolfram whirled and fled through the open doorway. "I shall find a way to renew the sleeping spell. Then it will most assuredly be I who awakens her the second time!"

Lightning flickering from his staff of theurgic power, he raced unimpeded down the stairway and back through the foyer. Outside the smashed main doorway, the bridge back to the rest of reality beckoned.

From the shadows there emerged a foot. A furry foot, sandal-clad. It interposed itself neatly between the sorcerer's feet.

Looking very surprised, Wolfram tripped down and forward, his momentum carrying him right over the side of the bridge. As he fell, he looked back up at a rapidly shrinking fuzzy face, astonished that he could have been defeated by something so common, so ordinary. As he plunged downward, he flailed madly for the staff he had dropped while stumbling. Though he never succeeded in recovering it, at least staff and owner hit the bottom of the canyon in concert.

Peering over the side of the bridge, Mudge let out a derisive whistle. "Bleedin' wizards never look where they're goin'."

By the time the otter rejoined his companions, Jon-Tom was facing a revitalized Stromagg and his new-found paramour. The paws of each grizzly were locked in the other's grasp.

"Sorry, guys," Stromagg was murmuring. "I think I'd kinda like to stay here."

Jon-Tom was grinning. "I can't imagine why."

A familiar hand tapped him on the arm. "You'd best lose that sappy grin now, guv, or they'll likely 'ang you for it back in Lynchbany. You look bloody thick."

"Be at peace, my good friends and saviors." Though rather deeper than was traditional, the voice of the restored princess was still sweet and feminine. "I have some small powers. I promise that upon your return home, you will receive a reward in the form of whatever golden coins you have most recently handled and that these shall completely fill your place of dwelling. As Mistress of the Namur, this I vow."

"Well, now, luv," declared a delighted Mudge. "That's more like it!"

It took some time, and not a small adventure or two, before they found themselves once more back in their beloved Bellwoods. Espying his riverbank home, a tired and dusty Mudge broke into a run.

"Time to cash in, mate! Remember the hairy princess's promise."

Following at a more leisurely pace, Jon-Tom was just in time to see his friend fling open his front door—only to be buried beneath an avalanche of gleaming golden discs. Hurrying forward, he dragged the otter clear of the mountain of metal.

"Rich, rich! At last! Finally!" The otter was beside himself with glee.

Or was, until he peered more closely at a handful of the discs. Doubt washed over his furry face. "'Tis odd, mate, but I swear I ain't never before seen gold like this."

Gathering up a couple of the discs, Jon-Tom regarded them with a resigned expression. "That's because it's not gold, Mudge."

"Not gold?" Sputtering outrage, the otter sprang to his feet. Which, given the shortness of his legs, was a simple enough maneuver. "But the princess bleedin' promised, she did. 'The last golden coin I 'andled,' she said. I remember! That were wot that slimy Wolfram character paid us with at the tavern back in Timswitty." His expression darkened. "You're shakin' your 'ead, mate. I don't like it when you shake your 'ead."

"She said 'golden coin,' Mudge. Not 'gold coin.'" His open palm displayed the discs. "Remember when we were fleeing my world? These are London Underground tokens, Mudge." At the otter's openmouthed look of horror, he added unhelpfully, "Look at it this way: You can ride free around Greater London for the rest of eternity."

Sitting down hard on the useless hoard, the otter slowly removed his feathered cap from between his ears and let it dangle loosely from his fingers. "I don't suppose—I don't suppose you 'ave a worthy spellsong for rescuin' this sorry situation, do you, mate?"

Bringing the duar around, Jon-Tom shrugged. "No harm in trying."

But Pink Floyd's "Money" did not turn the tokens to real gold, nor did all the otter tears that spilled into the black river all the rest of that memorable day . . .

Redundancy

This story was originally commissioned for UNIX magazine. New intelligent software had been developed that allowed a computer to make decisions not only based on a predetermined set of standards, but also by appraising and evaluating situations and reaching an appropriate conclusion on its own. Similar software helps the Mars rovers to navigate independently while out of the range of communication with Earth.

The tale never appeared in UNIX magazine because, according to the editor who commissioned it, his superiors felt that a science-fiction story was not appropriate for a venue that dealt with actual science. This would, I think, be news to several generations of scientists, engineers, and researchers who have ofttimes been inspired by the science-fiction stories they read while growing up.

In composing stories, I frequently have to try to put myself in the mental and physical position of various aliens. Though designed by humans, nonhumanoid machines still qualify as perfectly alien. What, really, is your computer thinking when you put it, and yourself, to sleep? Relying entirely on the standards and practices that have been programmed into it, how could one possibly make what in the last analysis amounts to a moral or ethical decision?

In Tom Godwin's classic SF story "The Cold Equations," a human is forced to make a life-or-death decision in a machine-like fashion.

What if the reverse were true?

*   *   *

Amy was only ten, and she didn't want to die.

Not that she really understood death. Her only experience with it had come when they had buried Gramma Marie. Now the funeral was a wisp of a dream that hung like cobweb in the corners of her memory, something she did not think of at all unless it bumped into her consciousness accidentally. Even then it was no more than vaguely uncomfortable, without being really hurtful.

She did not recall a lot about the ceremony itself. Black-clad grown-ups speaking more softly than she had ever heard them talk, her mother sobbing softly into the fancy lace handkerchief she never wore anywhere, strange people bending low to tell her how very, very sorry they were—everything more like a movie than real life.

Mostly she remembered the skin of Gramma Marie's face, so fine and smooth as she lay on her back in the big shiny box. The fleshy sheen mirrored the silken bright blue of the coffin's upholstery. Such a waste of pretty fabric, she remembered thinking. Better to have made skirts and party dresses out of it than to bury it deep, deep in the ground. She liked that idea. She thought Gramma Marie would have liked it, too, but she couldn't ask her about it now because Gramma Marie was dead, and people couldn't talk to you anymore once they were dead. Not ever again. That was the thing she disliked most about death: not being able to talk to your friends anymore.

Thinking about it made her shiver slightly. She knew she was in big trouble, and she didn't want to end up looking like Gramma Marie.

The potato vines and the carrots and the lettuce had not yet begun to die, though the leaves on the fruit trees were already starting to droop. Some had been killed by the explosion, torn to bits or ripped up and hurled violently against one another. One of the big pear trees had been blown to splinters. Smashed pears lay scattered across the floor like escapees from a Vermeer still life. Amy knew that the others would start dying soon, now that the hydroponic fluid that nourished their growth had stopped circulating and the special lights used to simulate the sun had gone out. The heaters were off, too, though some residual warmth still emanated from their internal radiant elements. The temperature was falling steadily, soaked up by the thirsty atmosphere of the rapidly cooling station module.

What really frightened her, though, was not the darkness or the gathering cold. It was the persistent, angry hiss that came from the base of the wall at the far end of the module. She couldn't see the leak, but she could hear it. She tried putting some empty sacks over the hiss and then piling furniture on them. It muted the noise, but did not stop it. So she backed as far away from it as she could, all the way back across the room, as if retreating from a dangerous snake. There were four safety doors in the big module, designed to divide it into airtight quarters in the event of a leak. Not one of them had closed. She didn't know why, but she guessed that the explosion had broken something inside them, too.

She wondered if she would know it when the air finally ran out.

She would have asked Mr. Reuschel about it, but he was already dead. He did not look at all like Gramma Marie had. His mouth hung open and instead of lying neat and straight on his back he was all bent and twisted on the floor where the explosion had thrown him. She didn't know for certain he was dead, but she was pretty sure. He did not reply to any of her questions and he didn't move at all, not even when she touched his eye. When she put her palm up to his mouth the way she had been taught to in school she couldn't feel anything moving against her skin.

He had been the gardener on duty when everything had blown up. Daddy called him a hydroponics engineer, but Amy just thought of him as the gardener. Ms. Anwalt was the other gardener. Like everyone else on the station she probably knew about the explosion by now and would be anxious to check on the garden, but she couldn't. No one could because the access door didn't work anymore. The explosion had broken it just like it had broken Mr. Reuschel.

The door led to the lock, that led to the service corridor, that connected the hydroponics module to the rest of the station. Amy knew it was still connected because her feet were not floating off the floor. If the module had broken away from the rest of the station then it wouldn't be swinging around the central core, and if it wasn't rotating around the central core then she would be floating in zero-g right now.

She wondered if Jimmy Sanchez was worried about her. She hoped so. Jimmy was twelve, the only other kid on the station. His parents were photovoltechs who spent their days drifting like butterflies around the huge solar panels that powered and heated the facility. Jimmy was pretty nice, for a boy. She liked him more than he liked her, but maybe, just maybe, he was thinking about her.

She knew Mom and Dad must be worrying about her, but she tried not to think about that because it made her sad. She thought of all the bad things she had done as a little girl and wished now she hadn't done them.

It was getting cold, and she knew she should keep moving.

She walked over to the rectangular port behind the tomato vines. Since all the overheads had gone out, the only light in the module came from the ports. Pressing her nose to the transparency allowed her to see the big blue sphere of the Earth outside, rotating slowly around the port. Doing geography helped keep her mind off the chill. She located Britain and Spain and the boot of Italy. There was no cloud cover over the Alps and she saw the snow on the mountaintops clearly. But the oceans were easiest to identify. They made her think of beaches, and the stinky-sweet smell of saltwater, and the warm summer sun.

She was able to see her breath by the light of the Earth. Mr. Reuschel still hadn't moved. He did not protest as she struggled to get his jacket off. He was a grown-up and heavy and hard to move, and it made her stomach feel queasy to try, but she kept pushing and shoving. His jacket was bulky-warm and covered her down to her knees.

Water dripped from a broken pipe, a comforting sound in the darkness. She drank and then did her best to wash the dirt off her face, the dirt from where she had landed. She understood enough to be thankful for it. If the compost pile hadn't been there to catch her and break her fall, she might be as twisted up as Mr. Reuschel.

After a moment's thought she decided to sit down by the door. All of its internal LEDs had gone out so she knew it still wasn't working. The big manual lever was bent and twisted and wouldn't move even when she put all her weight against it.

It was very dark next to the door and away from the ports but somehow she felt better sitting there. Pouring through the ports, Earthlight made shadowy silhouettes of the injured trees and bushes. The cabin in Residential Module Six with her stuffed animals and seashells and snug second-tier bunk seemed very far away. It would have been easier if Jimmy, or anybody, had been there with her. But they weren't. There was only poor Mr.

Reuschel, and he was worse than no company at all. She was alone.

Except she wasn't.

There was another presence in the module. It wasn't dead, but it was not really alive, either. Awareness is a matter of technical definitions and predetermined perceptive capability. Consciousness is something entirely more abstract.

Molimon was aware of her presence but could not talk to her, could not provide reassurance or comfort. It was aware of the damage that had occurred, of Mr. Reuschel, of the falling temperature and absence of light. It had detected the leak at the far end of the module and continued to monitor the rate at which air was being lost. It was aware of everything around it. That was the job it had been assigned to do. That was the job it did well.

Until now. It knew that the environment in which it operated had undergone an abrupt and drastic change. There was damage and destruction everywhere. Nothing was functioning within assigned parameters and try as it might, Molimon could not restore anything to normal.

That was because it had suffered considerable damage itself. A pair of memories were gone, and an IOP processor had been popped by the force of the explosion. Two molly drives had stopped spinning. Efficiently, effectively, Molimon distributed the responsibilities of the damaged sectors among the components of itself that continued to function. It was wounded, but far from dead.

Internal communications continued to operate, allowing Molimon to send details to Command Central of the damage it and the module had suffered. So far there had been no response. No doubt Central was concentrating on assessing the damage to those components and parts of the station that were unable to report on themselves.

Knowing that Molimon could take care of itself, Central would take its time responding.

Having reported the damage and requested instructions on how to begin repairs, Molimon rested and waited for a reply. It could not wait long. If no instructions were forthcoming, it would have to shut itself down while battery power remained, thereby preserving its programming and functions until full external power was restored. This caused it no concern. Anxiety was not part of its programming. It had no concept of unconsciousness. Shutdown was merely another state of existence. There was nothing to be concerned about, since all systems within the module were fully redundant.

It was aware of the damage to the hydroponics module only in purely quantitative terms: the absence of light, of heat, of equipment functioning efficiently and according to plan. Supervising the hydroponics environment was but one component of its mission, and it could not bring anything back online until power was restored. Knowing this, it completed its observations, allotted them a sector on one of its still-functioning mollys, and made a complete record of the situation. Programming now called for it to commence an orderly shutdown while sufficient reserve power remained for it to do so.

It did not. Unexpectedly an important component of the module still functioned.

Hedrickson studied the readouts and listened to the human static that filled his headphones. The various speakers were angry, frustrated, anxious. He worked at the console unaware that he was gritting his teeth. They were starting to hurt, but he didn't notice the discomfort.

Just as he did not immediately take notice of the hand that came down on his shoulder.

"How're we doing?"

Pushing the phones off his ears, he leaned back in the chair and stared dully at the monitors. "It's slow. Real slow. The corridor's a mess. They're clearing it as fast as possible but they can't use heavy tools in there or they're liable to hull the tube."

"Doesn't matter, if they're working in suits." Cassie's gaze flicked over the readouts. The figures were not reassuring.

"They're afraid any explosive decompression might weaken the tube's joints to the point where they could snap. Engineering already thinks that the initial explosion may have compromised structural integrity where the corridor attaches to the module's lock. If that goes, we could lose the whole thing." His tone was leaden, tired, indicative of a man who needed sleep and knew he was not going to get any. "How're the Maceks taking it?"

Cassie Chin shrugged helplessly. "Tina's in shock. They took her down to the clinic and put her under sedation. Iwato's watching her closely. I think he's pretty worried about her."

"Damn it. What about Michael?"

"Couple of the riggers volunteered to stay with him. They had to lock down the main bay to keep him from going out in a suit."

Hedrickson's fingers drummed nervously on the console. "How much do they know?"

"They've figured out Amy's in there somewhere. They know the lights are out and the heat is going, that the AV lines are down and that no one inside is responding to queries through the board."

The engineer exhaled slowly. "Do they know about the leak?"

"No." Cassie stared at him. "That I couldn't tell

them. Nobody else is up to that, either. They'll find out when the crew goes in. There isn't much hope, is there?"

"I'm afraid not. The rescue specs are working like maniacs, but even if the leak doesn't get any worse, the air in there'll be gone before they can cut the door. Morrie Reuschel was engineer on duty when it happened. We haven't heard from him. If he's that badly hurt, then the girl . . ." His words trailed off into inaudibility, foundering in despair.

"The only communication we have with the module is via its independent Module Lifesystems Monitor. It says it got wanged pretty good, but you know how much redundancy those suckers have built into them. It took stock of its losses and shifted all necessary functions to undamaged components outside the module. That's the only reason we have some idea of what's going on inside. One boardline survived the damage, so we're still getting reports."

The woman frowned. "But there's no power to the module."

"The section there is operating on standard multiple battery backup."

"I know." She leaned curiously over the console. "But it shouldn't be. It's designed to render a report and then shut itself down to preserve programming and functions if it loses primary power. Something else is wrong. Has it requested repair instructions yet?"

"I would imagine." Hedrickson checked a readout. "Yeah. Right here. Haven't been sent out, though."

"Why not?"

"Central's dealing with more serious damage elsewhere."

Chin straightened. "Instead of cycling through shutdown the way it's supposed to, it keeps requesting repair instructions. There's got to be a reason." She thought furiously. "Can you override Central from here?"

Hedrickson frowned at her. "I think so, but you'd better have a damn good reason for messing with prescribed damage-control procedure."

"As a matter of fact I don't have any reason at all. But it seems as if the Molimon does. If its internal diagnostics are functioning well enough to tell you what's wrong, can you send it the necessary instructions on how to fix itself?"

"Why bother? Just so I'll have something to tell the board of inquiry."

"I just told you: It's got to have a reason for not shutting itself down."

Hedrickson looked dubious. "You'll take the responsibility?"

"I'll take the responsibility. See what you can do, Karl."

The technician bent to work. Cassie stood staring at the wall. Halfway around the station the darkened, leaking module swung precariously on the end of its access tube, to all intents and purposes dead along with everything it contained. Dead except for one semi-independent device, which was disobeying procedure.

Computers do not act on whims, she thought. They respond only according to programming. Something was affecting the priorities of the Molimon unit that supervised the hydroponics module. But it could not proceed without apposite human directives.

Sometimes you just had to have faith in the numbers.

The darkness and gathering chill did not trouble the Molimon. It was immune to all but the most extreme swings of temperature. Reserve power continued to diminish. Still it did not commence shutdown.

Information on how to effect necessary repairs finally began to arrive. Gratefully the incoming instructions were processed. The problem with the critical downed memory was located and a solution devised. Memory reintegration proceeded smoothly, enabling the Molimon to bypass one of the downed molly drives.

The system component that most concerned the Molimon reported borderline functional. It sent out a command, to no response. Clearly the trouble was more serious than anyone, including its programmers, had anticipated.

That did not mean the problem was insoluble. It merely required a period of careful internal debate. The Molimon's internal voting architecture went to work. One processor opted for procedure as written, even though that had already failed. The second suggested an alternative. Noting the failure of the first, processor three sided with two. Having thus analyzed and debated, it tried anew.

This time the door responded. Like all internal airtights it contained its own backup power cell. Running the instructions exhausted the self-contained cell's power, but the Molimon was not concerned with that. It wanted the door shut. Opening it again would be a matter for future programs.

Internal alarms began to go off. It had spent entirely too much time operating when it ought to have been shutting down. There was insufficient power to preserve programming. When it shut down now, it would do so with concurrent loss of memory, even though all critical information would be effectively preserved on the surviving mirrored molly drives. The Molimon was not bothered by this knowledge. It had fulfilled another, more important aspect of its programming.

Enough reserve strength remained for it to send a last message to a slave monitor. Composition of the message caused the Molimon some difficulty despite the fact that it had been programmed to accept and respond in plain English.

Then its backup power gave out completely.

* * *

Amy was waiting patiently next to the mixing vats when they found her. The jammed lock door gave way with a reluctant groan. Shouts, then laughter, then tears filled the hitherto silent module. She looked very small and vulnerable wrapped up in the dead engineer's jacket.

Cassie Chin watched the reunion, wiping at her eyes as she listened to the wild exclamations of delight and joy. Mike Macek was tossing his daughter so high into the air, Cassie was afraid that in the limited gravity he was going to bounce her off the ceiling. Her expression turned somber as she watched others kneel beside the body of Morrie Reuschel.

Eventually her attention shifted to the rearmost of the module's airtight doors. Somehow the Molimon had managed to get it to shut, effectively sealing off the air leak in the section beyond. That action had preserved the remaining atmosphere in the other three-fourths of the module until the rescue team had succeeded in punching its way in. She regarded the lifesaving door awhile longer, then turned to business.

Karl Hedrickson was waiting for her.

"Look at the damn thing. It's half bashed in." He pointed at the debris-laden floor. "Looks like that big wrench hit it."

Cassie sighed. "Let's get the rear panel off."

Their first view of the Molimon's guts had Hedrickson shaking his head. "These mollys must've gone down first. Then I don't know what else."

"But after it fixed itself it figured out how to seal off the leak and stayed online long enough to get the job done." She shook her head in disbelief. "Batteries?"

Hedrickson ran a quick check, made a face. "Dead as an imploded mouse."

Chin pursued her lips. "Then the programming's gone. I don't mind that except it means we'll never learn why it didn't follow accepted procedure and commence preservation shutoff when the primary power went down."

Hedrickson turned to the nearest monitor, plugged in a power cell, and brought the Molimon unit online. "Nothing here," he told her after several minutes of inquiry. "No, wait a sec. There is a shutdown indicator. It knew it was going." He frowned. "The message is in nonstandard format."

Chin moved to join him. Lights were coming on all around them as repair crews began to restore station power to the hydroponics module.

"What do you mean, it's 'nonstandard'?"

Hedrickson ran a speculative finger along the top of the dead Molimon. His voice was flat. "Read it for yourself."

Chin looked at the softly glowing monitor he was holding. She expected to see the words *Shutdown procedure completed*.

Instead she saw something else. Something that was, after all, only an indication of programming awareness. Nothing more. What it said was this.

LITTLE GIRLS ARE NOT REDUNDANT.

Panhandler

The stories I tell tend not to be controversial. That doesn't mean I could not write a story about extreme sexual deviancy or serial murder or genocide or based on any one of a dozen other "dangerous" themes. In point of fact, I have written such stories. They are rejected with numbing regularity, like the one about the first humans to land on Mars. The crew is composed of multiple amputees afflicted with a variety of incurable terminal diseases, all of whom are eager volunteers for the one-way mission. Too much logic, I suppose, for the taste of editors charged with buying for the supposedly "daring" genre of science fiction.

Most of us have read about how really grim are the original versions of Grimm's fairy tales. The bulk of traditional children's stories, in fact, frequently contain mention of everything from bestiality to mass murder. The trend in retelling seems to favor sanitization over authenticity in order to protect fragile young minds. One exception is the TV show The Simpsons, *whose writers are intelligent enough to recognize that they, too, were once young and that contrary to the pious protestations of those who see their sacred duty as supervising the maturation of children not their own, children can handle grim fairy stories without being bludgeoned into gibbering insanity by such tales' perceived excesses. Or as Bart and Milhouse joyfully and innocently chant in one episode, "Car-toon vi-o-lence, car-toon vi-o-lence!"*

Itchy and Scratchy are contemporaneously copy-
righted, so I could not use them to illustrate my point.
The utilization of another older and even more famous
children's trope, however, still unnerved the publishers
of the anthology in which this story originally appeared.
Names had to be changed to protect, if not the innocent,
at least the perceived threat to the almighty corporate
balance sheet.

The title of the story, by the way, is a triple pun . . .

Harbison pulled the rear flap of the overcoat's
thick, heavy collar up against his neatly trimmed hair-
line so that it covered the fuzz and the bare skin on the
back of his neck. With the passage of time the morning's
icy rain was turning to sleet as the incoming storm lay-
ered the city with a cold, damp mucus. In response to
the glooming clouds, lights over storefronts and on bill-
boards were automatically warming to life. Some flickered uncertainly in the murk, as if confused by stalking
weather masquerading as night.

The park lay to his right, an oasis of dull green even in
winter. Awaiting still-distant spring, trees slept in silence, wooden obelisks scarred by switchbladed hiero-
glyphs. Bundled up like trolls, old ladies scuttled along
the slick sidewalks, heavy woolen mufflers making their
necks wrestler-thick. Businessmen preoccupied with affairs of the ledger long-strided between the heated
hobbit-holes of favorite luncheon spots and the bland-
ness of dead-end lives they knew no longer had meaning. At this time of midday you could tell which ones
were going to lunch and which ones returning to work,
Harbison knew. Those who had already eaten were
blushing from the effects of having consumed too much
rich food and depressed at having to repopulate their
myriad cubicles in the tall buildings, while those on their

way to indulge their expense accounts at fancy restaurants exuded anticipation like sweat.

He was on lunch hiatus, too, but it wasn't food he was after. Prowling the clammy streets, he sought satiation of a different sort. Striving to maintain as much anonymity as he could, he tucked his own muffler up over his chin and pulled the brim of his fedora lower on his forehead. That way, little more than his eyes and mouth showed. Both were eager.

The boys hung out on Eighteenth Street, opposite the park. There were not many of them, but there were enough. Practiced at pretending to be waiting for the bus, for friends, for a pickup game of basketball or street hockey, for anything but the tricks who sought them out, they worked hard at avoiding the attentions of the police. As a general rule the local cops did not bother them. In a city plagued by the attentions of genuinely bad people, hookers of any gender tended to be overlooked by the police until and unless some fool of a news reporter decided to guerrilla some video with a shaky, handheld camera so he/she could fill three minutes of the six o'clock report with human interest of the shameful kind. It was a cheap and easy way to sensationalize the news, maybe grab the attention of a few bored channel surfers and push those enervating reports about thousands dead of starvation in Ethiopia to the late-night closing minute.

Following the occasional police roundup, executed to show the powers-that-be that the boys in blue were On Top of the Situation, those boys and girls unlucky enough to be apprehended promptly got out on bail and went back to work. The cops—the ones of good sense and duty, anyway—went back to actually trying to protect the public.

Harbison didn't need any protection. He knew his vices and how to slake them. He was their prisoner, and the boys on Eighteenth Street were happy to fulfill his needs and take his money. Usually he found someone quickly, terms were agreed upon much faster than in his law office, and it was all over and done with in time for him to still grab a relaxed meal at Carrington's.

He did not have to approach anyone. All they needed to come flocking was to see the need and the hunger in his eyes. Impatient, he checked them out one by one, like a farmer evaluating prize calves at a country auction. This one too old, that one tweaking, the next too needy, his friend too mired in depression. Harbison ran through them by walking past them, having long since mastered the ability to ignore the filmy haunt that veiled their old-young eyes. They were nothing more than fruit in a market, and he had the time and the money to pick and choose the fresh from the rotting.

He was about to make a deal with a lanky recent immigrant from the heartland, all soulful brown eyes and agile midwestern hands, when he saw the boy in the back.

He was leaning up against the stone wall of the office building, one knee raised, foot propped against an outcropping of early-twentieth-century granite, and openly smoking a joint. He was short, maybe five-five or -six, lean but obviously muscular beneath his jeans and too-light-for-the-winter black leather jacket. The icy slush dribbling down from the sullen sky did not seem to bother him. Atypically, he was gazing off into the distance, ignoring the two or three other johns who were cruising the street offside the park. His eyes were a striking arctic blue. Wavy blond hair peeked out from beneath the brim of the backward cap that covered his head without warming it.

Harbison was drawn to him immediately.

The boy didn't snuff out the joint, but he did look over as the lawyer approached. His attitude was an in-

triguing mix of bottled arrogance and heartrending vul-
nerability. The latter was a quality Harbison was accus-
tomed to encountering in the boys he used, but the
former was not. He immediately got down to business.
He had to, if he was going to finish and still make lunch.

"How much?" he asked offhandedly. Those eyes. His
own eyes strayed elsewhere. The boy didn't object to the
blatant inspection. It was expected, and clearly he was
used to it.

"The usual?" The kid's voice was high, sweet, girlish.
Natural, somehow not yet broken, not a put-on. Better
and better. Harbison nodded, struggling to contain his
eagerness. "Twenty."

Fair, the lawyer thought. Good. He wouldn't have to
waste time bargaining. "Needs to be quick. I've got a
lunch appointment." He indicated his wrist without exposing his watch. This was not a prudent location to
flash a Piaget. "You got a place?"

The boy nodded. Flicking the stub of the joint onto
the street, where the gathering cold slush instantly extin-
guished it, he turned his head toward the nearby alley.
That made Harbison hesitate.

A grin creased the child-like face. Full of magic, it bor-
dered on the angelic. The boy looked even younger than
he doubtless was, Harbison mused. What an enchanting
discovery.

"Got a little box in back," the kid told him. "Propane
heater. Mattress, chair. Doorway locks. Nice and private. I'm okay with spending the night there. You don't
have to, but then you don't want to. It'll do fine for what
you want."

Harbison was not convinced, but there was no way he
was going to pass this up. He had to make a decision
fast. Lunch beckoned. And the boy was slim, couldn't
weigh more than 110, 120. An utterly adorable adoles-
cent. Remarkably his skin was as pale and unmarked as

a baby's, devoid of scars and needle marks. Not something one encountered every day on a less-traveled city street. Especially on this street.

"Okay, but no funny stuff." He put a hand in an empty pocket. "I've got a taser."

The grin lingered, humorless. "You ain't payin' enough for funny stuff."

Smart, too, Harbison decided as he followed the boy into the alley. Not that he was paying for smarts. "What's your name, kid?"

"Peter."

Harbison choked back something akin to an amused response.

"No, really," the boy told him. "Ironic, huh? Or poignant. Depends on your point of view, I guess."

Something about the reply struck Harbison as out of the ordinary. Natural suspicion being a hallmark of his professional as well as his private life, he slowed his stride. "Just out of curiosity, kid, where'd you learn how to use that word?"

The boy stopped too and turned to face the curious lawyer. "What word?"

"Poignant." Turning slightly, Harbison indicated the street behind them. "The kids I meet up with here usually can't get a handle on anything with more than four letters."

Blue eyes narrowed slightly and hands rested challengingly on narrow hips. "You want to fucking talk or you want to get it on? I thought you were in a hurry." The pose reminded Harbison of something, but he could not decide what. Then he saw the green shirt peering out from behind the battered leather jacket. It had a fringed hem. His gaze dropped. The shoes. They hadn't registered at first. Now they did.

"Your toes must be freezing in those."

Looking away, the boy muttered something obscene

under his breath before his gaze returned to meet the lawyer's. "What the fuck do you care about my friggin' toes, Jack? You into feet or something?"

"You're an actor, right?" Harbison wasn't sure why he continued with the questions. Maybe because he had always been one to act on hunches, even in court. "When you're not on the street picking up a few extra bucks for rent, you're in a play. Or trying out for one." He smiled reassuringly, confidently. "I think I know which play."

"Oh, shit," the boy muttered. His expression twisted. "Yeah, that's right. Only, you know what, Jack? I'm gonna tell you something. Because every once in a while, for some reason, I just feel like telling somebody. For the hell of it. I'm not an actor, see, and it's not a play. Not that it means anything, but my last name is one you already know. From the 'play.'"

Harbison's guard went up immediately. Either the kid was toying with him, and before time, or else he was going to prove difficult. The latter possibility did not concern Harbison overmuch. He'd had to deal with rants before. They rarely interfered with what he came for. Like all the others, the boy would eventually settle down. Because in the end, no matter how pissed off he got or for what reason, he would still want his money.

"It's all right," he said soothingly. "I don't care what you do once we've concluded our business. I just thought, seeing the shirt and the shoes and all . . ."

"Turns you on, does it?" The boy was watching him steadily.

"A little maybe, yeah."

"You don't believe me, do you?"

"Sure I do. Hey, I think it's great. Stay in character when you're off stage. Ought to be good for business, anyway. I know a couple of guys who'd pay double just to have you do them in full costume."

"I bet you do." Raising one arm, the boy gestured to take in the alley, the street beyond, the vast, uncaring city. "You know why I'm stuck here, putting up with this shit? Putting up with marauding, predatory assholes like you?"

"It doesn't matter." Time's a-wastin', Harbison realized. He could still do this and make lunch. Assuming the kid knew his business.

"It's all the fault of a certain fucking jealous little bitch. Since you're so confident of what role I'm 'acting' in, I'm sure I don't have to name her. Not the Brit twit, that's ancient history. But last New Year's I was in Times Square, and there was this little Puerto Rican chiquita and her friend, and they thought the hat and shirt and shoes were, like, oh so cute, you know? So, like, how about a threesome, to, like, celebrate the Neuva Año, *verdad*? Oh yeah, by the way, I'm bi. That bother you?"

"No," Harbison admitted honestly.

"So we, like, went back to her place, and I showed them how to fly, in a manner of speaking, and that mini-bitch I can never seem to shake no matter where I go or how hard I try showed up at just the wrong moment. Being kind of preoccupied at the time, I'd forgotten all about her. I thought she'd be out boogeying with the fireworks—that's one of her little SM things, you know? Man, was she pissed! So, no more fairy dust. I'm grounded until she gets her tiny little panties out of the knot they're in." Peering around, he took in his cheerless surroundings. "That was months ago, and I'm starting to wonder if she's ever coming back, and, like, even an immortal's got to eat, you know? I'm fucked if I'm gonna sling burgers for minimum. And with this not-growing-old thing, this fucking permanent youth, turns out I'm a boy-magnet to perverts like you."

Harbison bristled. "Calling clients names is bad for business."

"No shit?" Bold and completely unafraid, the boy approached until he was standing right up next to the older, bigger man. "You a lawyer or something?"

Harbison nodded. "Right now I need your services, but if you ever need mine . . ."

The lithe young male body spun around and back, a startlingly agile pirouetting leap that might have sprung straight off the stage at Lincoln Center. "Oh, right! That's it, that's the solution! We'll sue her! Haul her blond little ass right into civil court. Give new meaning to the term *small claims*. With you and her together there, facing each other, there'd be two fairies facing the judge." His tone darkened, like the weather. "Wouldn't work, dude. And you ain't licensed to practice where I come from." His gaze rose skyward. "Damn but I miss the place. Forest, mermaids. No fucking snow. No pathetic, lonely bastards like you to have to squeeze for enough wampum to get a decent meal. Even that miserable homicidal son-of-a-bitch nemesis of mine at least has his crew to help him out of a jam."

Despite having begun with promise this encounter was souring rapidly, an unhappy Harbison saw. As a lawyer, he knew when to pursue a case and when to settle and get out. It was time to get out. Plainly, the poor, beautiful kid was seriously disturbed, maybe strung out on crystal or Ecstasy or who knew what. He had suppressed his personal problems just well enough to fool Harbison. Until now. Regrettably the lawyer decided he would have to take a pass on his singular pleasure today. But there was still lunch to look forward to. The street, with its fluctuating complement of ready, accommodating, doe-eyed melancholic urchins, would still be here tomorrow. And the next day, and the day after that.

"On second thought, Mr.—Peter, I think we've wasted too much time talking and not enough doing. Now it's too late. I've got an appointment I have to keep." He turned to go.

He was not sure what they hit him with. It might have been a stick, it might have been a brick. Too early anticipating the night, stars filled his vision. He hit the alley pavement hard, his head bouncing off the wet asphalt like a mud-filled sock. Blinking, trying to clear his vision, he saw them standing over him. There were four, maybe five. A couple of them pretty big, all of them armed with potentially lethal detritus scavenged from the alley's battered, oversized Dumpsters. Reaching around behind his throbbing head, his hand came back bloody.

"Don't hurt me," he mumbled weakly. "I've got money."

The boy was bending over him, unsympathetic, thoughtfully checking the bleeding face. To the others he snapped, "He'll be all right. Joey, Arturo—get his wallet. Just the cash." The lawyer felt grubby fingers fumbling at his pockets. "Don't forget his watch." Crap, Harbison thought. Insurance would cover part, but not all, of the expensive chronograph's replacement cost.

He saw the boy straighten, open the ostrich-skin wallet, and pull out the couple of hundred bucks Harbison always carried with him. Another boy admired the glint of the Piaget on his own dirty wrist. His face flush with contempt, Peter let the wallet fall on Harbison's face.

"Come to my home, you self-important, condescending fucker. I'll turn you over to our local felon and his crew. They'd use you up. But you'd probably get off on that." He gestured to the other members of the gang before sparing the man on the ground a last, disdainful look. "I don't want to see you here again. Meanwhile, me and the local version of my homeboys are gonna go and get us something to drink and something hot to eat."

Turning sharply, he and the other kids, laughing and joking, headed for the street. Pushing himself up on one elbow, a dazed but still gratefully alive Harbison watched them go, sniggering and cursing and shoving one another playfully in the manner of arrogant street kids everywhere. Superior and self-confident in the shadowy, misty murk, their leader seemed to float along just above the ground.

Slowly, painfully, Harbison picked himself up. His clothes were a mess, smeared with street grit and dirty snow, but the red oozing at the back of his head seemed to have slowed. He needed medical attention. Any legitimate doctor or hospital emergency room would demand the details of his encounter. As he staggered toward the street, his afternoon trashed, he was already hard at work putting together the lie he would have to tell.

He could hardly confess to having been mugged by a boy named Peter.

The Last Akialoa

A number of years ago a friend and I had the opportunity to spend a week on the Hawaiian island of Kauai, which is known as the Garden Isle. The top of the island is a volcanic caldera. Over the millennia, the caldera has filled up with decaying organic matter, like a giant planter. Within can be found some of the most unique biota in the world—a swamp in the sky.

Determined to hike across at least part of this wondrous landscape, we drove up past Waimea Canyon one cloudy summer morning, parked our rented car in the last lot, and set out on our hike. It quickly became clear that when it came to describing the actual conditions and terrain, all the guidebooks woefully understated the actual conditions. Most Hawaiian hikes do not involve repeatedly sinking, sometimes up to one's waist, in a thick, gooey sludge of organic mulch. Nevertheless we made it to our destination, a lookout on the pali (a steep cliffside) high above the little town of Hana.

Meanwhile the cloud cover had thickened dramatically. Wind and rain had been intensifying for hours. I decided to hunker down for the night with our emergency tarp and let the weather blow through. My younger companion, however, declared tersely that "I'm not going to freeze to death up here!" and started back. As he was my responsibility, I felt I had no choice but to accompany him. By the time we reached our car, barely before darkness settled in, it was the only one left in the *parking lot. Being well-prepared for the hike, it had never occurred to us to check the weather forecast.*

As it happened, Kauai was in the process of catching the trailing southern edge of a passing tropical storm.

Back in our hotel, I spent two hours in the shower. Ten minutes to wash the gunk off myself, and the remaining time attempting to get it out of my sneakers. The latter task proved impossible, so ingrained had the organic matter become. Regretfully I had no choice but to throw away the unsalvageable shoes. Had I planted them, I have no doubt they would have sprouted a fantastic variety of flora.

Some small literary controversy attended the publication of "The Last Akialoa" in The Magazine of Fantasy & Science Fiction. *There are those who think it does not qualify as either a fantasy or science fiction.*

A nice leisurely afternoon stroll in the Alakai would, I think, change that perception . . .

The first thing Loftgren noticed was the rain, coalescing out of the air as mist, then sifting gently to the already sodden earth. He smiled to himself. They could hardly have expected otherwise considering they were about to enter the wettest place on Earth.

He didn't mind bringing up the rear. Fanole, their guide, was out in front, probing the feeble excuse for a trail, occasionally calling back to his two companions warnings and advice in equal measure. Behind him and just ahead of Loftgren was young Sanchez, the graduate student who had worked so long and hard to be included in the expedition. At the moment he resembled a runaway candy bar, enshrouded as he was in the transparent plastic sheets that shielded both him and his gear from the all-pervading damp.

Back down the road they had just left and four thousand feet below them lay the Kauai coast, with its warm tropical sunshine and chattering tourists and full-service hotels. Ahead lay thirty square miles of the most improbable and impenetrable terrain in the United States, if not the world. Equally remarkable, much of it was still unexplored.

The Alakai Swamp occupied the bowl of a gigantic caldera that formed the top of the Hawaiian island of Kauai. Trade winds slamming into the flanks of its highest peak, Mount Waialeale, were shoved upward into colder air where they were forced to drop their load of moisture day after day, month after month, year after year, with a benumbing, saturating regularity. Four hundred and eighty inches of rain a year. Six hundred and twenty-four inches in the record year of 1948. Cherrapunji in India occasionally had more during the monsoon, but Cherrapunji also enjoyed a dry season.

In the depths of the Alakai, the swamp in the sky, the dry season was measured in hours.

By late morning they were making their way down one of the knife-edged ridges that slice up the Alakai like razor blades planted in a pie. The Forest Service had hacked notches out of the solid rock, and while the going was slippery, by choosing his handholds with care Loftgren was able to keep all but the soles of his Gore-Tex-lined boots out of the stream that tumbled down the crack in the mountain. The temperature hovered in the sixties, and he was still dry and comfortable.

Fanole had warned him that no matter what he wore he wouldn't be able to stay dry for more than a day or two. They'd laid a small wager on the matter. Thanks to the university's beneficent largesse, Loftgren had been able to outfit Sanchez and himself in the latest in tropical gear, modified to take into account the fact that at this time of year temperatures in the Alakai often dropped into the forties at night.

Their guide wore comparatively little: shorts and a light cotton sweatshirt, cheap ankle-high sneakers and socks. His pack weighed more than those of his companions because he carried the tent, but that was only proper. He was being paid well for his exertions.

Loftgren hadn't really wanted to engage Fanole, but the number of men who knew anything about the deepest parts of the Alakai could be counted on the fingers of one hand, and when they found out where the ornithologist wanted to go, every one of them had turned him down. When asked why, an old half-Hawaiian, half-*haole* had quietly responded, "Because I want to live to enjoy my grandchildren." Fanole was the guide of choice because among the knowledgeable only Fanole had agreed to take on the expedition.

Such caution—fear, even—surprised Loftgren. Having carried out important fieldwork in both Papua New Guinea and the western Amazon, he was hardly about to be intimidated by the prospect of working on Kauai, with a profusion of Sheratons and Hyatts sprawling not two hours' drive from where they'd parked the rented van. He'd been planning this trip for more than a year and had prepared himself by reading everything extant in the limited literature about the Alakai.

He'd also encountered the stories—true, apparently. About the honeymooning couple whose car had been found at the nearby Kalalau Lookout a few years ago and who had never been seen again, alive or dead. About the US Geological Survey engineer who died of a heart attack three hundred yards from the summit of Mount Waialeale in 1948 and because of the difficulty of the terrain had to be left tied to a tree until his companions could return with adequate help to bring him out. It took sixteen men three days to get his body off the mountain. About the attempt to push a road through the swamp back in the 1950s. The construction crew had smashed their way into the forest and quit for the day, only to return the next morning to find their bulldozer missing. A brief search revealed that it had simply sunk out of sight.

Then there were his unsuccessful predecessors. Kinkaid of the University of Hawaii first, and two years ago Masaki of UC Riverside. Brazen to the end, Kinkaid had gone in alone, while Masaki had wandered away from his companions one day, never to be seen again. Kinkaid had been too brash for his own good, and Masaki—well, it was felt that Masaki had been the victim of either bad judgment or bad luck, neither a fault to which Loftgren was heir.

It was raining harder now and he found himself having to concentrate more closely on the trail. They were off the ridge and advancing through dense forest. Uluhe and ekaha ferns grew thickly in the underbrush, and the occasional flash of brilliant red ohiʻa lehua or waxy yellow-white lobelia flower flared like strobe lights among the green walls through which they were moving. Occasionally he picked out the bright orange berries of the Astelia lily gleaming among the sodden verdure.

"Starting to get a little sloppy. Watch your step," Fanole called back to them.

An instant later Sanchez slipped off the rotting log along which he had been tiptoeing and plunged waist-deep into thick, soupy, organic muck. Fanole edged carefully around the inadequate pathway, clinging for balance to the overhanging branches of dripping trees, and reached down to give the embarrassed student a hand up.

Beneath the transparent rain slicker the young man's waterlogged jeans were now stained brown from the waist down. Shreds of bark and leaves and other unidentifiable macrobiotic matter in various stages of decomposition clung to his legs and shoes.

An unsympathetic Fanole offered one of his typically terse observations. "Warned you. In here if you don't get soaked from the top down, sooner or later you get soaked from the bottom up." With that he turned and started back up a trail that had already diminished to little more than a narrow tunnel between the trees. "Might as well get used to it!" he yelled back.

The now saturated graduate student looked unhappy. "Sorry. I thought I could keep dry for one day, at least."

Loftgren tugged the brim of his slicker down over his forehead. His face was wet, but the rest of him still held back the best efforts of the swamp to drench him. On the other hand, he was already soaked with sweat.

The Alakai was where dryness went to die.

"Don't be too hard on yourself, Julio. Both Fanole and I have a lot more experience in this kind of country than you do."

Twenty minutes later Loftgren stepped over a log and onto a seemingly solid patch of ground that turned out to consist of cloying thigh-deep sludge. Fanole and Sanchez stood off to one side, looking on as he slowly pulled himself out and worked his way through the trough. No one said a word.

By nightfall they'd reached the junction of the Pihea and Alakai trails. Here the Forest Service had helicoptered in thick beams and wood planks. Securely strapped together, these formed a level, solid, platform at the trail juncture.

Fanole set up the tent, somehow managing to keep the interior halfway clear of rain. Beneath the extended, oversized storm flap they stripped nude and deposited their equipment outside on the redwood six-by-sixes.

"Any other wood'd rot out inside a month," their guide pointed out unnecessarily. "Except cypress and mahogany. But we can't get cypress here, and mahogany's too expensive. So we have to import the red-wood."

Using clean towels they dried themselves, then crawled into the tent to settle down around the camp stove Fanole ignited. By the time dinner was ready it was darker outside than the inside of a cave. A drenching, dripping, soaking dark. Steady rain pattered like dancing mice on the top of the tent, falling harder at night than it had during the day. Except for the monotonous thrumming of the continuous downpour—the heartbeat of the Alakai—it was dead silent outside the shelter.

Fanole poked leisurely at his reconstituted freeze-dried supper, looking on as Sanchez ravenously devoured his and Loftgren made a more considered go of his own. The guide was nearly fifty, with a receding forehead of thinning brown hair and dark eyes the color of aged bourbon that seemed to pierce whatever crossed their path, be it human or rock or tree. His sun-seared appearance left his ancestry open to some question, but he was certainly at least part Hawaiian. He had a slight bulge around his middle: spare tire for a bicycle rather than a sedan. Otherwise he was surprisingly muscular.

"You don't mind my saying so, I think you're both crazy."

Loftgren grinned. It wasn't the first time that opinion had been expressed in regard to the expedition. "You're entitled to your opinion. If you feel that way, why did you agree to guide us?"

Fanole finished the last of his dinner and set the plate carefully to one side. "Because no one else would. I know you academic types. If you couldn't get any help, you'd eventually have tried it on your own." He glanced up at the roof, listening to the rain tap-dancing relentlessly outside. "You'd never have gotten out of this place alive."

"Don't bet on it," Loftgren told him. "I've been in

rougher places than the Alakai. There are no snakes here, no hostile natives. Not even any dangerous bugs, and the mosquitoes quit climbing at the thirty-five-hundred-foot level."

Fanole nodded. "That's right. Nothing dangerous here but the place itself. Don't need any snakes or tigers. The swamp'll kill you all by its lonesome." He looked toward the entrance and nodded knowingly. "No landmarks, either. No sky overhead; only clouds. No ground underfoot; only a bottomless pit of composting plant matter. Even compasses act funny in here."

Sanchez felt compelled to speak up. "Begging your pardon, sir, but we got through the first of the bogs okay." He smiled apologetically. "Didn't stay very dry, but we got through." Reaching over, he tapped his pack. "Hard to get lost with a GPS."

Fanole shook his head once. He didn't smile. " 'The first of the bogs'? We haven't even reached the bogs yet, kid. That was just muddy trail. I've personally sounded bogs here that were twenty feet deep. There are deeper still, but they ain't been plumbed yet."

"How come?"

"Nobody's ever brought in a long enough measuring probe. Remember: we're walking across the throat of an old volcano. Might be bogs a hundred feet deep. Maybe a thousand. Nobody knows. In the whole swamp there's only two barely-there east–west trails and nothing at all running north to south. Your plan is to head off-trail and follow the line of the Wainiha Pali. Nobody's ever gone in there and done that." He snorted softly. "With or without a GPS."

"Kinkaid went in," Loftgren corrected him, "and Masaki."

"Nobody knows that for certain." Fanole's eyes burned into those of the ornithologist. "Masaki got to the Kilohana Lookout. Nobody's sure about Kinkaid. If you try to go north from there, you've got sheer cliffs on one side and unplumbed bogs on the other. I give you *haoles* about a day before you give up on it. If we make it that far."

"I once spent a month in the highlands of New Guinea, Fanole. Don't try to scare me."

"I'm not." The guide leaned back on his light sleeping bag. "You hired me for advice. I'm giving it. Just think it's a lot to go through for a glimpse of a bird that's probably been extinct since the 'seventies."

"There have been reports of song-sightings since then," Sanchez pointed out. "The survivors of Masaki's party all confirm it."

Fanole rolled onto his side, propping his head up on one big, weathered palm. "You stay out here long enough, it's easy to start hearing things as well as seeing them."

"Masaki vanished while tracking a singing akialoa," Loftgren insisted stubbornly.

"Maybe."

"Those with him heard it, too. The weather and the terrain got so bad, they all gave up and fell back, except Masaki. But they heard it."

"Maybe." The guide was incorrigible. "Next you'll be telling me you expect to find an o'o'a'a, too."

"No." Loftgren's voice dropped. "No, I'm afraid the o'o'a'a is gone. But not the akialoa. I won't accept it. It's too beautiful to not exist any longer."

From his file pouch he drew forth a folded eight-by-ten. Like every other picture he carried, like every map, it was laminated to protect it from the all-pervasive, all-destroying moisture. Unfolded, it revealed a painting of a small bird with a distinctive brown patterning and a lighter buff underbelly. Attractive but hardly spectacular.

Except for the downward-curving sickle-beak, which

was fully one-third the length of the creature's body. It was this remarkable protuberance that set the akialoa apart from its immediate relatives and for that matter, from all but a few other birds in the world. It had last been seen in the Alakai in 1973, and the possibility of its continued existence was the reason for Loftgren's university-sponsored expedition.

To find the akialoa, he mused as he gazed at the painting, the details of which he knew as intimately as those of his own body. Finding it would guarantee publication in *Science, Natural History,* the *Smithsonian, National Geographic*—they would be fighting one another for the right to be first to publish his words and pictures. A coup for the department and for the entire university. Perhaps a chair dedicated in his name. Promotion to professor emeritus of ornithology. The world would be his—or at least that small portion of it that concerned itself with birding.

Kinkaid had plunged into the Alakai seeking the elusive scimitar-billed bird and had vanished. So had the esteemed Masaki. Now it was his turn, and he fully intended to succeed where they had failed. If the akialoa still lived, it would be left to professional ornithologists such as himself to devise a scheme for ensuring its survival. Only they had the knowledge and ability to do so.

But first he had to find one.

The rain was lighter when they awoke. Carefully, they packed their equipment and set out again. Halfway up a steep, slippery, moss-bedecked slope he was delighted to find an outcropping of ohi'a trees. Fully mature at eight inches high, they were all more than a hundred years old. Later he spotted a thriving specimen of gunnera, the world's largest herb, with its unique eight-foot leaves.

Miniature trees and giant herbs. Reversed proportions, he reflected, were the norm in the Alakai.

Later that day the sun came out and they saw their first birds. Sanchez picked up a pair of bright red apapane, but it was Fanole who pointed out the endemic anianiau and the rarer i'iwi. Loftgren felt left out until he saw a tiny elepaio sheltering from the sun beneath a palapali fern.

Of the akialoa, however, there was no sign.

It was raining seriously when they entered the first bogs, edging around them where possible and wading through—sometimes up to their waists—when it was not. Fluttering fragments of fluorescent tape tied to tree branches were all that marked the trail, and these were hard to see in the fog that had settled over the swamp. Several times Loftgren had to admit he would have been lost without Fanole to lead the way.

On the third morning they turned off the intermittent trail and plunged into abject wilderness.

No one bothered to comment on the damp anymore because they were all soaked from head to foot. It was a distinctive, all-pervasive dampness that made you feel as if your skin were slowly sloughing off your body. White ridges appeared on palms and fingers; it felt as if at any minute your flesh would burst into flagrant, pustulant bloom. Forward progress was now measured in yards instead of miles.

By the end of the week the formerly resolute Sanchez had had enough.

"I want out, Martin." Despite the protection offered by the battered but still-intact slicker, water trickled down the graduate student's sensitive face into his eyes and mouth and ears.

Loftgren regarded him sternly. "There's no 'out,' here, Julio. This isn't a library research project. We stay until

we've found what we came for or until we run out of
supplies."

Fanole materialized silently at the frustrated student's
shoulder. "The kid's right. We're in too deep as it is. If
we keep going this way and don't manage to hook up
with the Mohihi Trail, we won't get out of here."

"You'll find the Mohihi."

"Maybe. I've never gone this way before. No one ever
has. We could step right off the damn Pali or stumble
into Waialeale. You know damn well nobody's gonna
spot us from the air because the cloud cover only breaks
fully maybe once, twice a year. No emergency helicopter
pickups in here, mister. I say it's time to leave. You got
what you paid for."

"I paid for an akialoa. We have plenty of food left."

"We've been slogging and bogging for four days and
we haven't seen a hint of one. Nobody knows exactly
where we are, and in an emergency it wouldn't matter if
you could raise someone on that satellite phone tucked
in your pack anyway. It's time to go."

"If we don't save the akialoa, no one will. Even in the
academic community people are losing interest."

"You can't save what doesn't exist," Fanole replied
evenly. "People have been reducing the native birds'
range and food supply for hundreds of years. You know
that. Even if there are a couple left, we don't know if
there's enough of whatever they specialize in feeding on
to support them. Long-petaled flowers, bugs, whatever.
There's so little information about the akialoa that we
don't even know for sure what the hell they eat. But that
hook of a bill evolved to feed on something specific. We
don't know anything about it from the old Hawaiians
because they almost never came up here. Country's too
rough, too many dangerous spirits. Too many feather-
hunters who never made it back. Birds like that don't
just switch specialized feeding habits to lobelia or ohi'a

in a few decades. The o'o'a'a had a better chance in that respect and it didn't make it. Be reasonable, man."

Loftgren regarded his companions. Fanole was unyielding. Sanchez's expression was a mixture of pleading and anger. Bits of dark, decomposing plant material clung to his forehead and hair, giving him the aspect of a drowned Hispanic dryad.

"All right. But first we finish out the day and then camp. We can start back tomorrow."

Fanole grunted, willing to concede an afternoon. An exhausted and relieved Sanchez merely slumped to the ground where he stood. Beneath him, the spongy earth immediately began to give way, oozing up around his hips and shoulders. Hastily he rose to search for more solid ground. With the intensifying rain shrouding them in wet shadow, they made camp.

The song woke him. It was sharp, piercing, utterly distinctive. At first Loftgren thought it might be an akepa, but decided the concluding notes were too high.

Hauling himself to the front of the tent, he unzipped the flap and crawled outside. Fog swirled around the temporary shelter, coiling smoke-like through the trees, reducing visibility to a few yards. An errant shaft of sunlight shining momentarily through the clouds briefly pearlized the drifting fog.

It sat in a tree not ten feet away, singing energetically, that remarkable bill parting slightly to emit each series of notes. He stared breathlessly, hardly daring to move. Then it turned to regard him momentarily out of tiny blinking eyes before flying off into the enveloping mist. Alighting somewhere unseen, it resumed its cheerful song.

Loftgren flung himself back into the tent and pawed at his camera bag until he'd extracted the digital unit.

Fanole sat up and blinked at him as the ornithologist struggled feverishly with a fresh storage card. Sanchez stirred sleepily nearby.

"Nude Menehune nymphs cavorting in the bogs?" the guide inquired.

"I saw it." Trying to steady shaking fingers, Loftgren slid the camera into its protective housing, checked the telephoto, then began to tighten the knobs on the aluminum strip that would make the plastic airtight and waterproof. "I heard it first and crawled outside, and I saw it."

Fanole sat up sharply. "What do you mean, you saw it?"

"On a branch, right outside the tent. It was still singing when I came in for the camera." He rose, checked to make sure the card was more than half empty, and started for the tent flap.

"Hey!" Naked, Fanole scrambled out of his bag. "Where the hell do you think you're going?"

Loftgren paused in the entrance. "Can't wait. Might never see it again."

"You idiot, hold up!" Fanole lurched to the opening and outside, where it was beginning to rain afresh. On hands and knees, Sanchez blinked out from behind him, trying to wake up.

"What's happening? Where's Professor Loftgren going?"

Fanole stared into the intensifying shower. "He said he heard his damn bird. Says he saw one."

"Saw one?" Sanchez emerged, arms wrapped across his naked chest, shivering slightly in the early-morning chill. "An akialoa?"

"I guess." The guide turned and reentered the tent. Sanchez gazed into the fog and drizzle for a moment longer, then retreated.

"Aren't we going after him?"

The guide's eyes were unblinking, hard. "Without our equipment? Without planning? Not me, kid. Not me. If he has an ounce of intelligence left in him, he'll be back within an hour."

Sanchez hesitated in the doorway, wavering. "And if he's not?"

Fanole said nothing. He was heating coffee.

Loftgren ran on, pushing through the trees and brush, ignoring the brilliant red flowers that occasionally cropped up in his path. Once, an apapane trilled close on his left. He ignored it, concentrating only on the song that stayed just ahead of him but never disappeared entirely. The bird was moving, perhaps in search of the particular long flowers it needed to feed on that were nearly extinct elsewhere in the swamp, perhaps toward a nest. A nest! What a discovery that would be!

All he needed was a picture; one lousy picture. A single decent clear shot. Then he'd pick his way back to the tent. They could search farther for the bird or return to civilization if Fanole and that simpering Sanchez still insisted on going back. He'd expected better of his most committed graduate student. It was apparent he had the brains but not the dedication. Great discoveries were not made by the cautious or the reluctant.

A second time, the bird lighted in a tree in front of him. He aimed the camera, but the creature flew off as he thumbed the release and he couldn't be sure he'd gotten the shot. A check of the LCD screen showed that he had not. Damn! It was almost as if the bird was leading him on, deeper into the swamp. Absurd notion. Rare as it was, it would be nothing if not highly skittish. He plunged furiously onward, once wading through a bog that reached up his waist to his chest, then his neck, then to his very chin. You couldn't swim through a bog, he knew. It was too thick, too dense with organic components. But it wasn't quicksand, either, fighting to drag you down.

Out of breath, muscles aching, he flailed at a protruding root, got a grip, and pulled himself out. Just ahead the akialoa sang on, its song bright and strong.

Broken branches and thorns tore at his rain gear, at the sweatshirt beneath, and finally at his exposed skin. He ignored it all just as he ignored the profound dampness, just as he ignored the waning light. Dimly he realized that it would be impossible for him to find his way back to the camp by nightfall. Concentrating as he was on listening for the bird, he had no time for mere personal concerns. But he was strong and experienced. He would find his way back tomorrow.

In the brief, bright, burning fury of discovery, he had forgotten about the cold.

There was just a light breeze, but once the sun went down it was enough to drive the chill through his flesh and into his very bones. At times, he found himself remembering from his reading, the temperature in the Alakai could drop to levels that approached freezing. Ordinarily that would not have mattered, despite his light attire—except for the fact that he was soaked to the skin. Curled by the side of a bog, he started shivering as soon as the sun disappeared completely. By the time it was dark he was trembling violently.

He had nothing to light a fire with, even if any of the sodden pulp that passed for wood around him could have been persuaded to nourish a spark. For a while he tried shouting, gave it up when he realized no one would dare come looking for him in the dark.

Eventually the shivering began to subside. He lay on his side, his breathing slow and shallow, realizing what was happening to him. All because he wanted to help a single, rare bird to survive. His greatest fear was not of death, but that no one else would come after him. The public would forget about the akialoa without dramatic rediscovery and intercession by trained ornithologists. Without the support of dedicated scientists like himself, there was no way the species could survive.

An eternity later he became feebly aware that the light around him was strengthening. Had the night passed so quickly? Or was his perception of time failing faster than his other senses? The omnipresent fog and drizzle prevented the sun from reaching the surface, from warming him. Closer to Heaven he might be, but here it was wet and gray.

Searching for more solid ground, he dragged himself with infinite patience away from the bog until his hand wrapped around something hard and almost dry. A solid piece of wood at last. But when he struggled to pull himself higher it came apart in his fingers. Blinking, he examined it weakly in the saturated light. It was not brown, but white. With a great effort he managed to raise his head.

Not one, but two deteriorating skeletons lay just above him, entangled in the trees where they had collapsed. Scraps of rotting, disintegrating clothing clung to the bone-white shoulders and hips. Like desiccated string, a few vestiges of tendons hung slack from the limbs. Exotic mosses and small ferns flourished in the vacant body cavities, having fed well on the now decomposed flesh.

Kinkaid, he thought. Masaki. Or maybe just a pair of disoriented, unlucky hikers. Without a detailed forensic analysis, there was no way to know. Had they been drawn here, too, by the song of the akialoa? Drawn to what? A nesting place, perhaps. Or maybe a courtship ground, where hopeful males displayed their most colorful feathers and warbled their most enchanting songs.

From somewhere very close by, an akialoa greeted the morning with the rarest song in the world.

Kinkaid, Masaki, and now him. Everything risked for fame and modest fortune. All to try to help a wonderful, unique bird, and all for naught. How ironic it was that a man should die of hypothermia in the midst of a swamp. He pushed on, staggering and falling, struggling to his feet, always following the song.

He did not know how much time had passed when the sun finally came out. The warmth was as unexpected as it was welcome. With dryness came a rush of renewed strength and determination. Knowing he ought to turn back, he pushed on. Not the wisest of decisions, perhaps, but having come this far and endured so much, he felt he had no choice.

Then he saw them.

They were perched in a cluster of trees green with epiphytes and bromeliads, bejeweling the branches with the brilliance of their plumage. His jaw dropped in wonderment. A pair of black momo sat preening themselves, their own shorter sickle-bills digging parasites from beneath their wings. Nearby, a flock of greater amahiki chattered away like so many lime-green mockingbirds. With its thick, heavy beak, a greater koa finch was plucking caterpillars from the trunk of an isolated tree, while overhead a trio of o'o' flashed their extraordinary tail feathers and brilliant gold wing tufts. Crow-sized kioea yelled at diminutive red-and-gray ula-ai-hawane. It seemed as if all the extinct, beautiful birds of Hawaii had gathered in this one place, just waiting for the sun to come out in the Alakai. Waiting for him.

Then he heard the song again, and there they were. Not one, not two, but three pairs cavorting in the tree directly ahead of him, singing their approval of the rare appearance of the sun. The males were seven to seven and a half inches long, bright olive-yellow above and yellow below, the gray-green females slightly smaller. And those amazing, astonishing bills, unequaled anywhere in the kingdom of birds. There was a nest, too. Hearing the peeping of chicks, he hardly dared to breathe. Ever so slowly, he reached for his camera.

It wasn't there. He must have dropped it while running and slogging through the swamp, he realized. No matter. With such a sight as no ornithologist of his generation could dare to dream of spread out before him, it was enough simply to sink to his knees and stare, and stare. Spreading his arms out to his sides, he drank in the sight and the sun. And smiled.

Sanchez wasn't with the search party that stumbled across Loftgren's body early the following year, but Fanole was. The guide recognized the remnants of the ornithologist's boots as he rechecked his group's position on the new GPS he carried. He had to check it three times. Each time, his amazement grew. Without food or proper clothing, the haole researcher had somehow made it halfway up the side of Mount Waialeale itself.

Two of the Forest Service rangers on expedition with the guide peered over his shoulder. "Know him?"

Fanole nodded, resting an arm across one thigh. "Bird prof. Went running off into the depths by himself last year. His graduate student and I spent a day searching for him before we turned and got out. Barely made it." He thought back. "That was two days before Tropical Storm Omolu hit the island."

"Poor son-of-a-bitch." The taller ranger wiped moisture from his face beneath the rain hood. "What a way to die."

"I dunno." His companion cocked his head slightly to one side. "He looks kind of peaceful to me."

Fanole grunted, straightened. "We'll have to mark the location. Another crew can haul out the body."

"That's for sure." The first ranger started to turn

away, hesitated, looked back and frowned. "What's that he's holding in his right hand?"

The other ranger squinted. Fanole had already started back toward their bivouac. "Plant stuff. Fern leaf, I think. I don't guess that he's holding anything. Fingers contracted while dying." He sighed and shook his head sadly. "Rigor mortis."

Still, the taller man hesitated. Then he shrugged and started after his companion. "Funny. For just a second there I thought they were feathers."

Growth

An awful lot has happen to the characters of Flinx and his pet minidrag, Pip, since they first appeared in The Tar-Aiym Krang *thirty-five years ago. Having matured both physically and mentally, Flinx has gone from being a pretty aimless teenager to someone (or perhaps something) of immense importance to everyone around him. It's not a destiny he sought. But like so many of us, he can't escape the inexorable. That does not mean he wouldn't like to do so.*

As a consequence of who he is and what he may yet become, all manner of individuals and even entire societies have acquired an interest in what happens to him. Sometimes even without him being aware of it . . .

There was no denying that there were times when Flinx enjoyed being alone. One of the few times he could allow himself to relax was in transit. Because when traversing the immense distances between the stars he was spared the constant, puerile emotional babble of supposedly sentient individuals who collectively gave "higher intelligence" a bad name. Though interstellar travel did not entirely relieve him of his recurring headaches, the debilitating attacks were considerably reduced in number when he was by himself.

Of course, he was not entirely alone on the ship. Pip, the empathetic Alaspinian minidrag and his constant companion since youth, was with him. He could also count on the presence of the *Teacher*'s advanced AI. For an automaton, it was a pleasant, sophisticated presence—and unlike the interminably gibbering mass of humanxkind, one he could simply shut down whenever he grew tired of the conversation.

Man and machine were chatting now as Flinx relaxed in the lounge. With its artificial pond, waterfall, and small forest, it was his favorite part of the ship. The Ulru-Ujurrians who had presented him with the craft had left the relaxation chamber comparatively bare and utilitarian in both content and design. Employing the ship's automatics, Flinx had modified it repeatedly over the years.

Now as he reclined on the couch-lounge, he allowed music and the remnants of a good meal to slowly overtake consciousness. As he slipped sleepward, the AI's thoughtful voice grew fainter and fainter. Gliding toward him from her perch in one of the many decorative live plants that composed the tiny woodland, Pip furled her wings as she landed on his chest. Coiling against his ribs, emotionally surfing his current wave of contentment, she shut her own eyes and joined him in sleep.

The lounge forest was home to a small but exceptionally varied collection of flora and fauna drawn from different worlds. Before being transferred to the enclosed, climate-controlled chamber, their individual biologies and backgrounds had been thoroughly vetted by the vessel's Shell. Otherwise Flinx would not have felt comfortable going to sleep inside the lounge. He knew that none of the diminutive creatures that dwelled therein were capable of or inclined to do him harm.

It was not an animal, however, that was now advancing silently toward him.

The single oversized leaf split and split and split again into innumerable subsidiary tendrils, not unlike the singular twin leaves of the uncommon Terran desert plant *Welwitschia mirabilis*. The suddenly motile growth was one of many that had been given to Flinx by the adapted human inhabitants of the edicted planet known in restricted Commonwealth files as Midworld. The primitive human colonists who lived there had developed a capacity for empathetic foliation: the ability to sense, on a very simple level, what much of the planet's globe-girdling flora was "feeling." As an empath himself, Flinx to a certain degree shared that ability.

But he was asleep now. Not empathizing, not projecting, not receiving or feeling. Like his thoughts, his emotions were in stasis. The multiple tendrils that were twisting and weaving their way in his direction were doing so entirely on their own and without any prompting or tempting from their objective. The unanticipated activity did not, however, go unobserved.

The *Teacher*'s AI monitored the leaf's fracturing approach via multiple lenses embedded in the walls and ceiling that were capable of scanning the entire chamber simultaneously. Though it could have sent mobile devices to intercept the squirming branchlets, it did not react immediately. Its history showed that whenever a serious threat to its owner presented itself, Flinx had invariably been stirred to wakefulness. The same was true of his winged pet. Both continued to sleep, ignoring the floral advance. Their indifference, even in sleep mode, caused the AI to dither.

By the time it decided that regardless of a lack of responsiveness from its master it ought to take some action, it was too late.

By now the diameter of the smallest of the continuously subdividing tendrils could be measured in nanometers. Entering Flinx via his right ear, they proceeded to worm their way deep into his cranium without damaging the delicate tympanum of the hearing organ or stimulating it to generate potentially awakening noise. Knowing exactly where to penetrate, they entered the cerebrum at points that would have struck a human neurosurgeon as not only harmless, but useless. A normal human brain would not even have been affected. Flinx's mind, however, was far from normal. His closest human companion, Clarity Held, knew this. So, too, did a pair of longtime mentors, the human Bran Tse-Mallory and the thranx Truzenzuzex.

So also, it appeared, did certain highly specialized and abnormally active botanical xenophyta.

Once again Flinx found himself in that peculiar state of conscious sleep that periodically afflicted him. He was aware of himself and, to a certain extent, his immediate surroundings as well. He knew that he was safely on board his ship, in the lounge, but asleep. In this singular state of awareness but not wakefulness someone—or rather something—was attempting to converse with him.

Intermittent contact is wasteful. The sexless voice in his mind was vast, enfolding, luxuriant. *Greater intimacy will facilitate progress.*

Flinx did not argue. How could he, being asleep? Nor could he ignore what he was perceiving. He could no more blot out the voice in his mind than he could reach up and pull out the infiltrating tendrils of which he remained utterly unaware. Even if he could, there was no reason to do so. Their existence inside his head, inside his brain, caused him no pain, no discomfort. In fact, their presence was soothing, generating a kind of cerebral balm. As he remained motionless and unobjecting, the tendrils set themselves more deeply. He was aware that something was being done to his body but found himself unable and unwilling to oppose it.

As awareness dawned of what was taking place, the ship finally decided that it had to do something. But in order to safely counteract what it now perceived to be an unsolicited intrusion into the body of its master, it first had to ascertain exactly what was happening. Analysis always precedes action.

Alongside the couch-lounge a floor panel popped open. A cable emerged. The end of the cable split into smaller cables, which in turn divided into smaller and still-smaller metallic filaments. These gave birth to hypoallergenic wisps of silicaceous cilia. Ascending the lounge, they twisted and curled and found their way to the head of the recumbent, sleeping human. A small number of cilia entered his left ear, penetrating, questing. Looking for answers. Searching for connections.

The world-mind of Midworld that was present on the *Teacher* in the form of several decorative growths could not communicate with the ship's AI. The purely mechanical AI could not talk to the wholly organic representation of that immense green world-mind. But to the very considerable surprise of each, they discovered that they *could* communicate through the matchless, inimitable mind of the human dozing dreamily on the lounge. Genetically modified ganglia served to link plant and machine. It was not a function that had been envisioned by the rogue gengineers who had conceived the blueprint of the young man's mind. Conditioned to think of himself as receptor of emotions and possibly a kind of trigger for something incalculably greater and as yet undefined, a quiescent Flinx now found himself serving as the unconscious facilitator of an unprecedented link between plant-mind and machine.

Having unexpectedly established this rudimentary contact, the *Teacher*'s AI ventured a typical terse query. *What are you doing? Your presence here was not requested.*

Not requested, artificial mentality, but necessary.

The ship mulled this response. *I monitor the human's condition on a more than hourly basis. I have not detected, nor do I now, any need for the intrusion of another life-form. This plainly includes you.*

The botanical vastness replied, *Time passes. Events advance. It is thought a more intimate connection will help to speed, streamline, and facilitate certain essential decision making on the part of the human that is vital to the continued survival of all.*

Since Flinx was in no condition to object, the ship did so for him. *At times it may appear that the master hesitates unreasonably, or makes determinations that are contradictory or even counterproductive, which he then proceeds to follow. I have learned that this is necessary to the optimal functioning of his kind.*

That is contradictory. How can following counterproductive decisions improve function? The plant-mind was clearly confused.

One would have to be human to understand. It is true that I am not. However, I have spent all my conscious existence in the presence of or responding to the actions and thoughts of this one individual. You are, I perceive, a group consciousness. Not individual. It is not expected that you would understand.

The intimacy we have just forged will improve the human's functioning.

The *Teacher* was unhesitating in its response. *In the absence of empirical precedent I can neither refute nor verify that judgment. But I can tell you that while your intimate presence and consequent influence may possibly enhance his health and even extend his physical life span, it will only inhibit his decision-making ability.*

Another contradiction. Can you elucidate?

The *Teacher* tried. Being wholly human, the concept was not one that was easy for an artificial intelligence to explain. *When it comes to rendering rapid decisions on matters of great importance, safety and health are often inhibitors, whereas stress often proves to be the most important stimulant.*

The plant-mind was quiet for a long moment. *Yet it*

seems that all other living things function better in the absence of such stimulation. What proof of this theorem can you offer?

Only an opinion that is based on knowledge accumulated from my years of attending to, observing, and working with the organism under discussion. If it is more rapid and intuitive decision making that you seek to augment, you will find that your physical and mental intrusion, no matter how temporally copacetic, in the end has the opposite effect.

Another pause, then: *We seek only to support. It was not considered that self-evidentiary improvements might produce contradictory consequences. Until this paradox can be resolved, we will withdraw to ponder your interpretation.*

The curled green leaf that was protruding from Flinx's right ear quivered slightly as it began to withdraw. Within moments the last of the microscopic tendrils at its tip had slipped out, sliding wetly down the side of Flinx's jawline. Slowly the leaf pulled back across the floor, contracting, until it lay coiled against its parent plant: just one more innocuous decorative growth among the dozens of other exotics that made up the lounge's carefully maintained landscaping.

From his left ear, a glistening cable withdrew. Its retreating diameter shrank toward invisibility as smaller and smaller fibers slid into view. The last of them were far too minuscule to be visible to the human eye. As the last of the cable vanished into an open port in the floor, Flinx blinked and sat up. Her rest summarily disturbed, a mildly irritated Pip uncoiled, spread her wings, and flew off to land on a favorite platform set among the trees where she could resume her rest undisturbed by her indecisive companion. Unaware that anything out of the ordinary had transpired, she promptly closed her eyes

and went in search of the sleep that had just been interrupted.

Swinging his long legs off the lounge, Flinx yawned,
stretched slightly, and used his right palm to rub at a
slight itch that was irritating his right ear. It was too early
to eat again, the *Teacher*'s intended destination still lay
some days far-distant through space-plus, and he was not
in the mood to read, view, or listen to anything intended
as a recreational distraction. Standing, he found himself
not for the first time faced with budding boredom. He
knew he need not succumb to it. On a vessel as elaborate
as the *Teacher*, there was always something to do.

Without exactly knowing why, he decided it might be
a good time to prune the plants.